BabOon!™

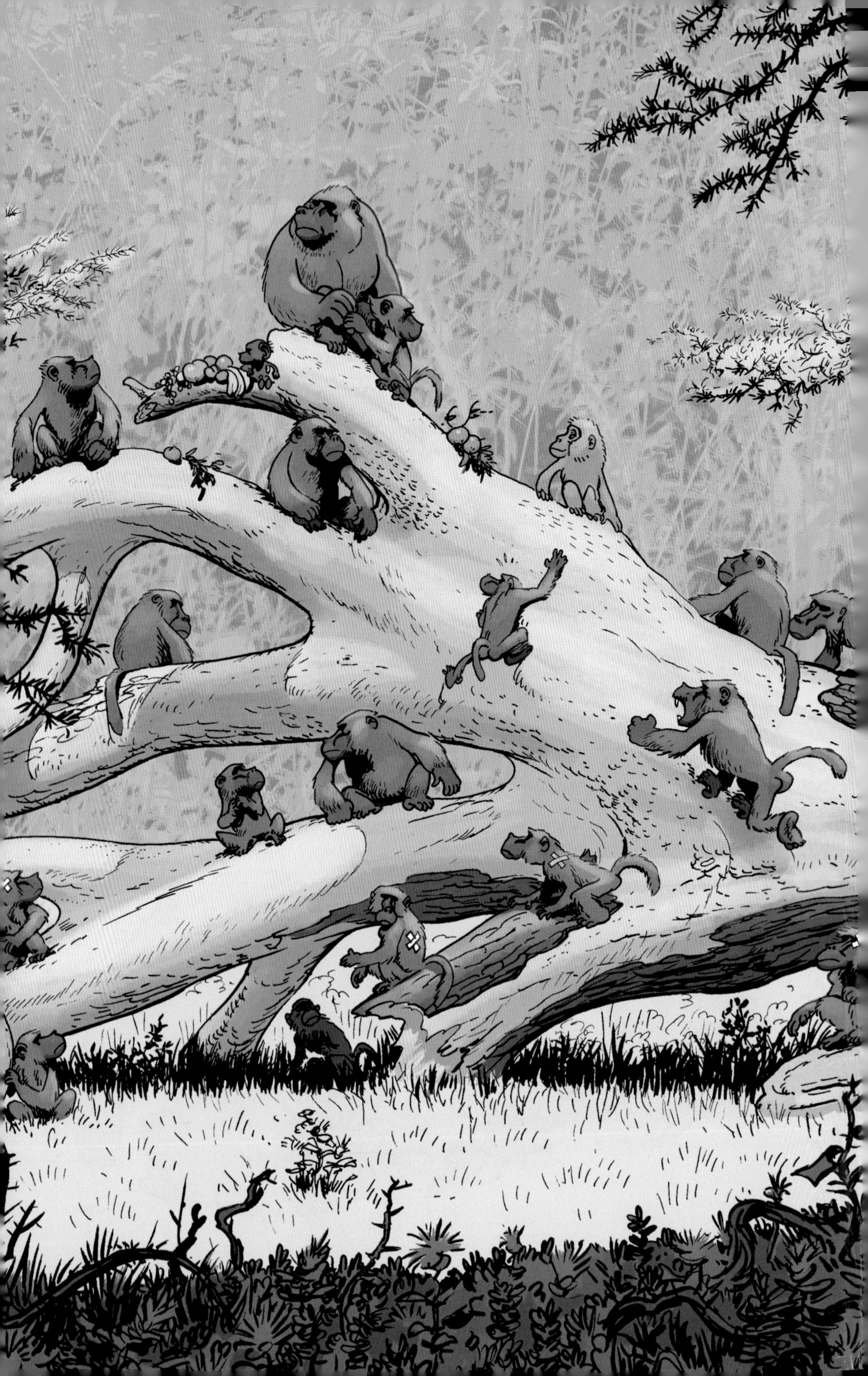

WRITTEN AND ILLUSTRATED BY

PAU

DARK HORSE BOOKS

President and Publisher
MIKE RICHARDSON

Editor
MEGAN WALKER

Assistant Editor
JOSHUA ENGLEDOW

Designer
SCOTT ERWERT

Digital Art Technician
ADAM PRUETT

Published by Dark Horse Books
A division of Dark Horse Comics LLC
10956 SE Main Street, Milwaukie, OR 97222

DarkHorse.com

 Facebook.com/DarkHorseComics
 Twitter.com/DarkHorseComics

Advertising Sales: (503) 905-2315
To find a comics shop in your area, visit comicshoplocator.com

First Edition: October 2020
ISBN 978-1-50671-795-1
1 3 5 7 9 10 8 6 4 2
Printed in China

Library of Congress Cataloging-in-Publication Data

Names: Pau, 1972- author, illustrator.
Title: Baboon! / written and illustrated by Pau.
Description: First edition. | Milwaukie, OR : Dark Horse Books, 2020. |
    Audience: Ages 12+ | Audience: Grades 4-6 | Summary: "After the death of
    its adopted leopard mother, an orphaned baboon wanders the wild in
    search of companionship and a sense of identity. Stumbling upon the
    troop of baboons from which it was originally stolen, the baboon falls
    in love with the troop's head female. Initially rejected, beaten, and
    discarded by the alpha baboon of the troop, the orphaned baboon trains
    to fight and earn its respect in the animal kingdom!"– Provided by
    publisher.
Identifiers: LCCN 2019060119 | ISBN 9781506717951 (trade paperback)
Subjects: LCSH: Graphic novels. | CYAC: Graphic novels. | Baboons–Fiction.
    | Stories without words.
Classification: LCC PZ7.7.P29 Bab 2020 | DDC 741.5/973-dc23
LC record available at https://lccn.loc.gov/2019060119

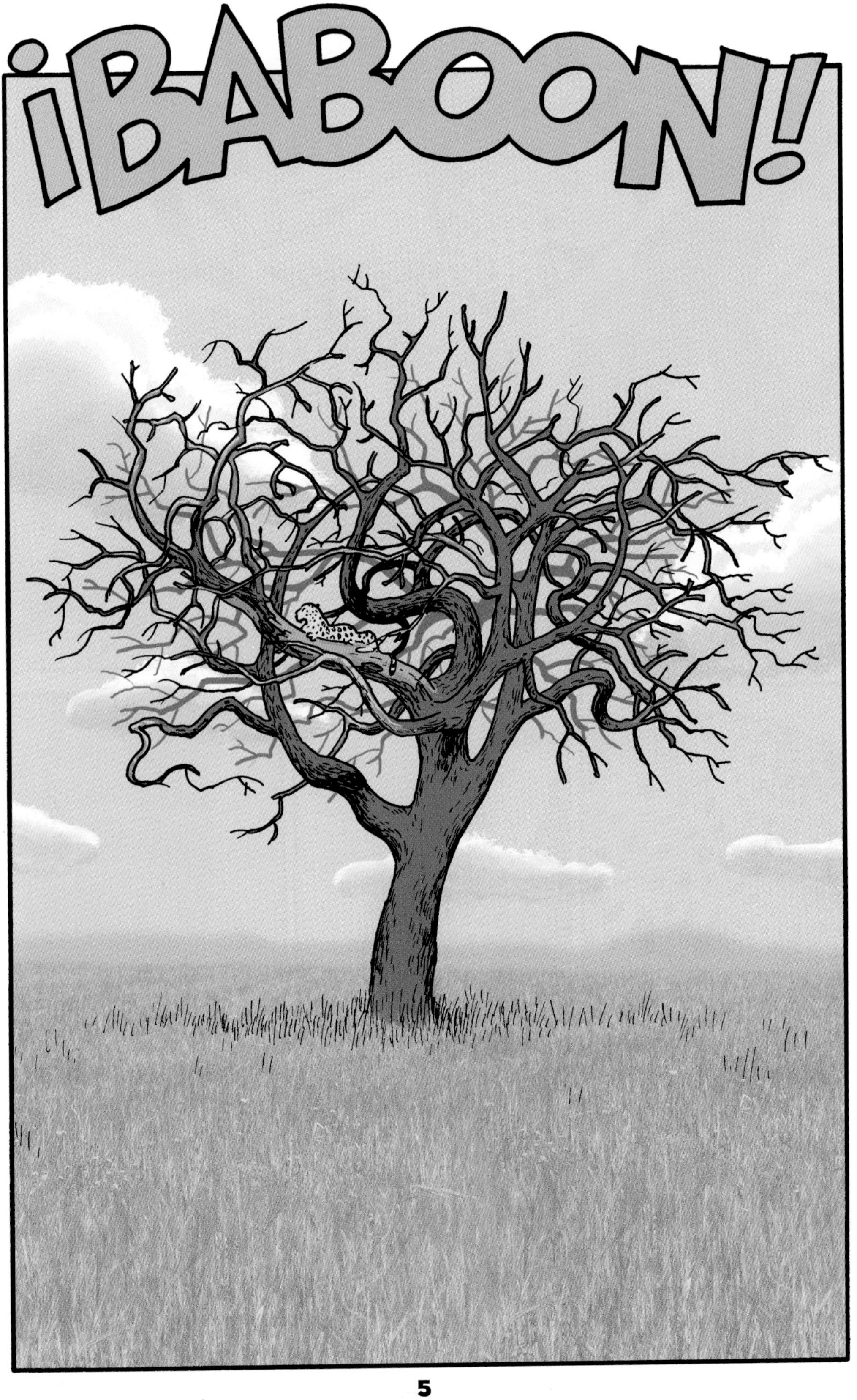
¡BABOON!

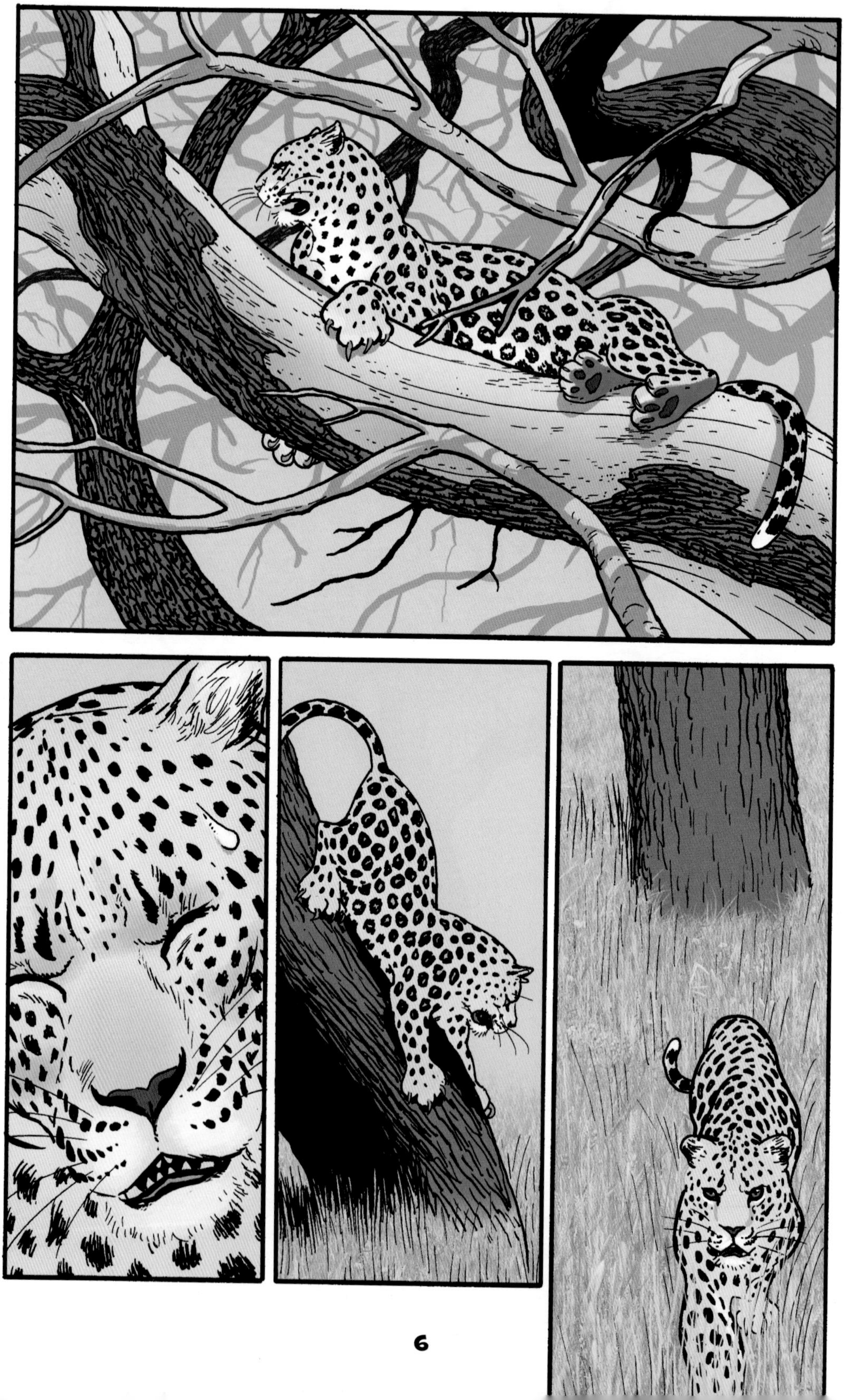

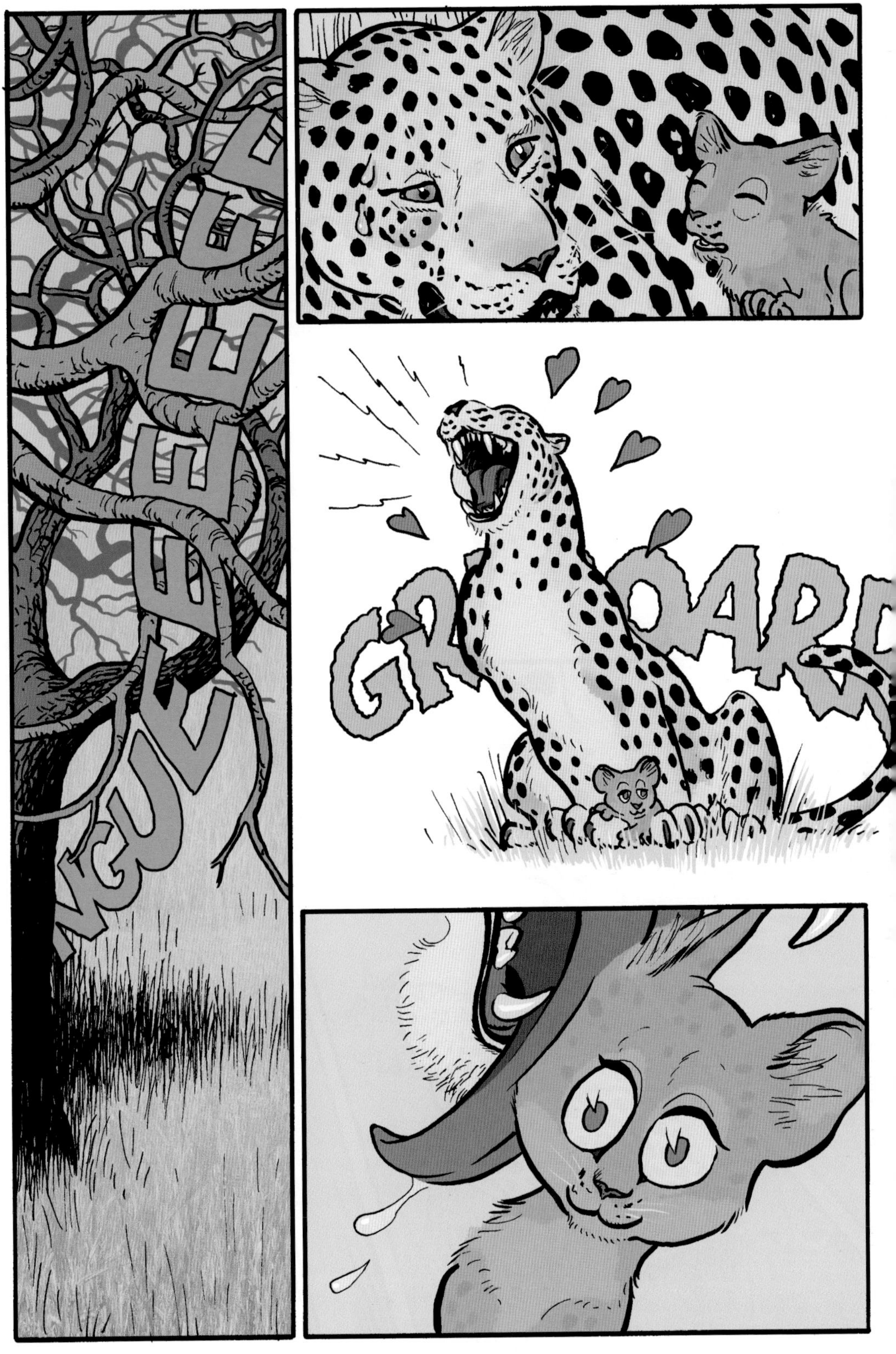
NGUEEEEEE
GROAR

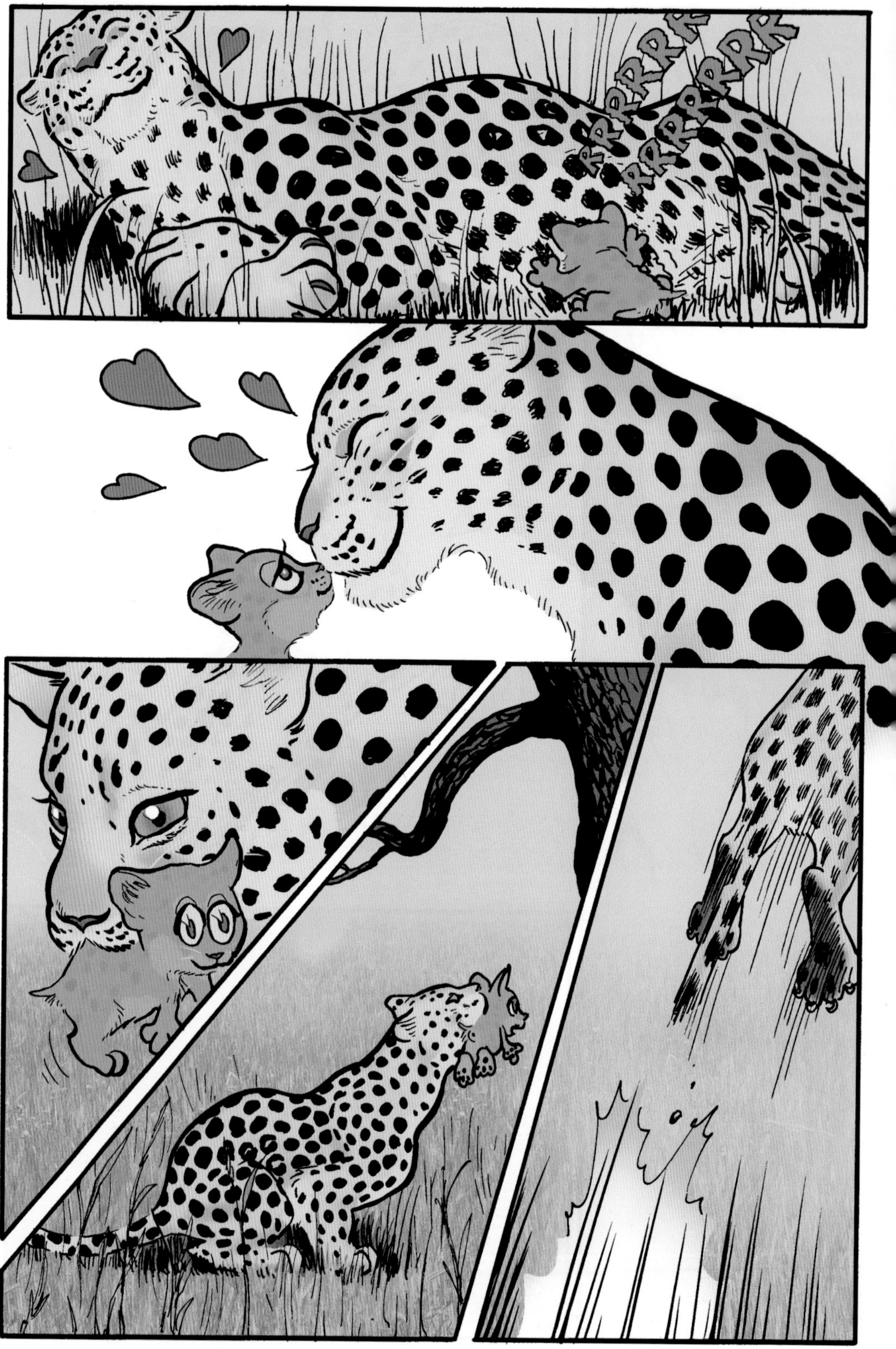
RRRRRR
RRRRRR

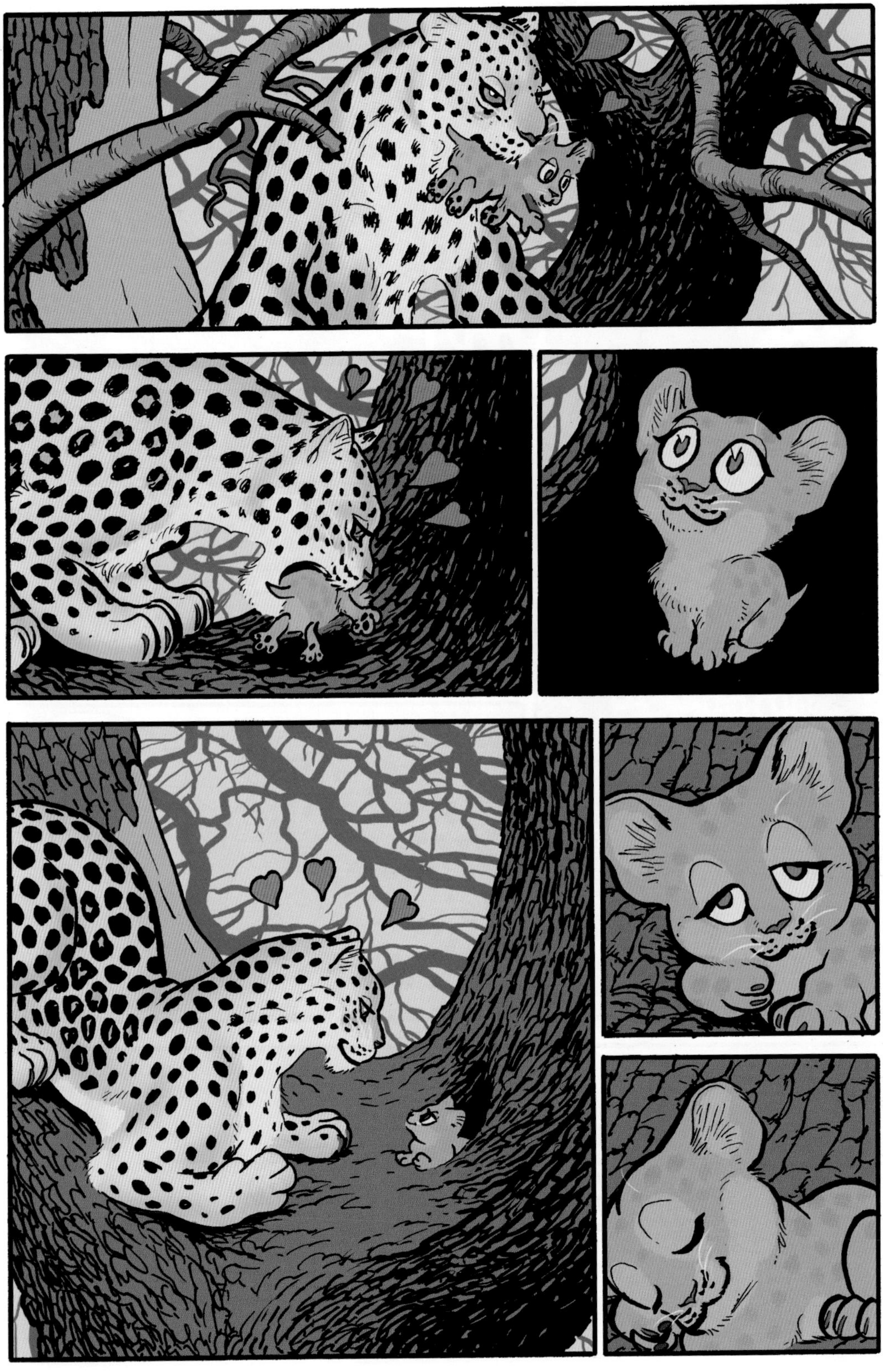

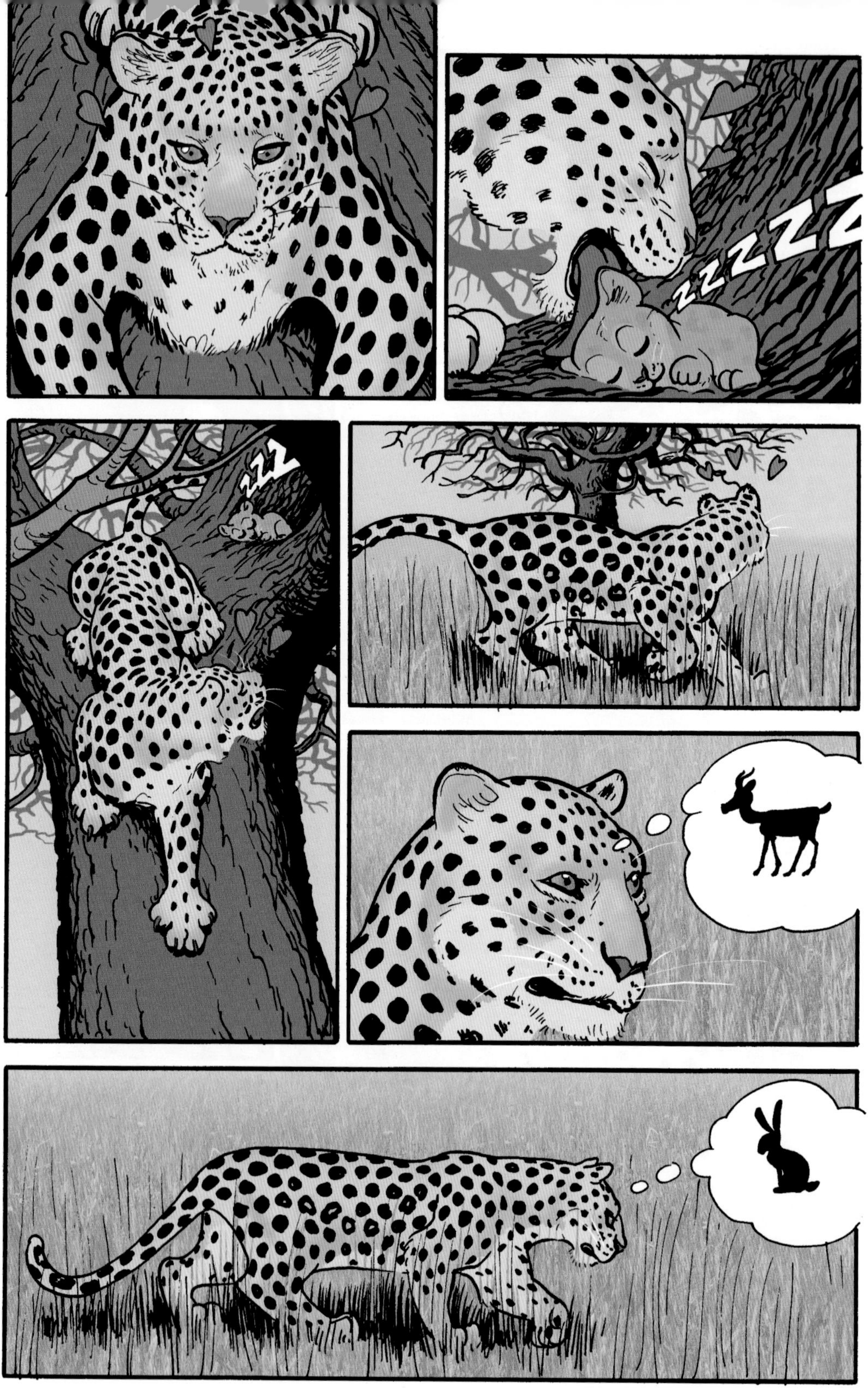
ZZZZZZ
ZZZ

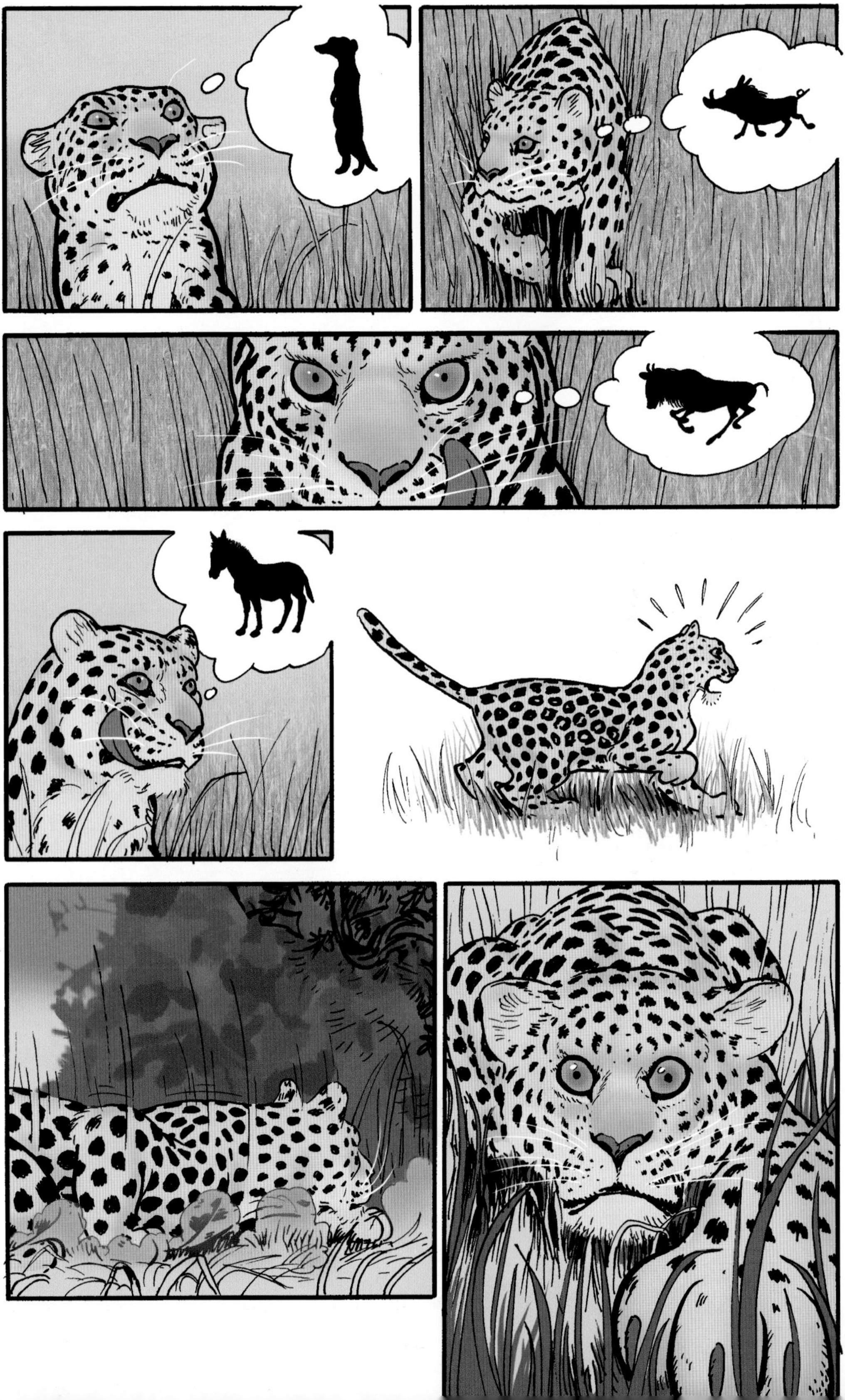

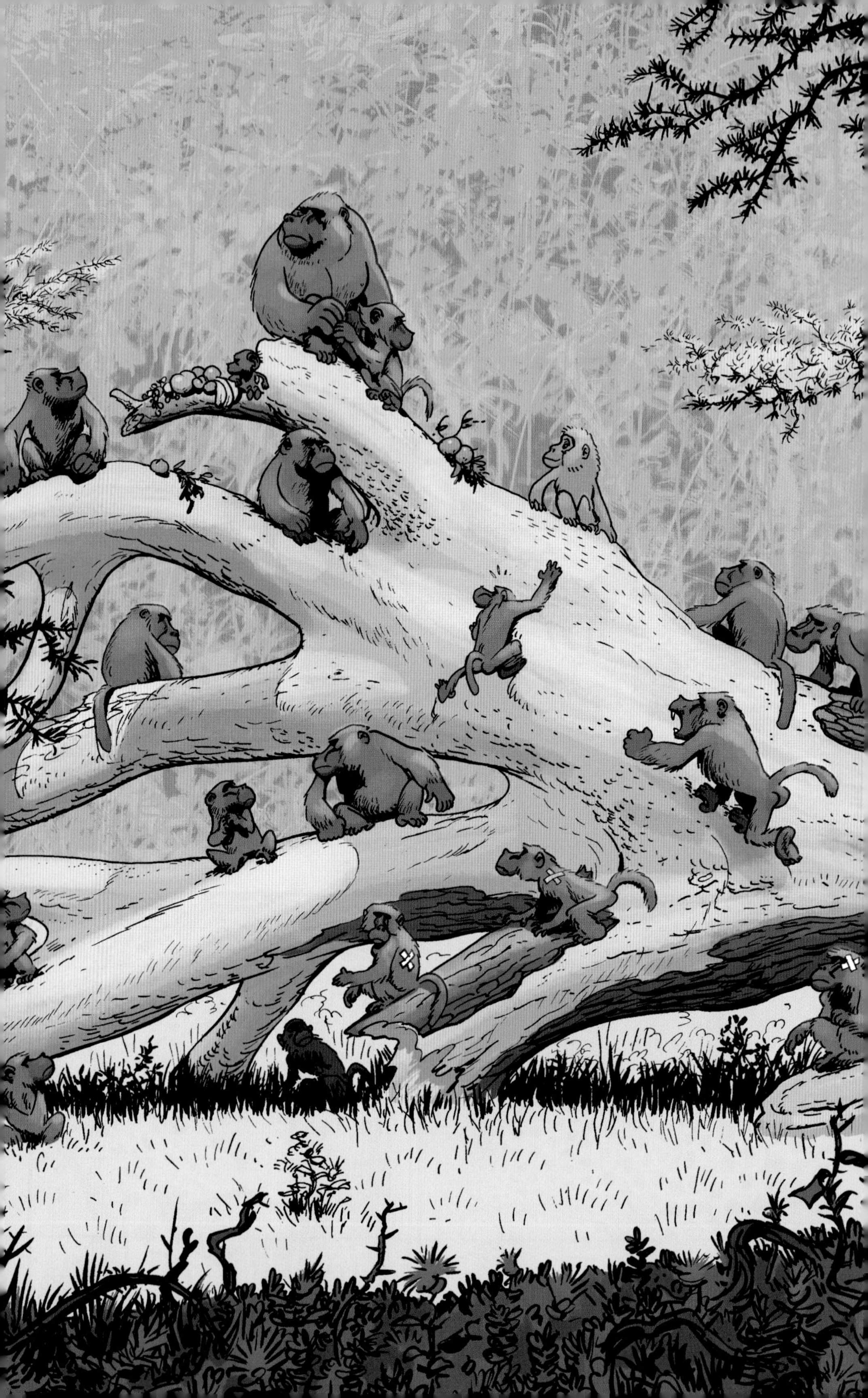

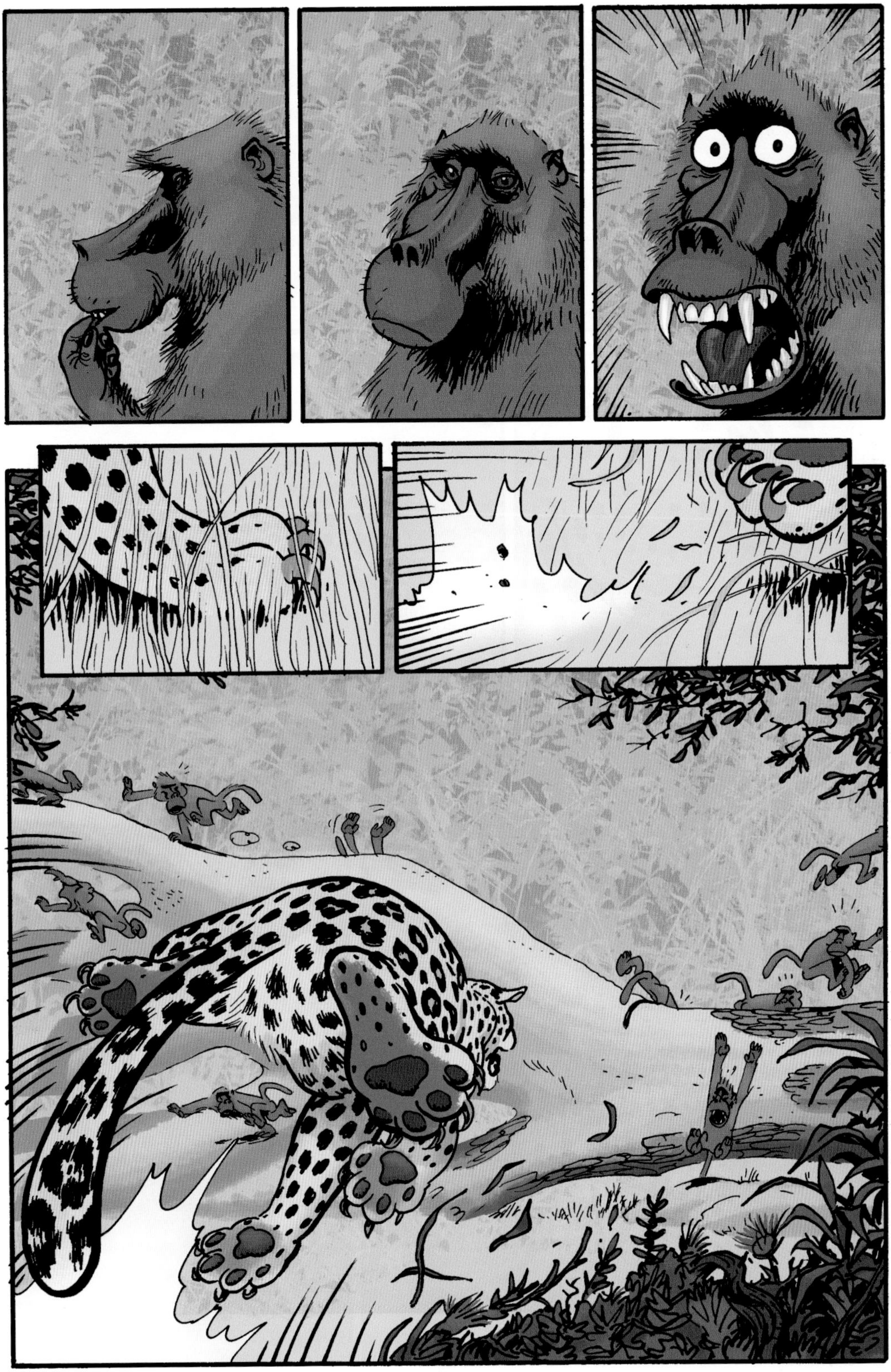

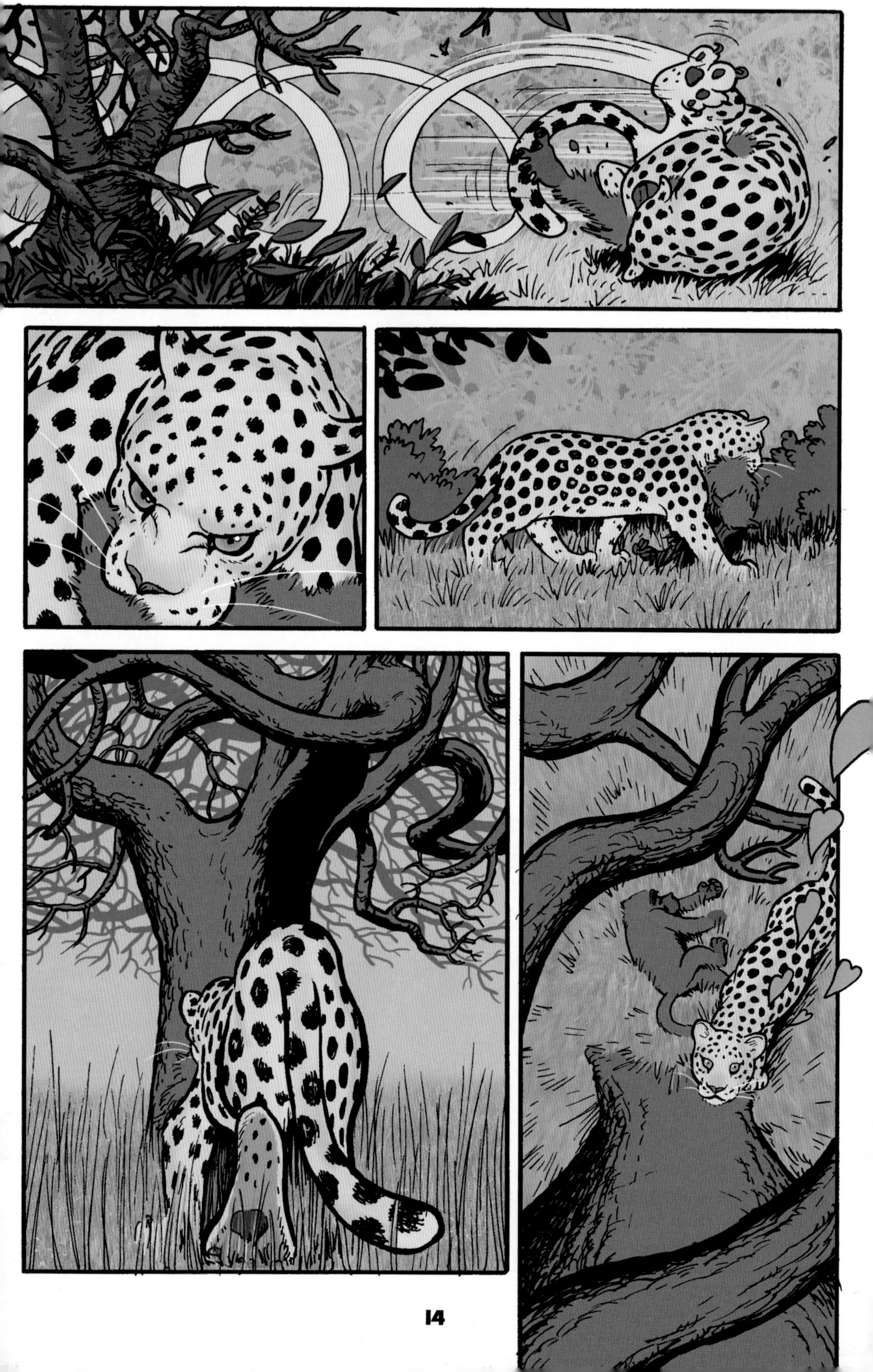

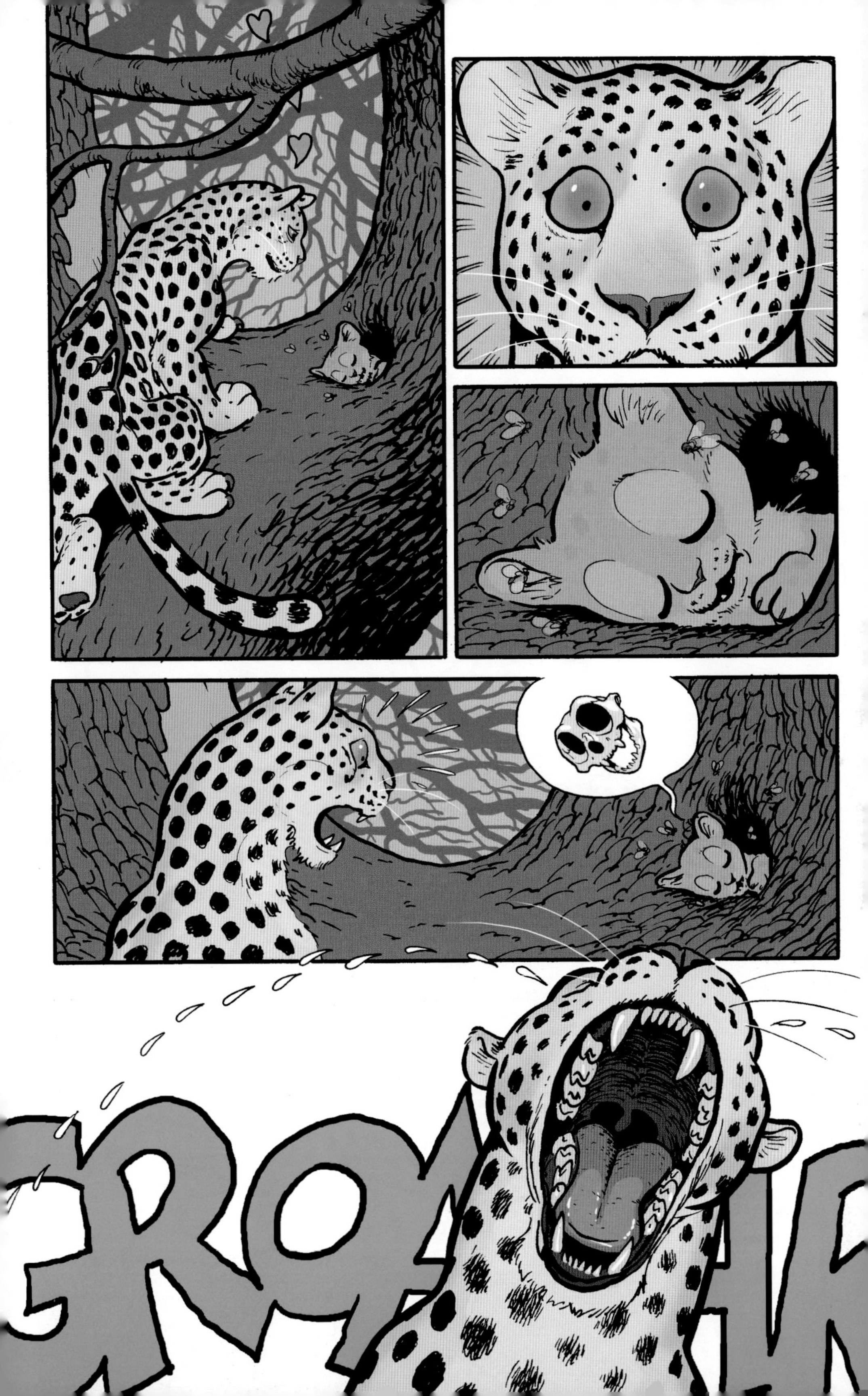

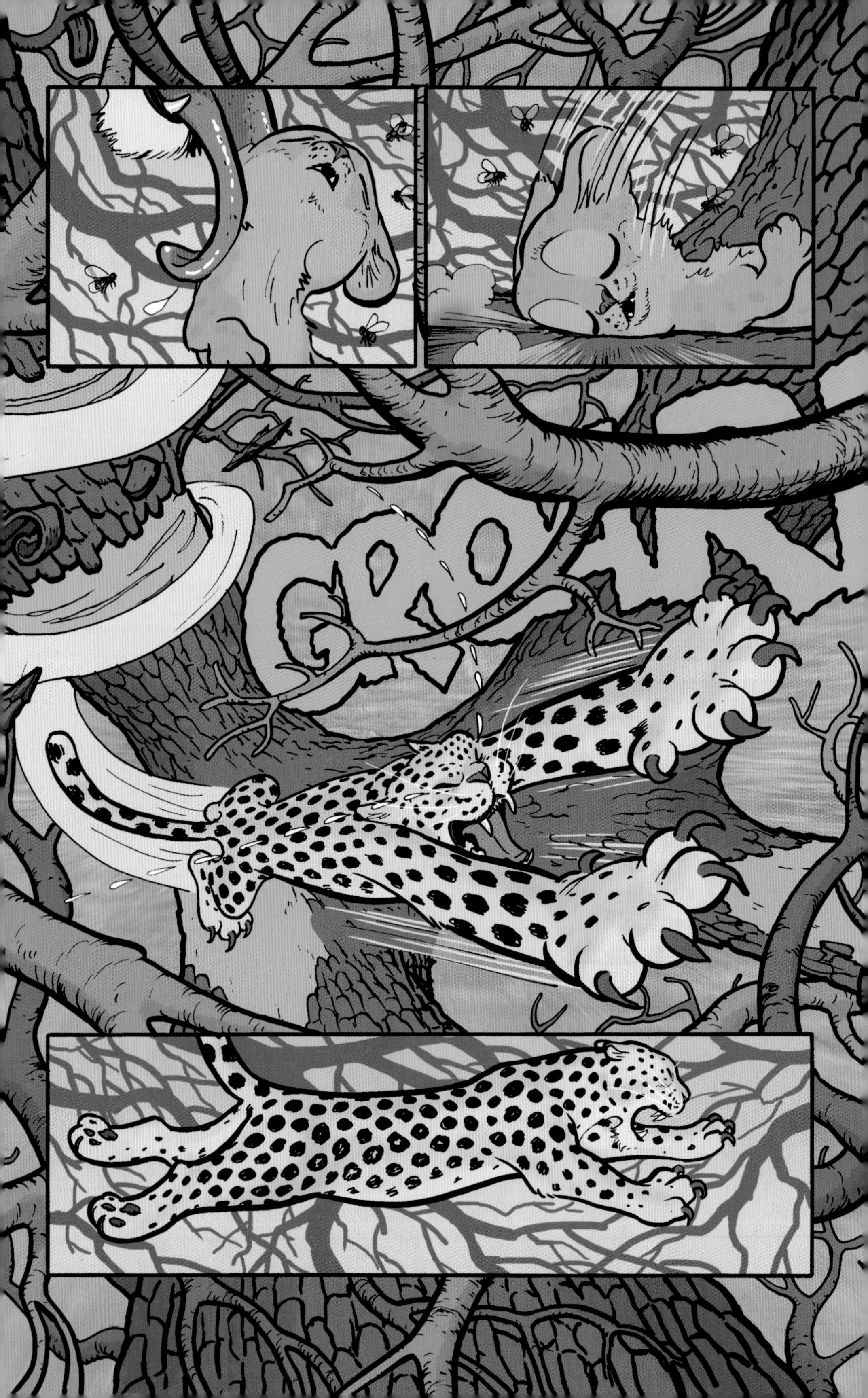

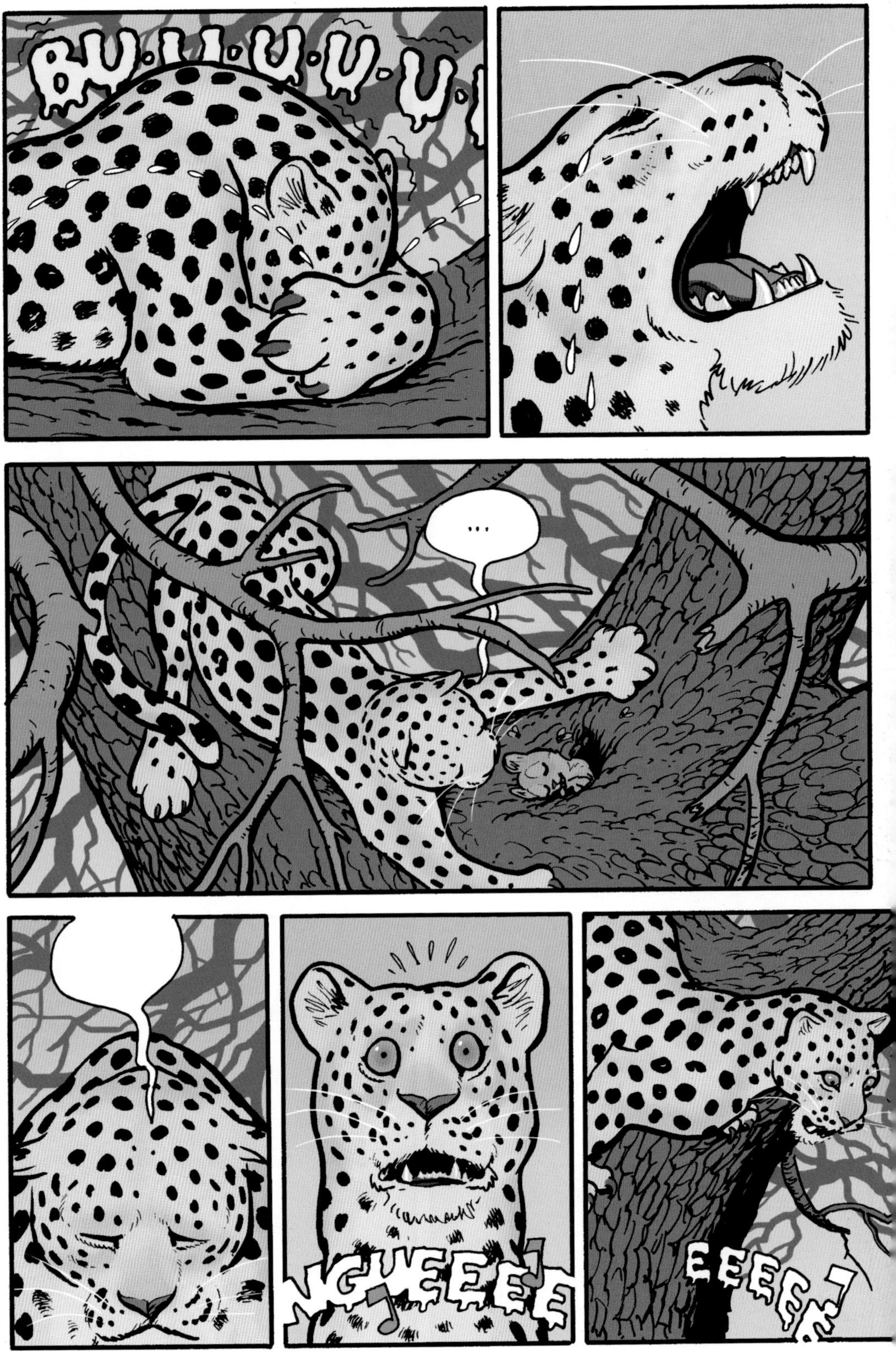
BU·U·U·U·U·U·
...
NGEEEE
EEEEE

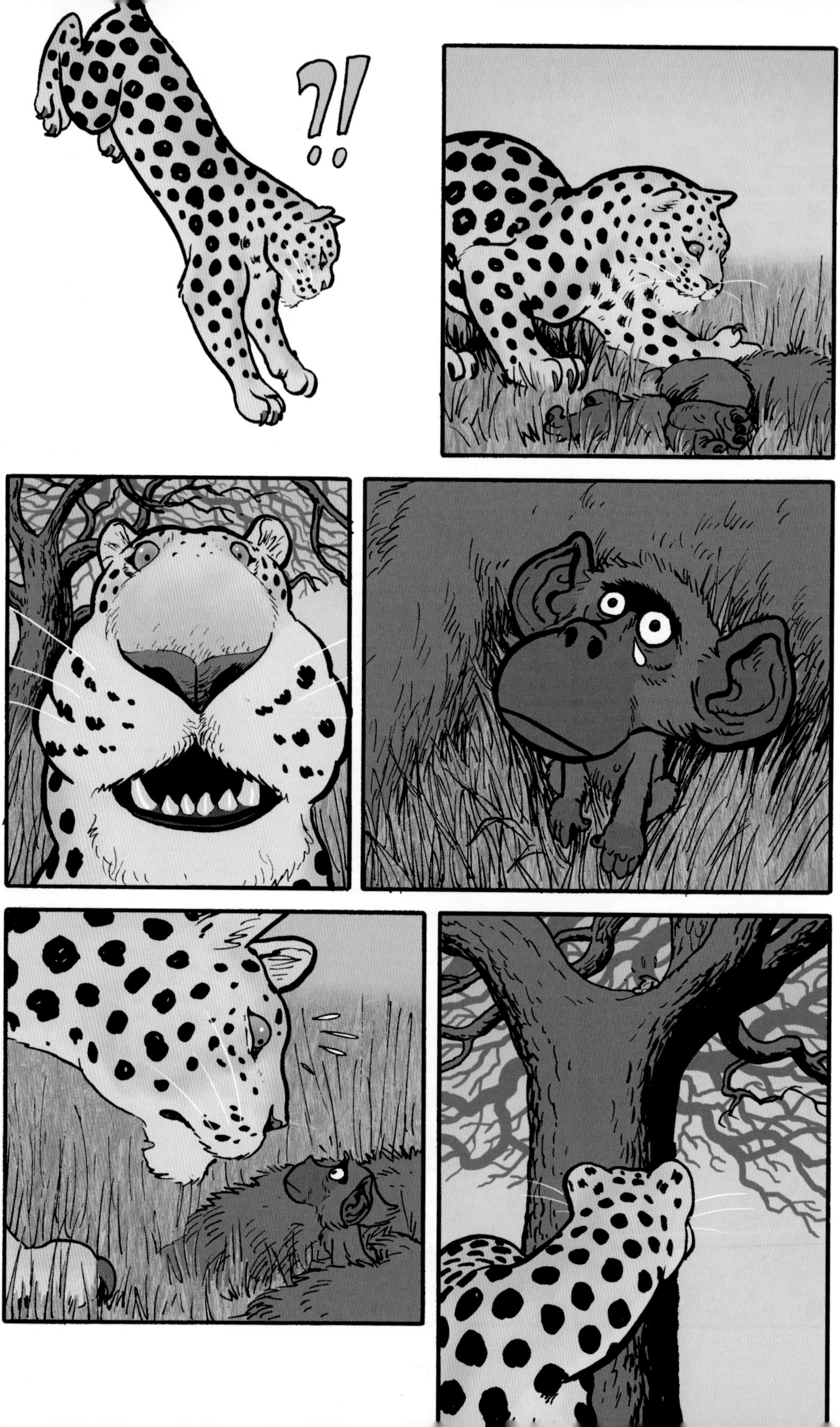
?!

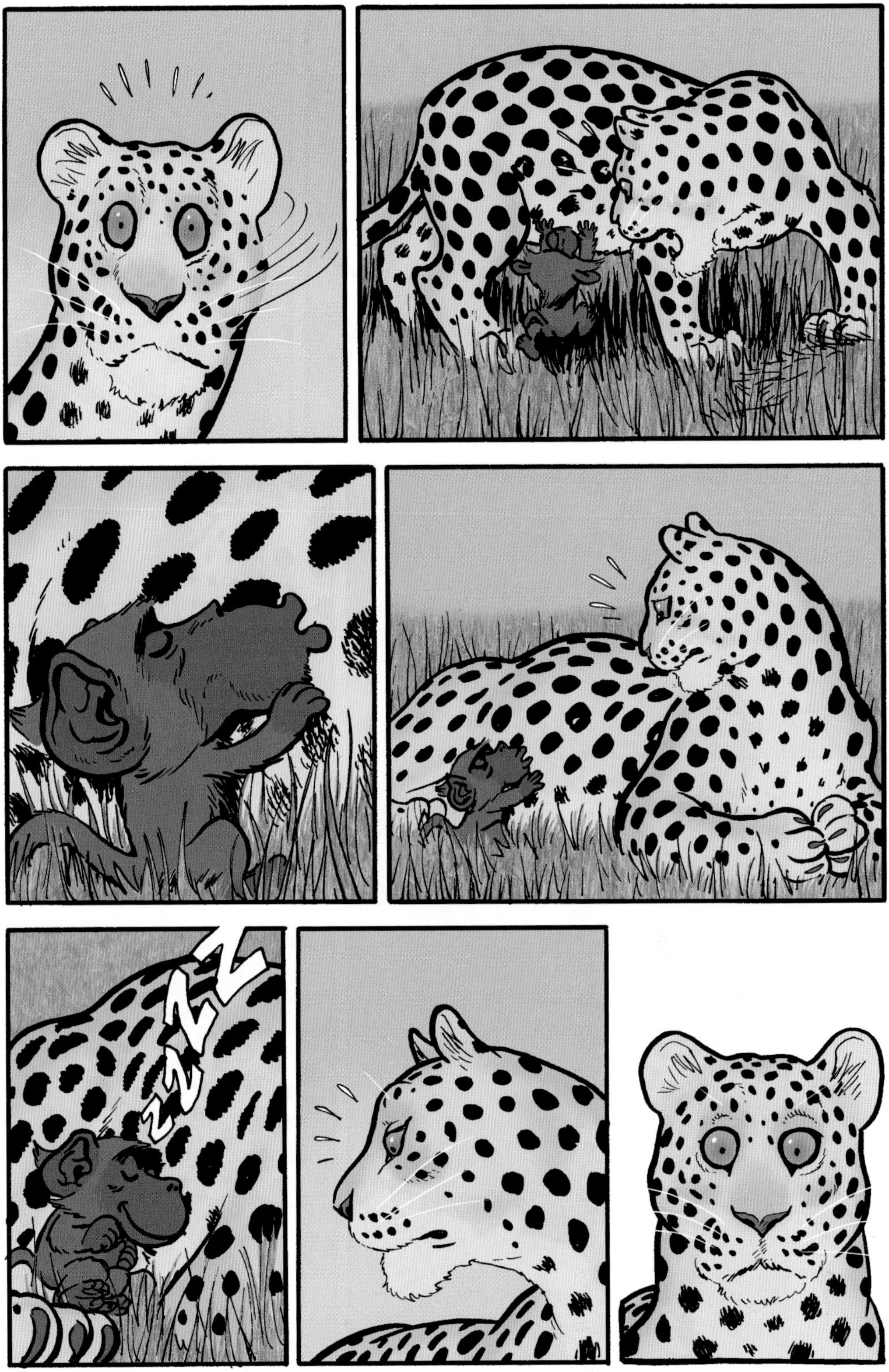
ZZZZ

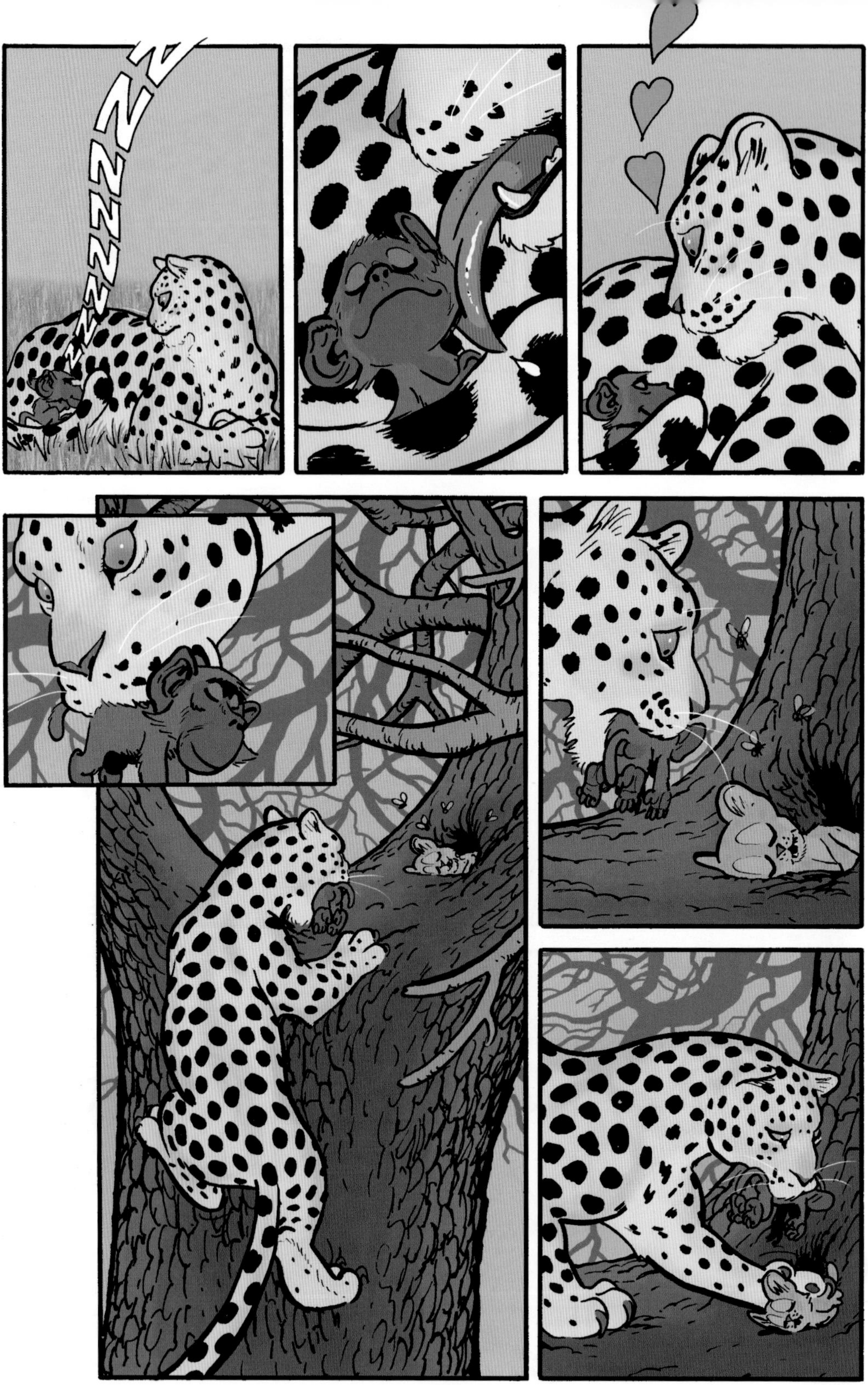
ZZZZZZZZZ

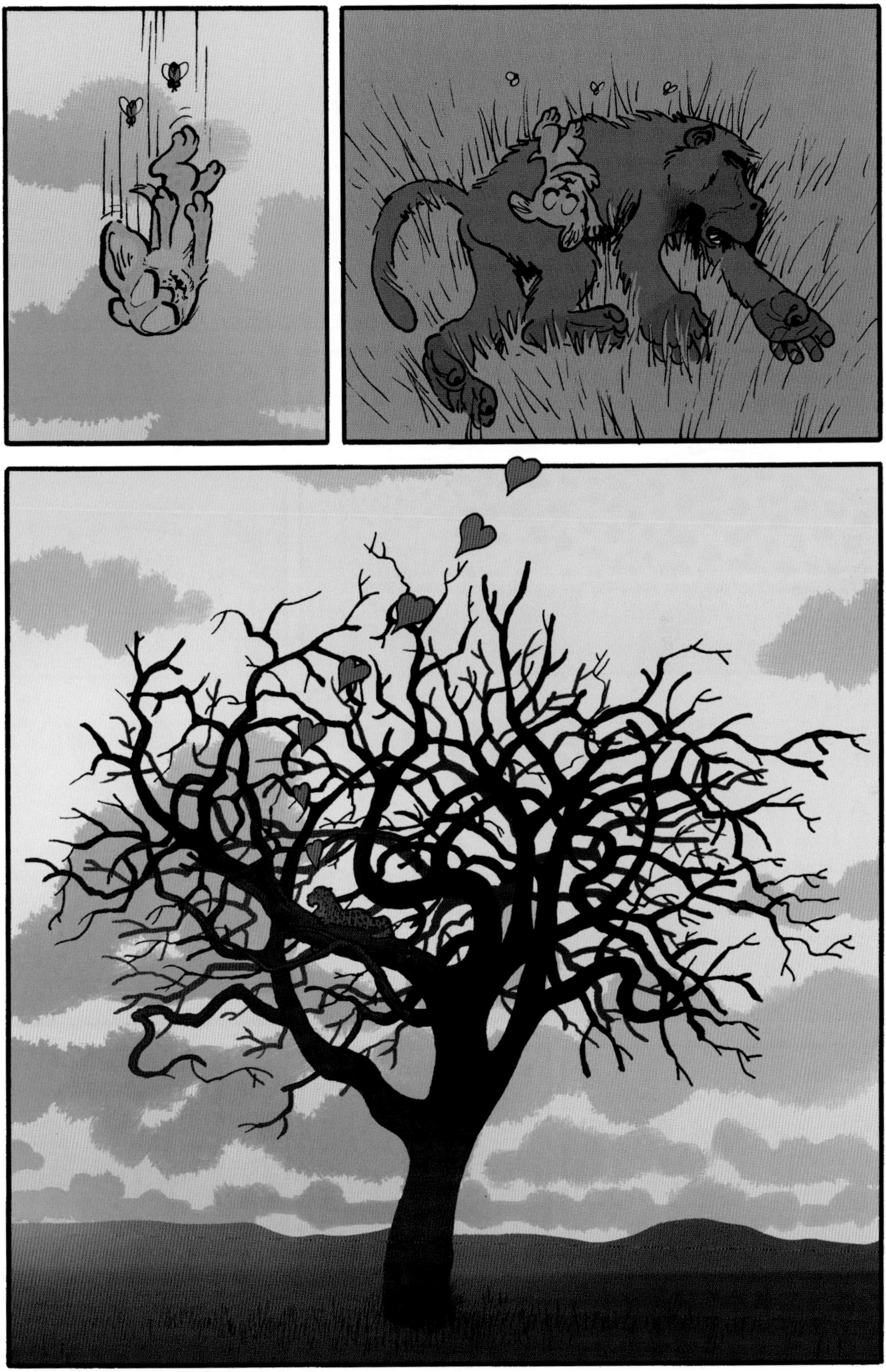

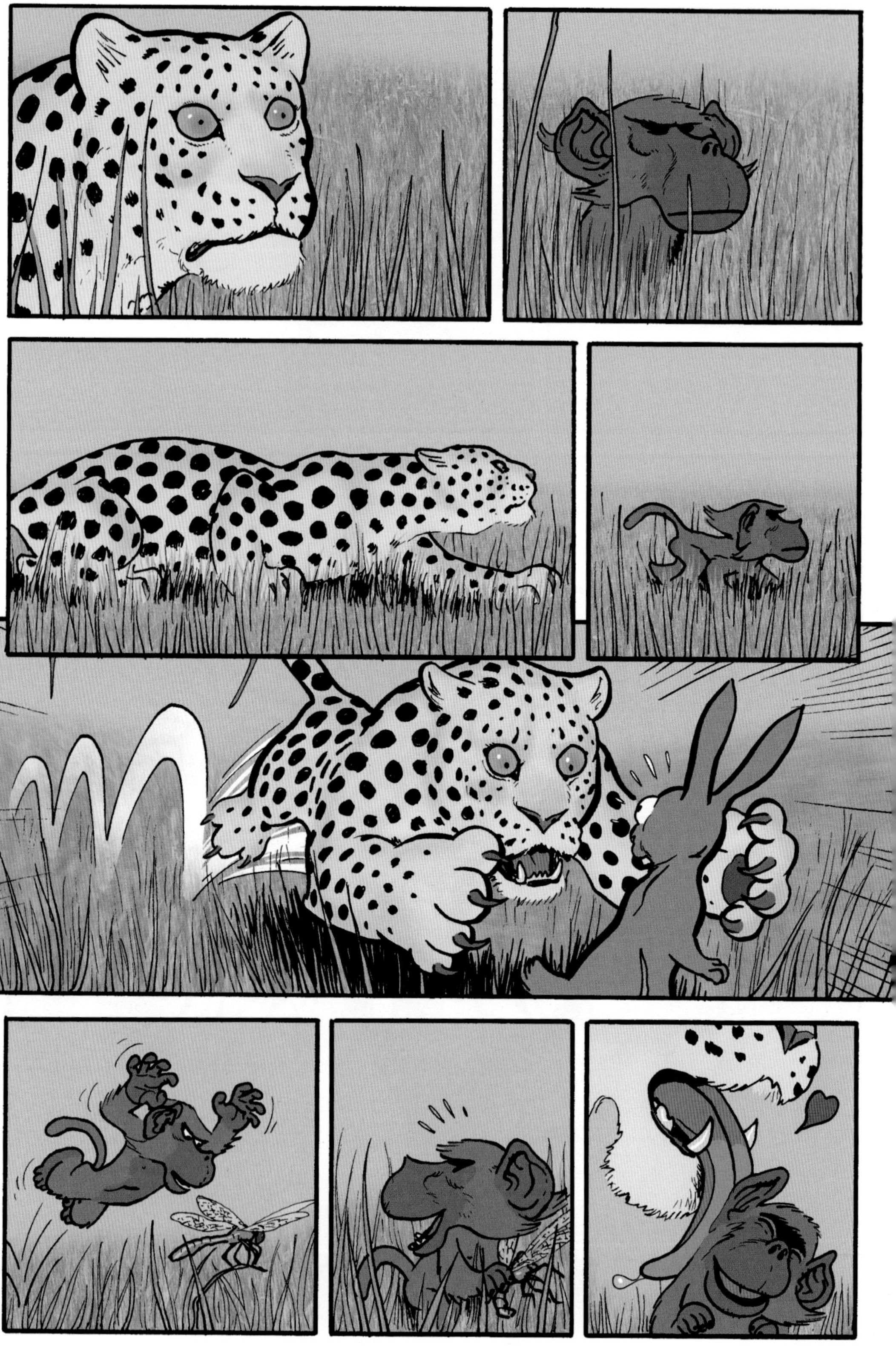

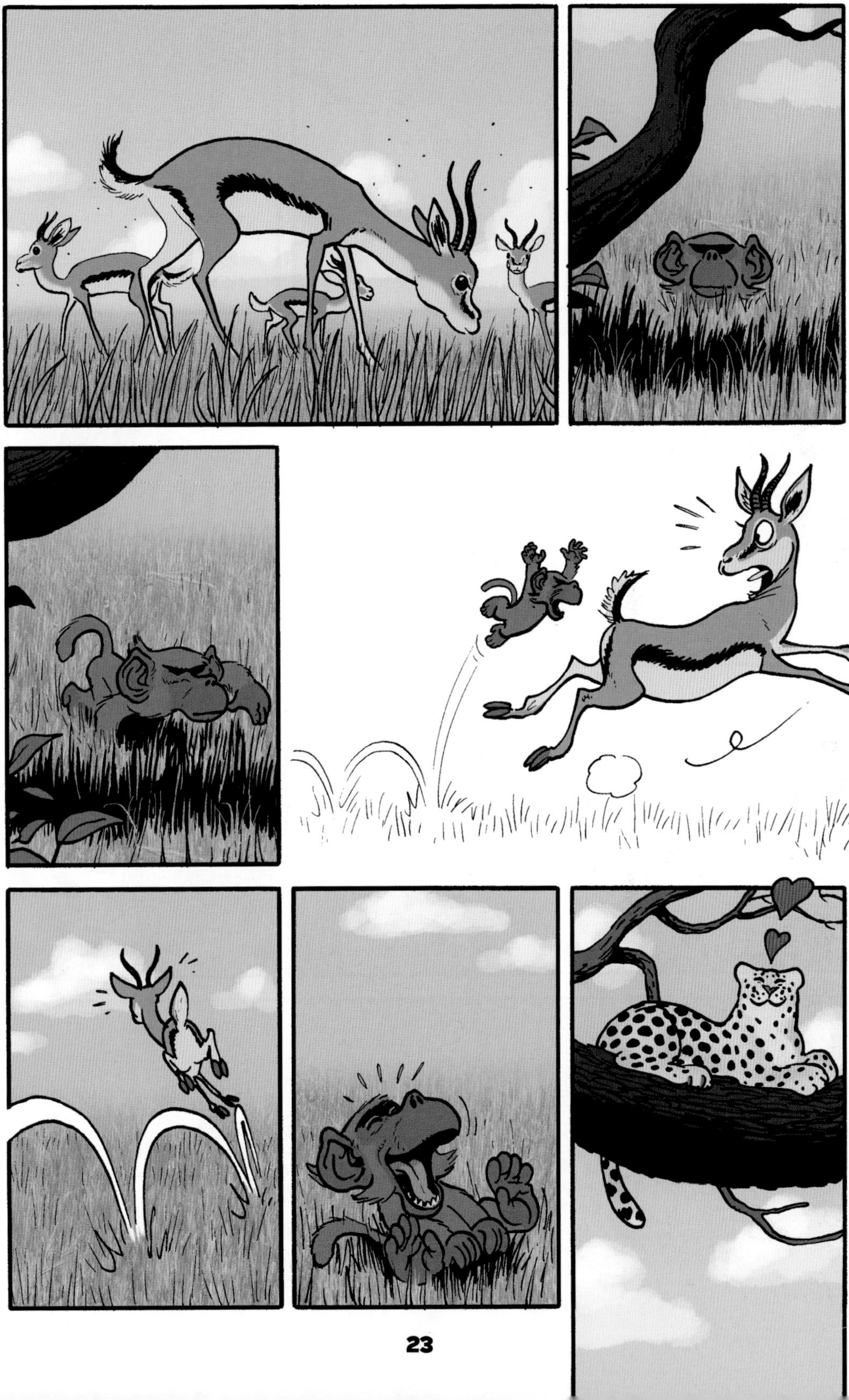

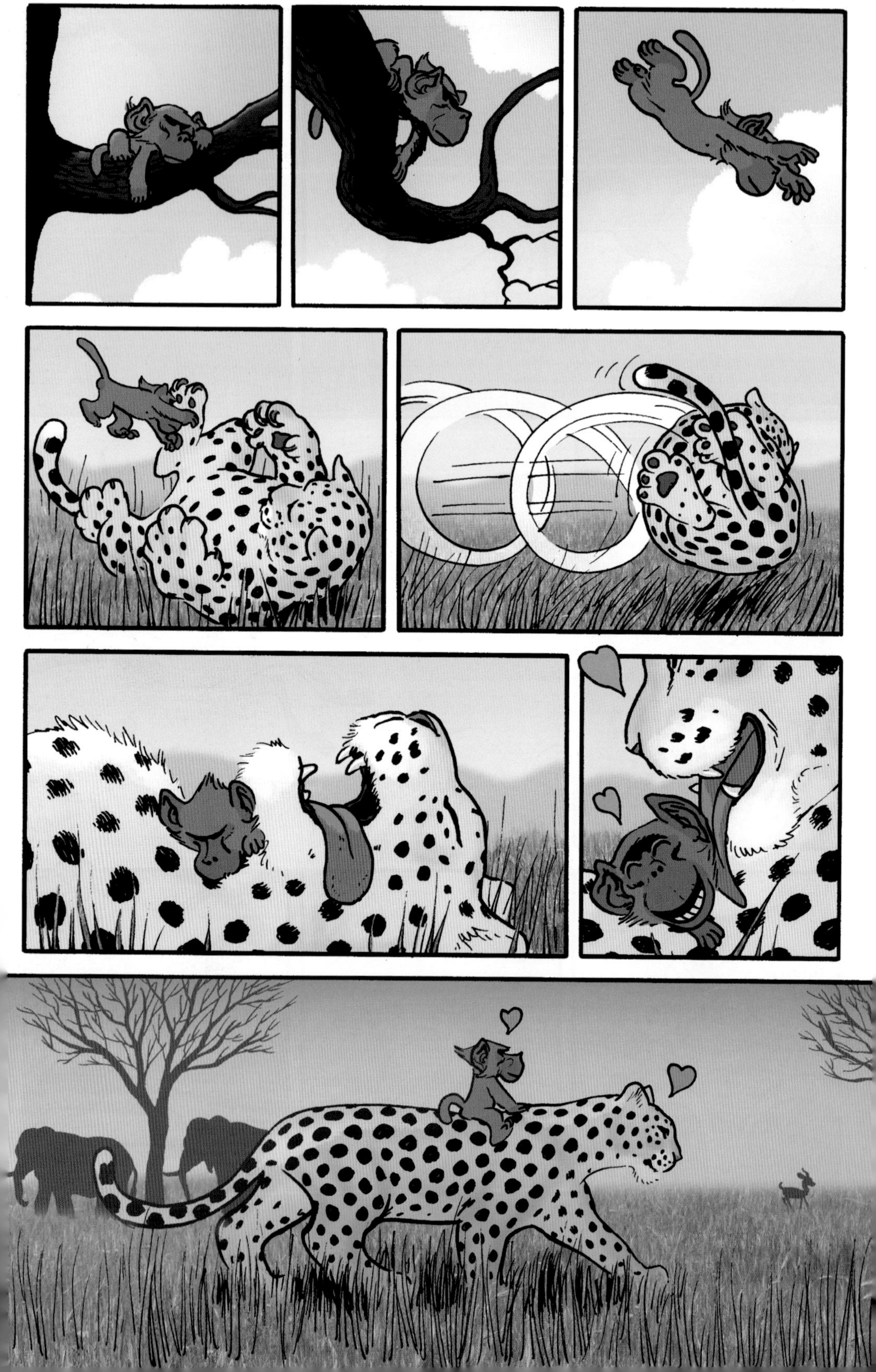

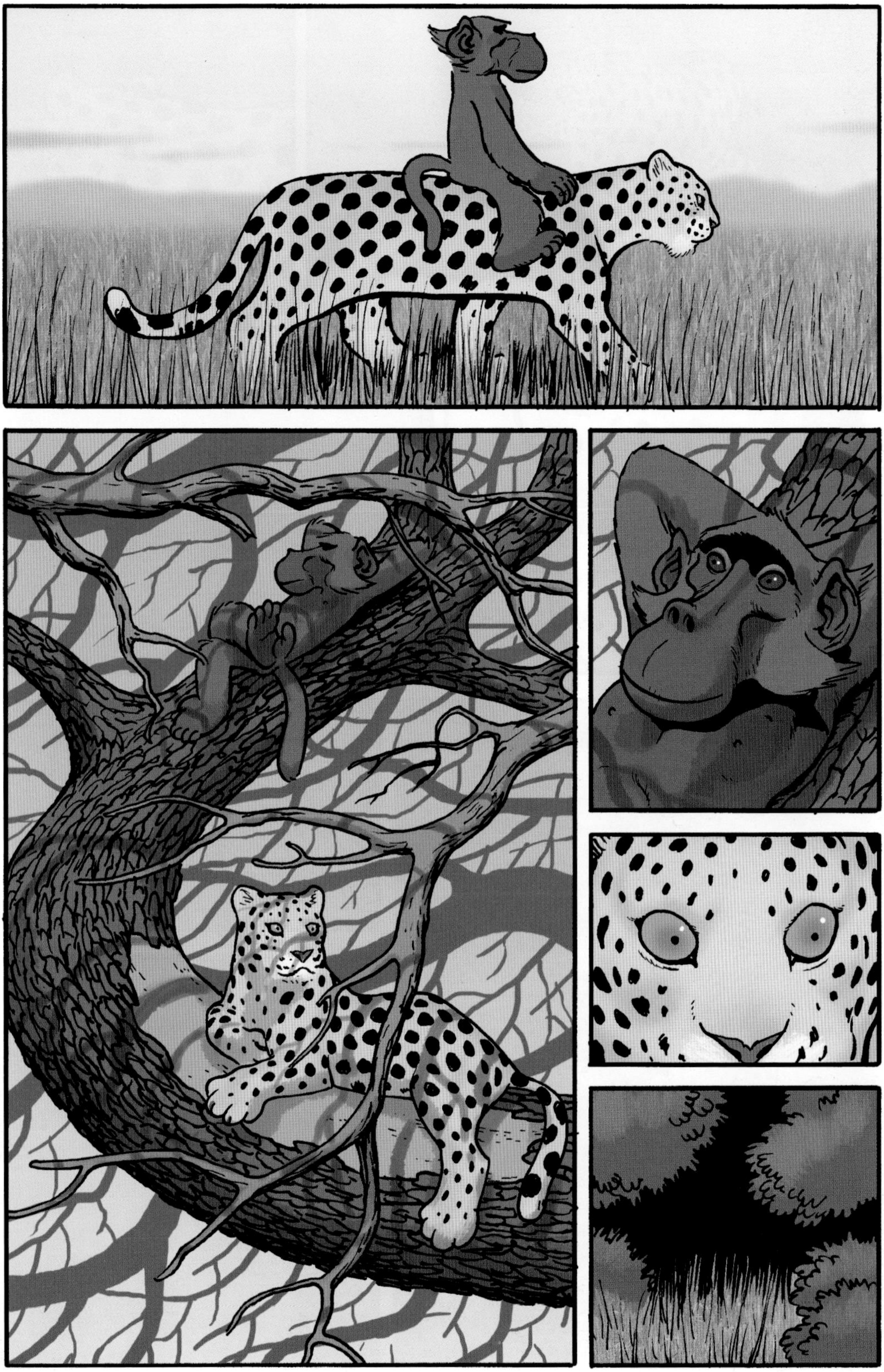

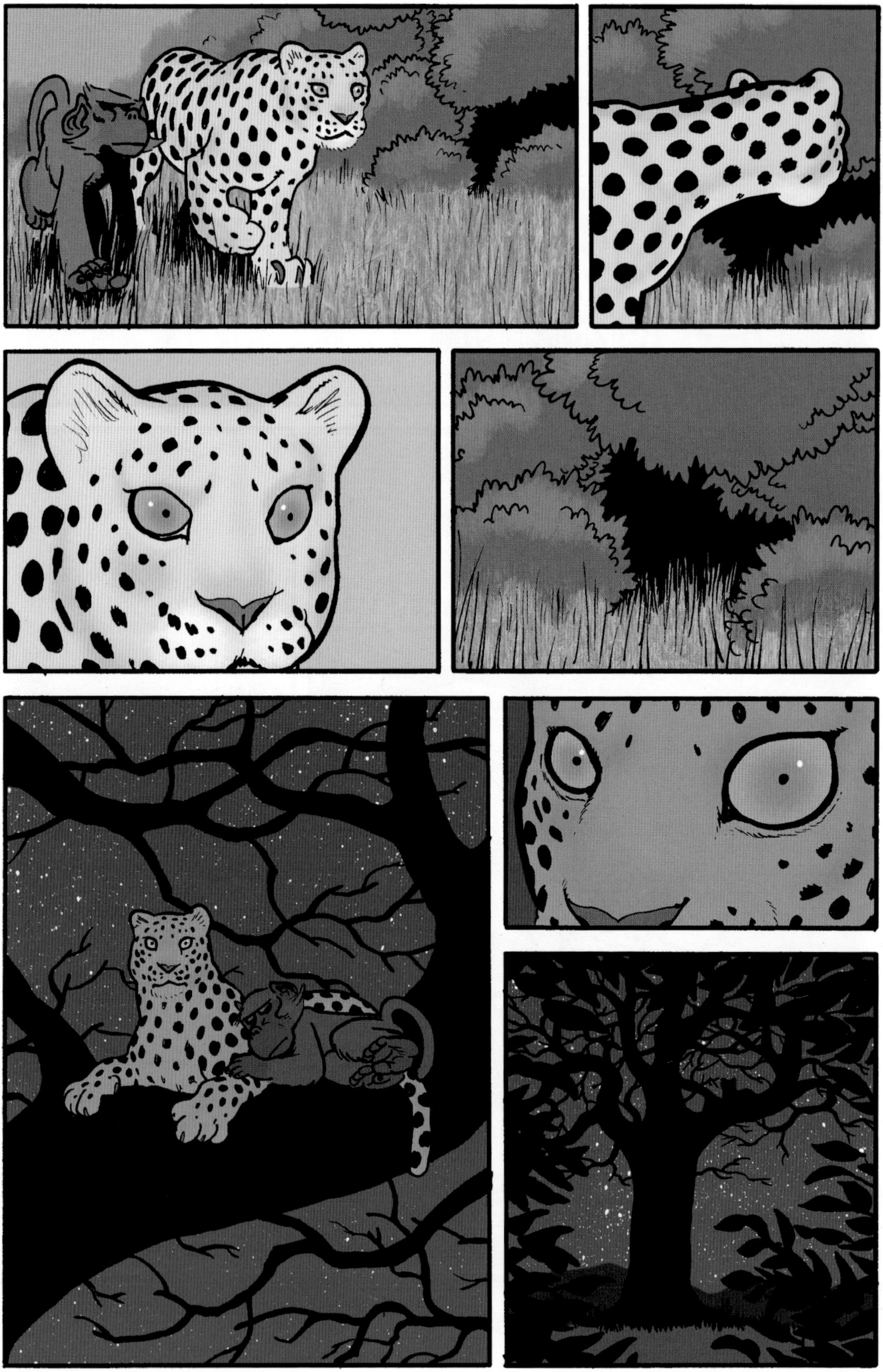

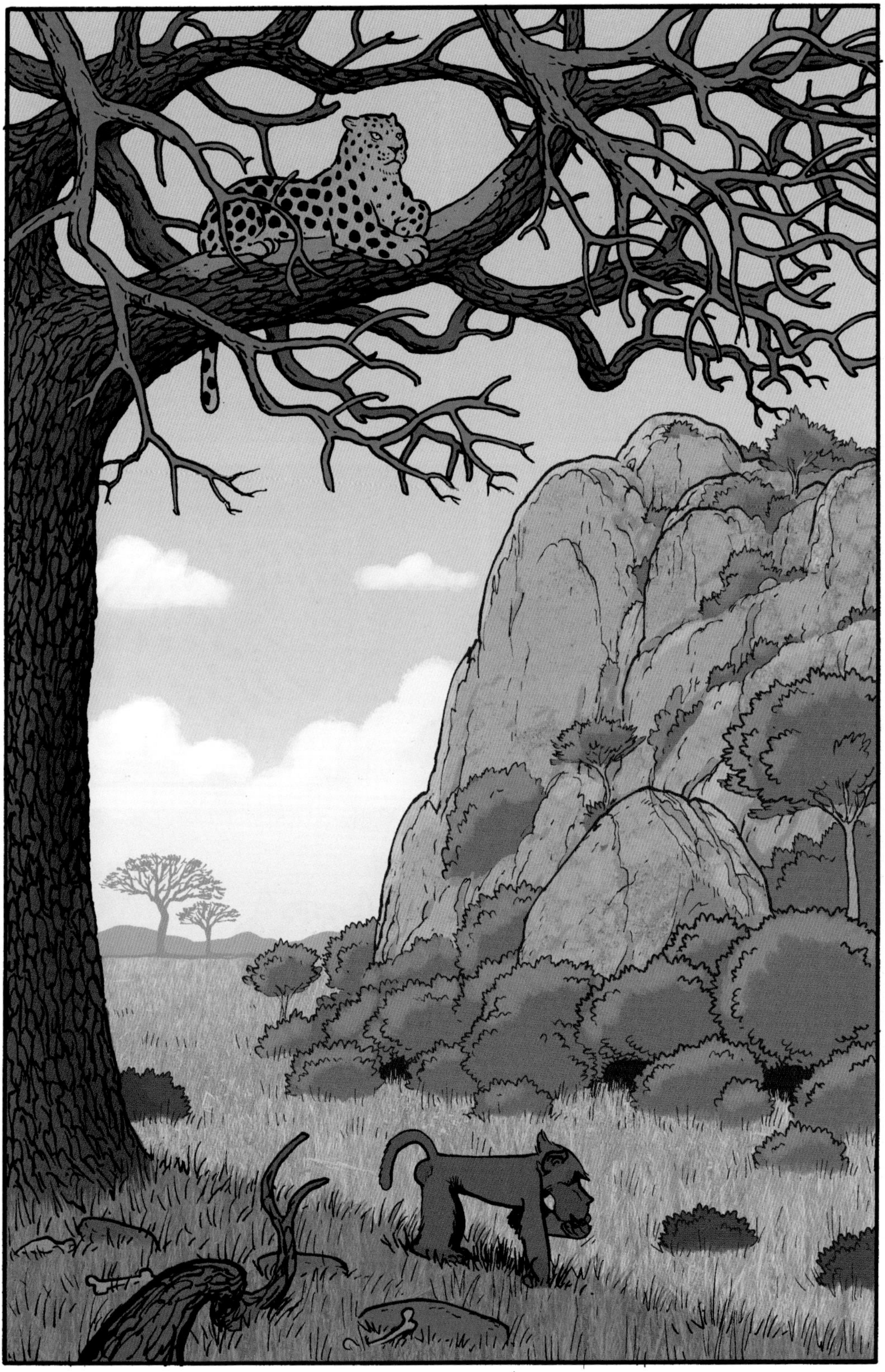

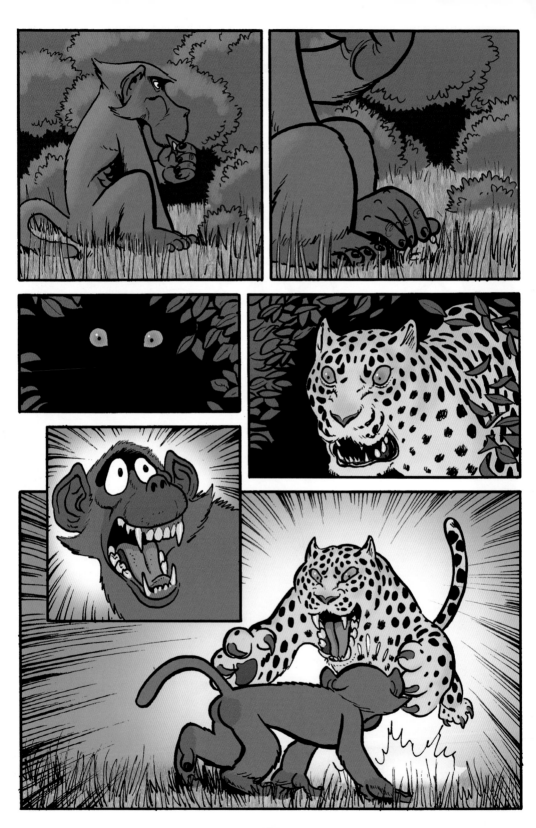

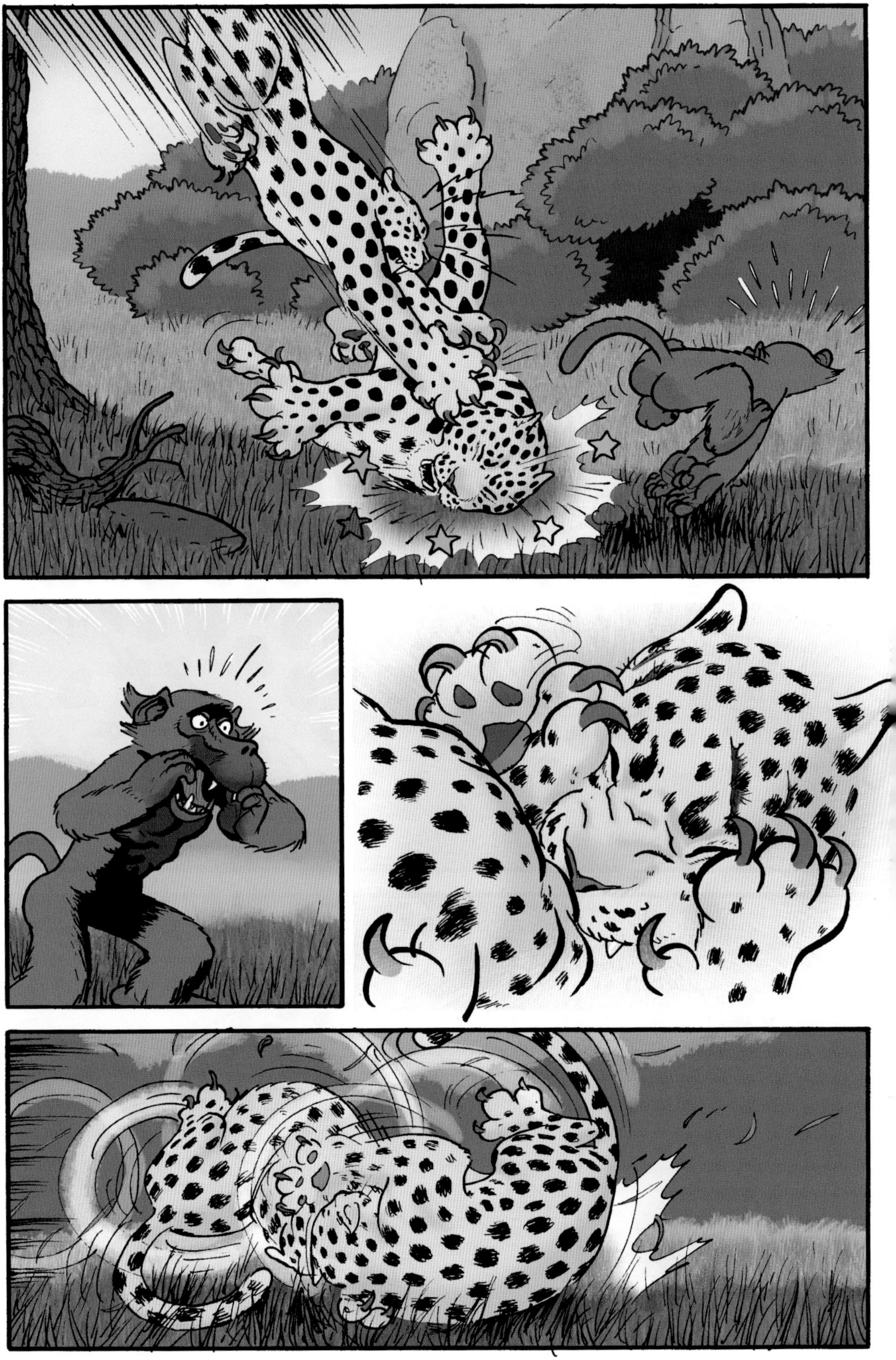

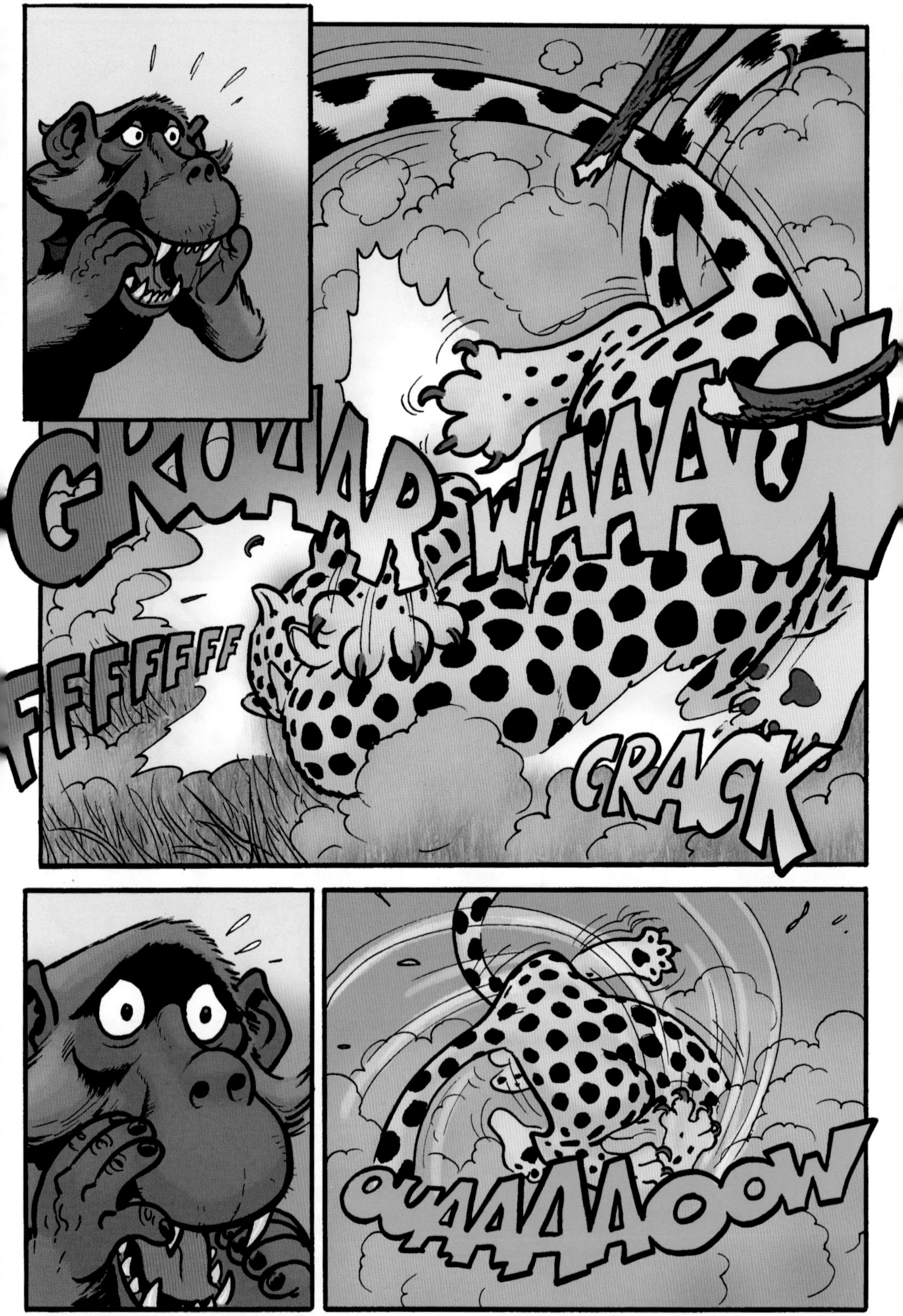
CRACK

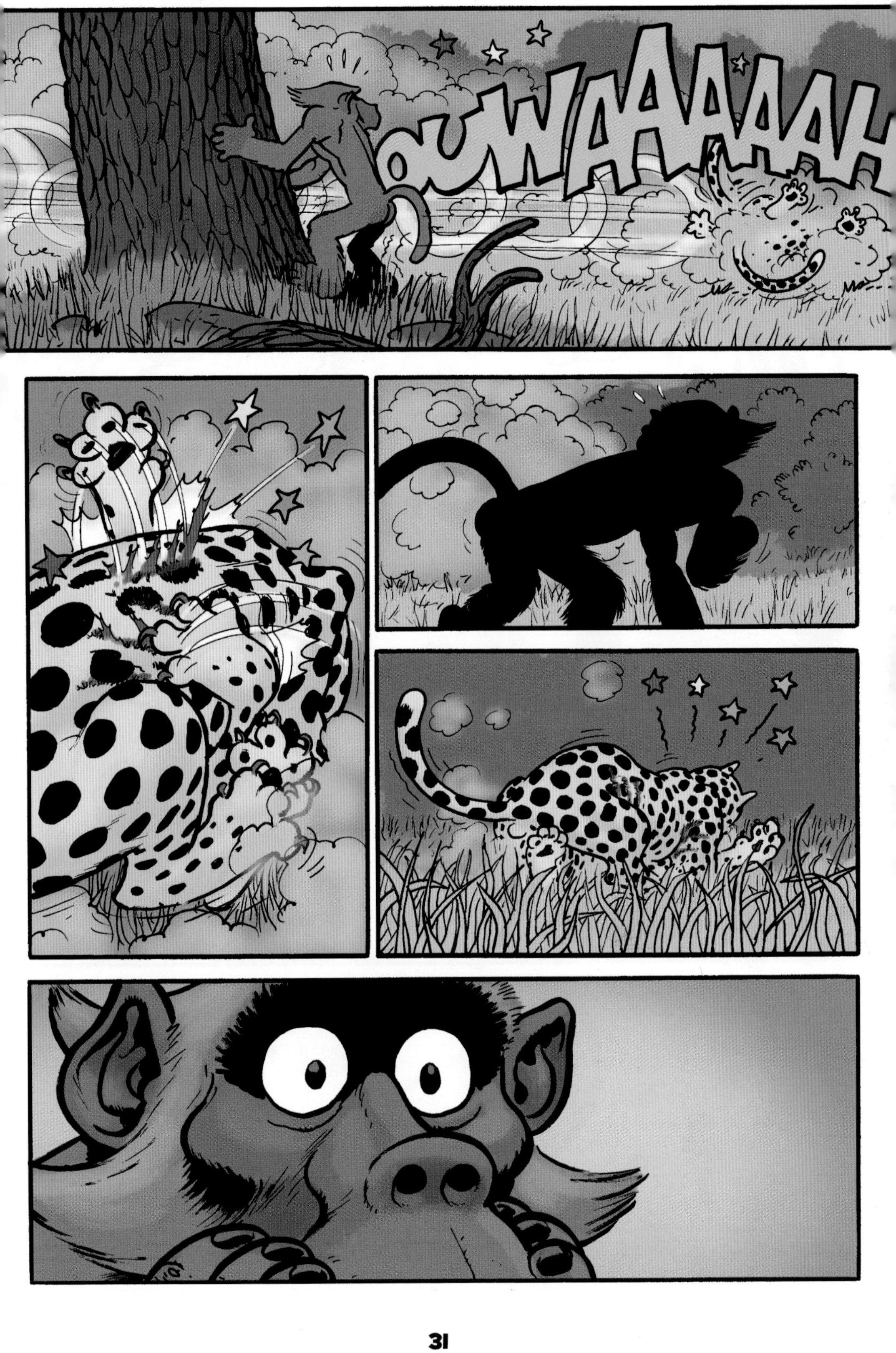
OUWAAAAAH

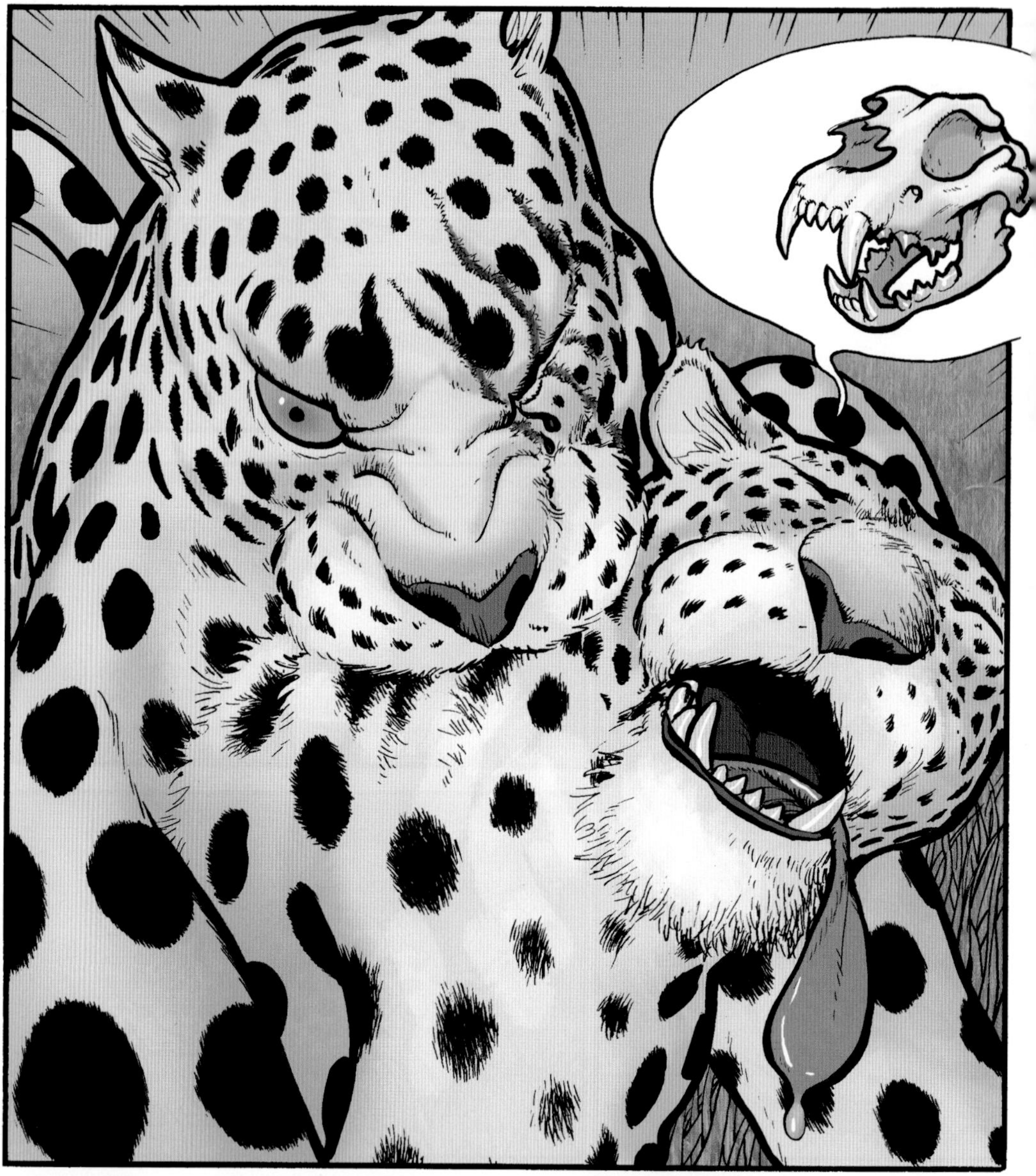

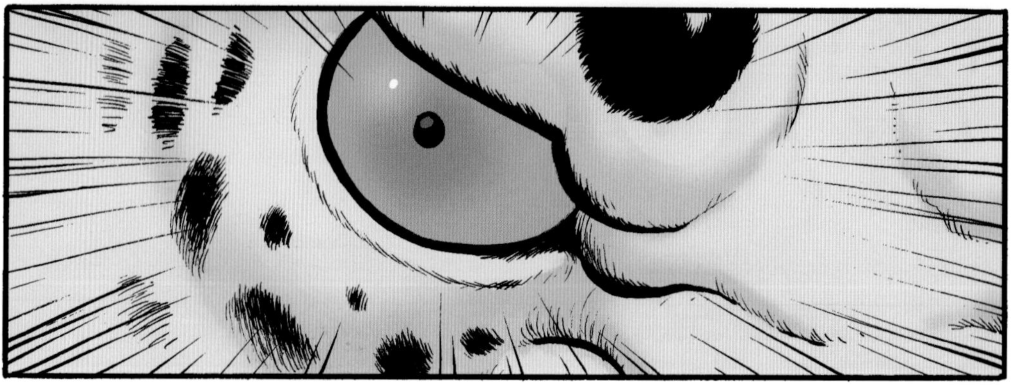

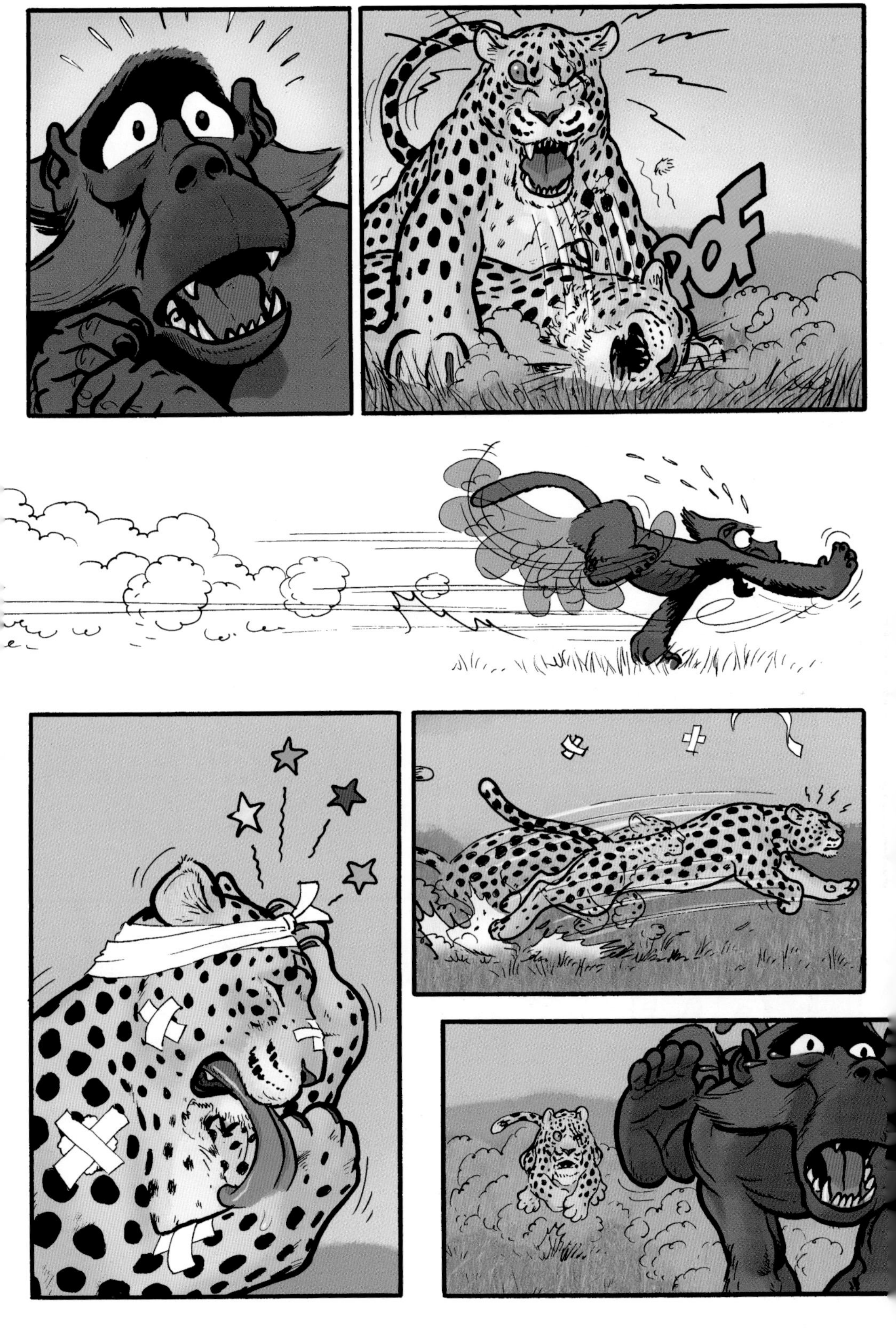
POF

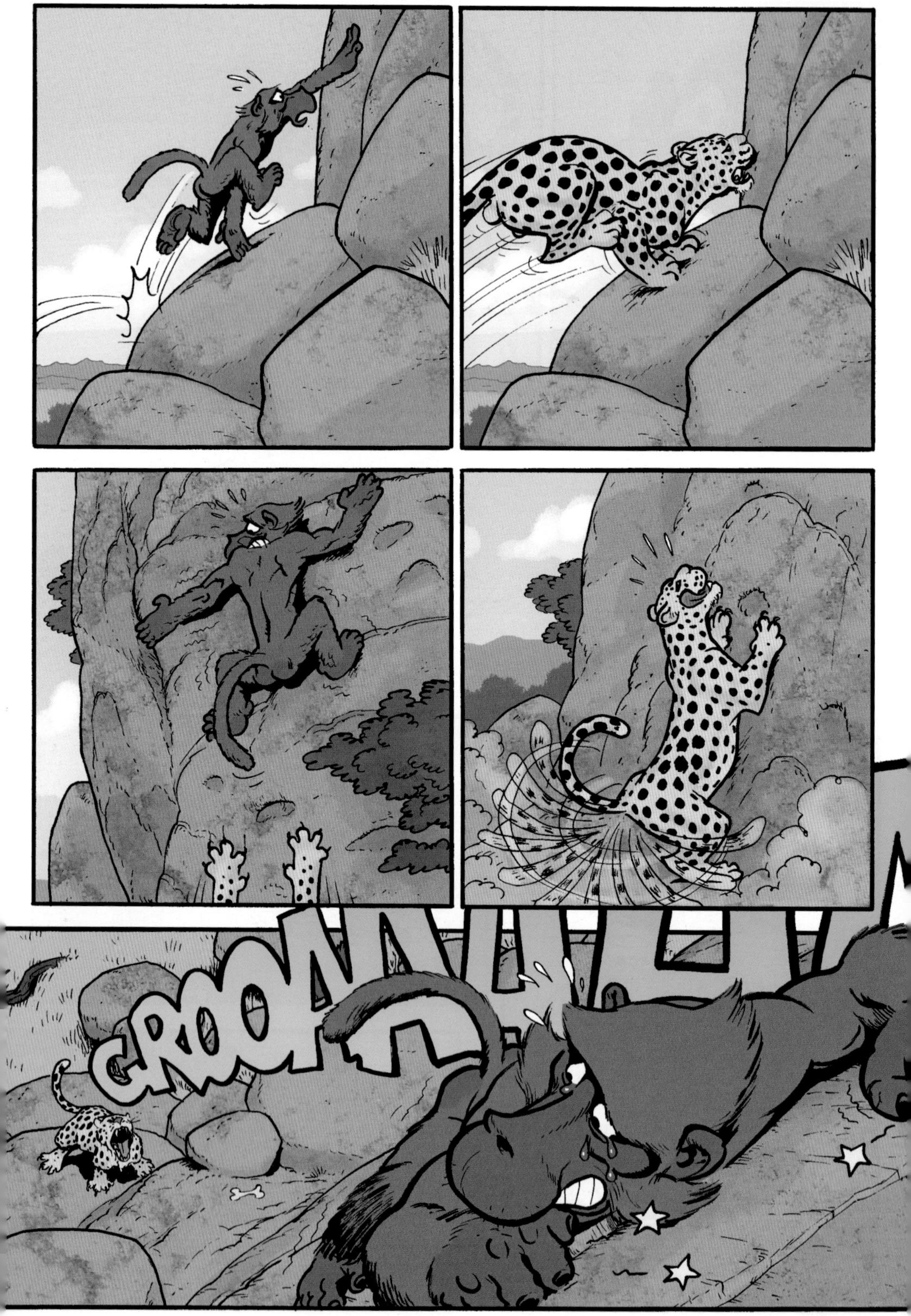
GROO

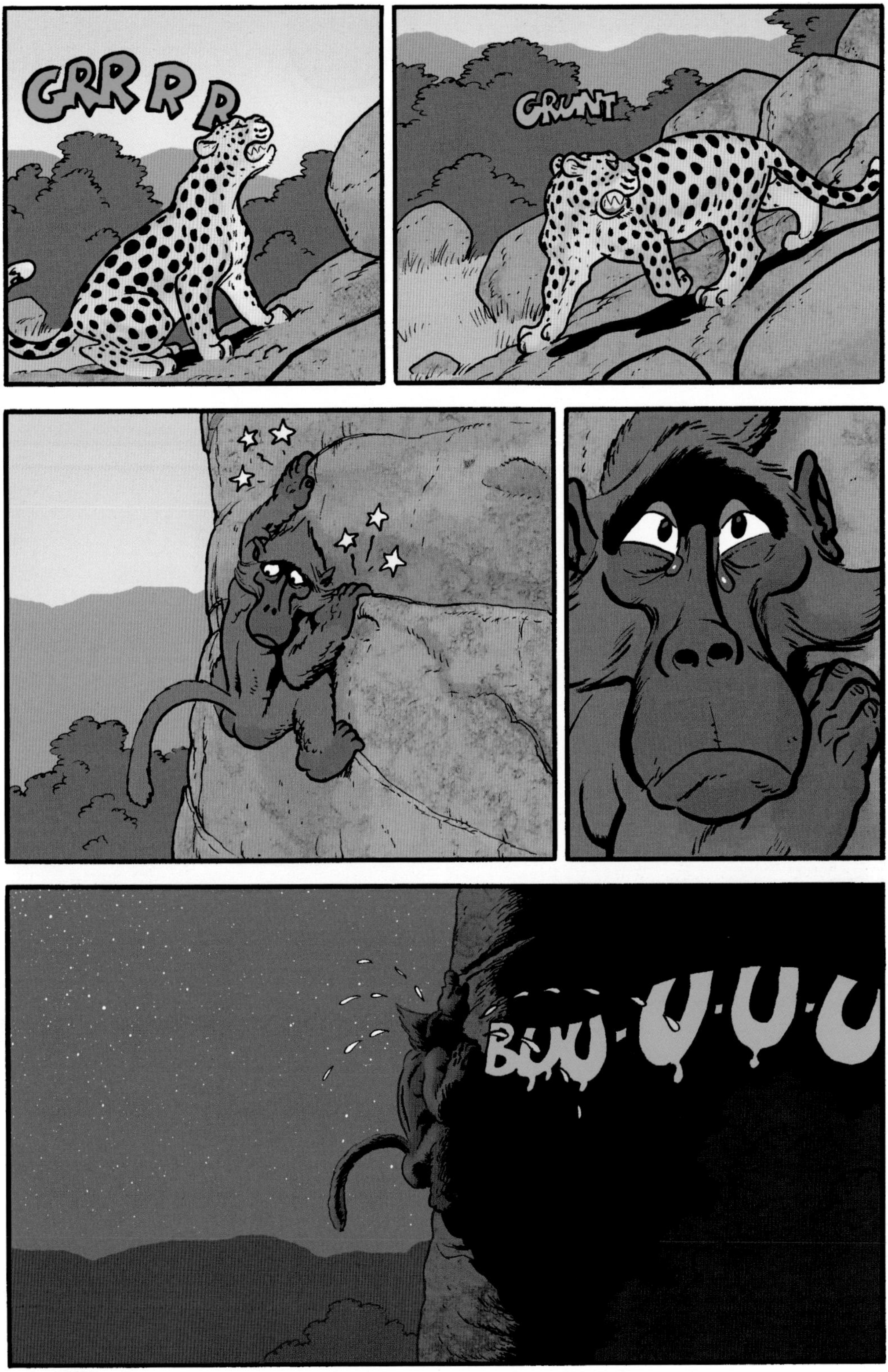
GRRRR
GRUNT
BUU-U-U-U

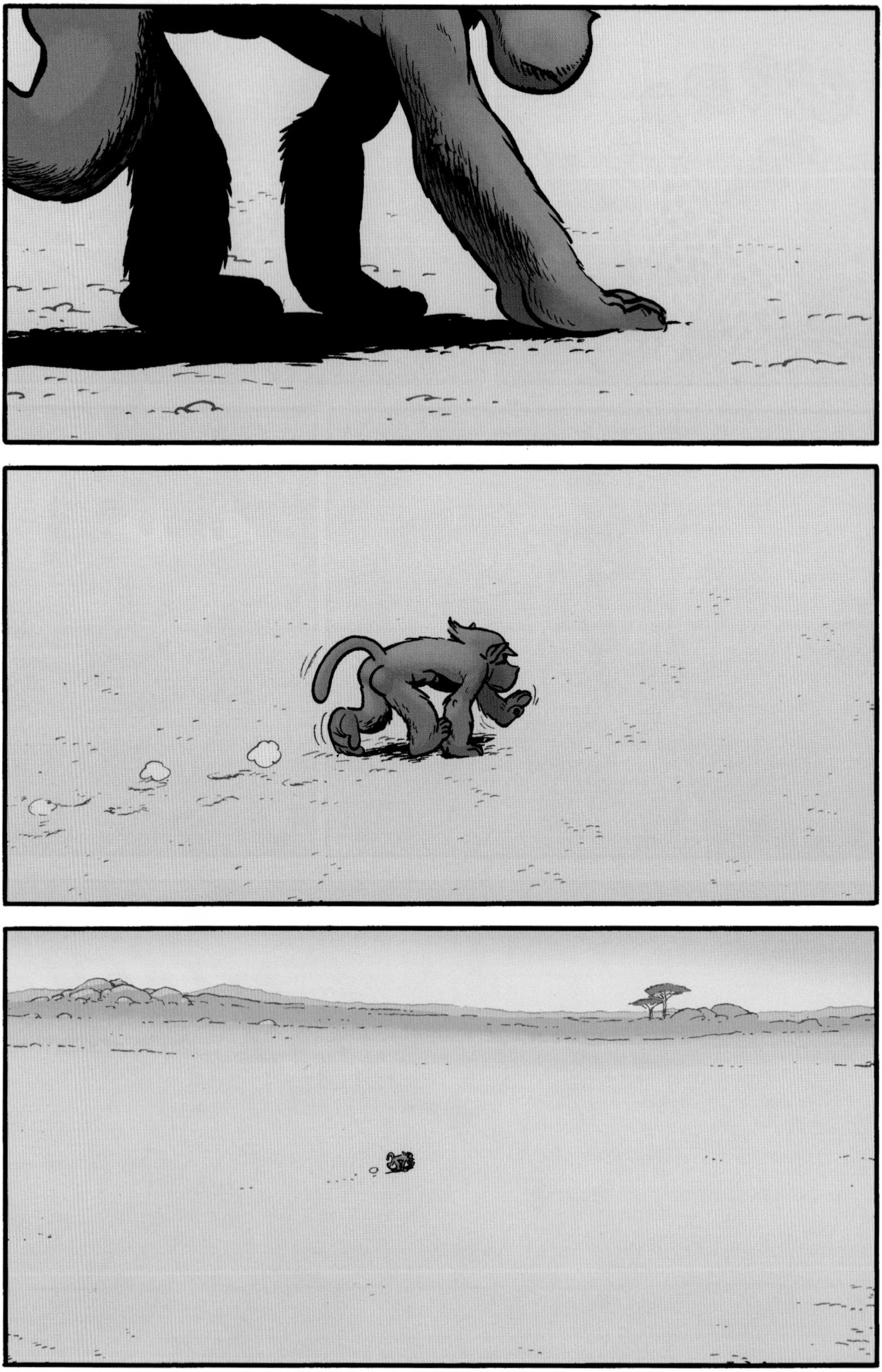

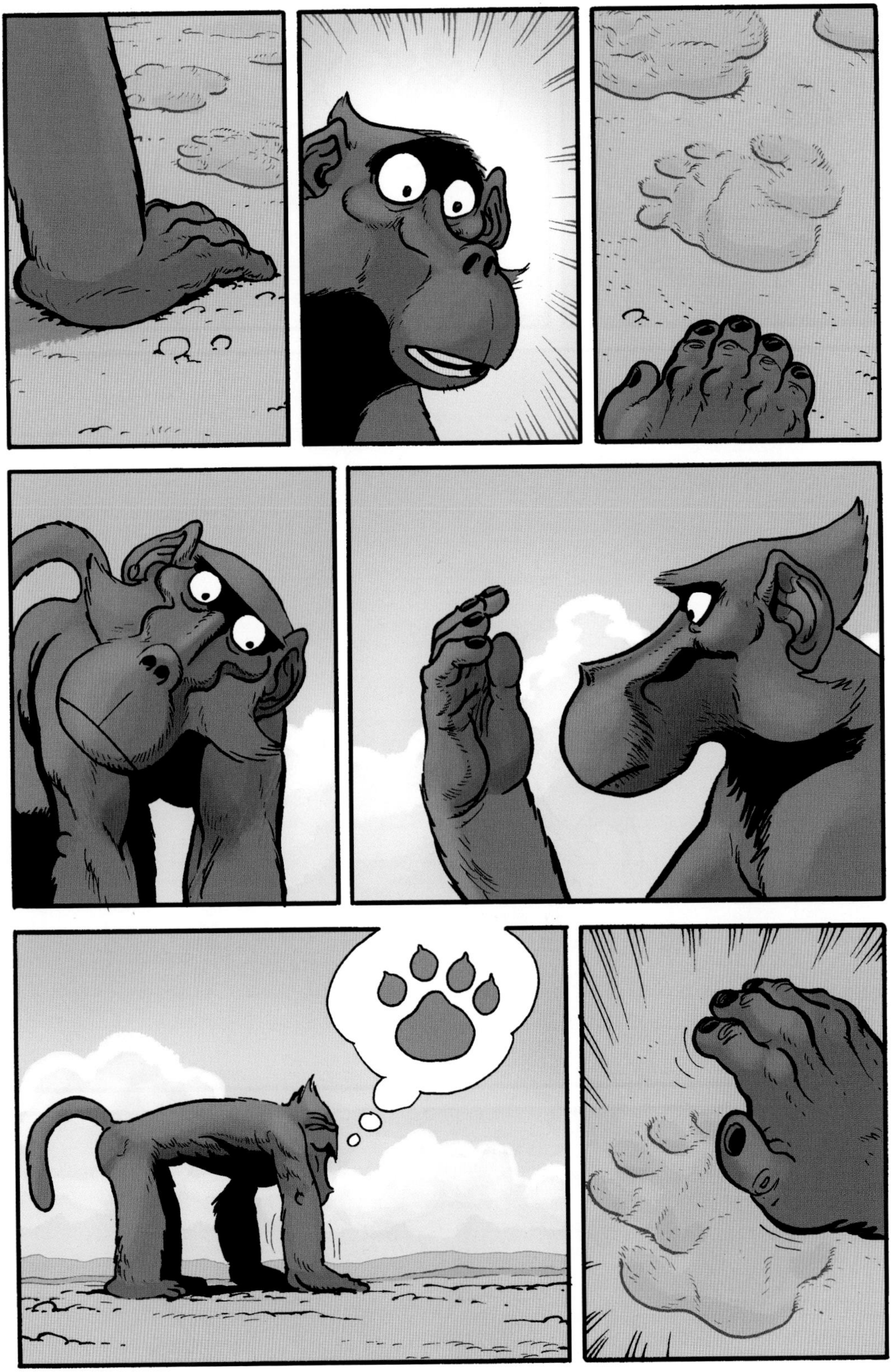

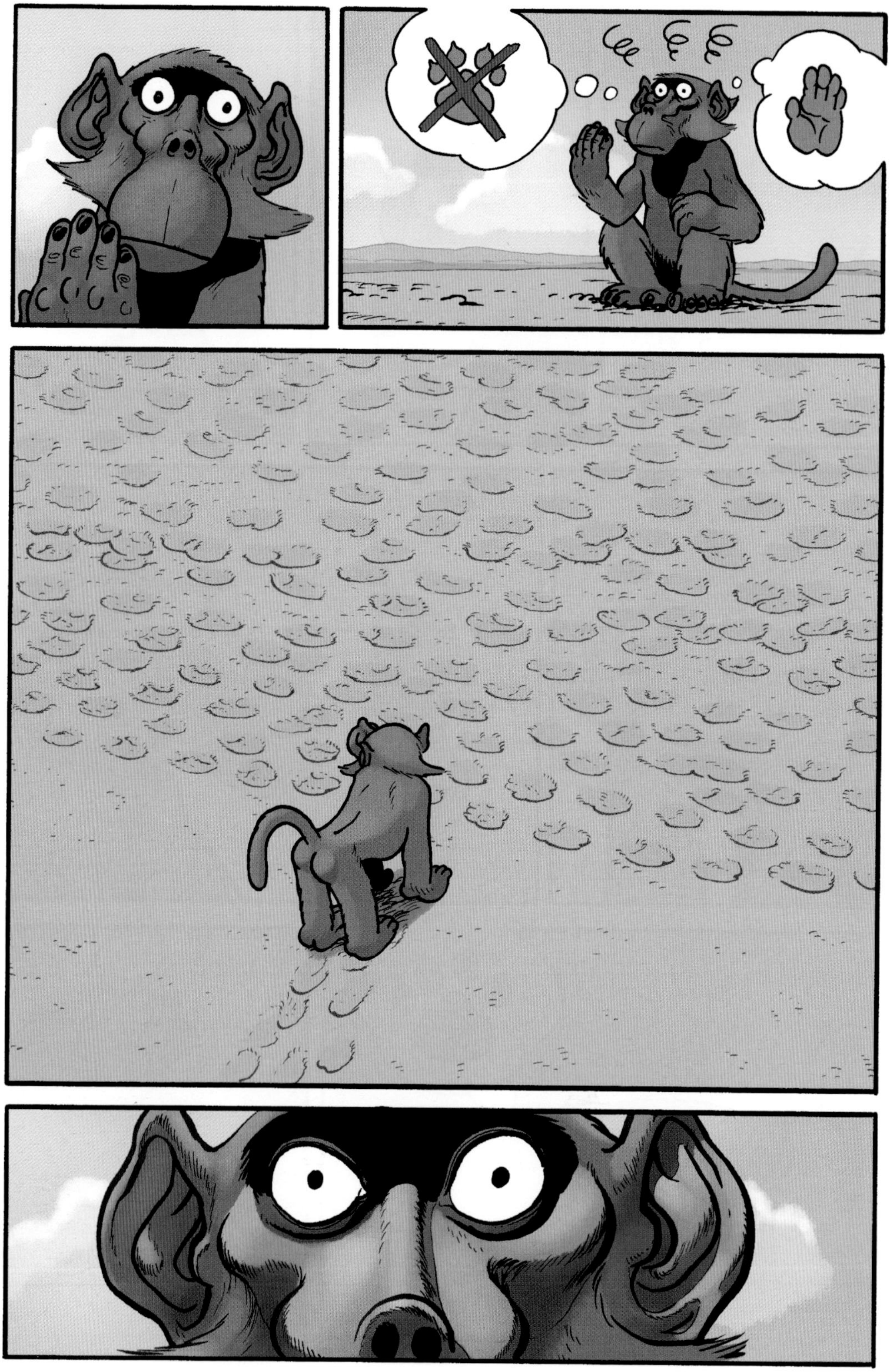

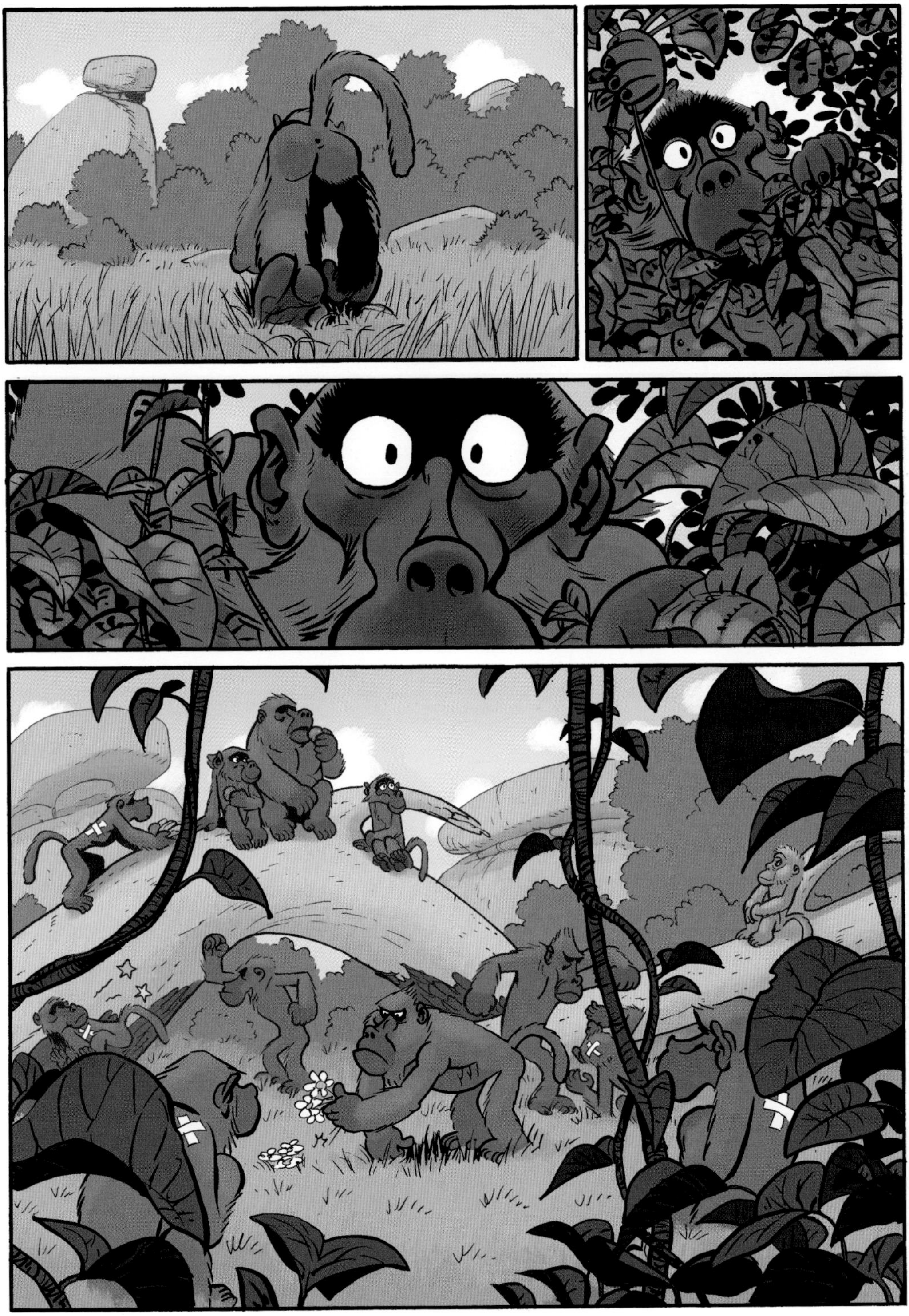

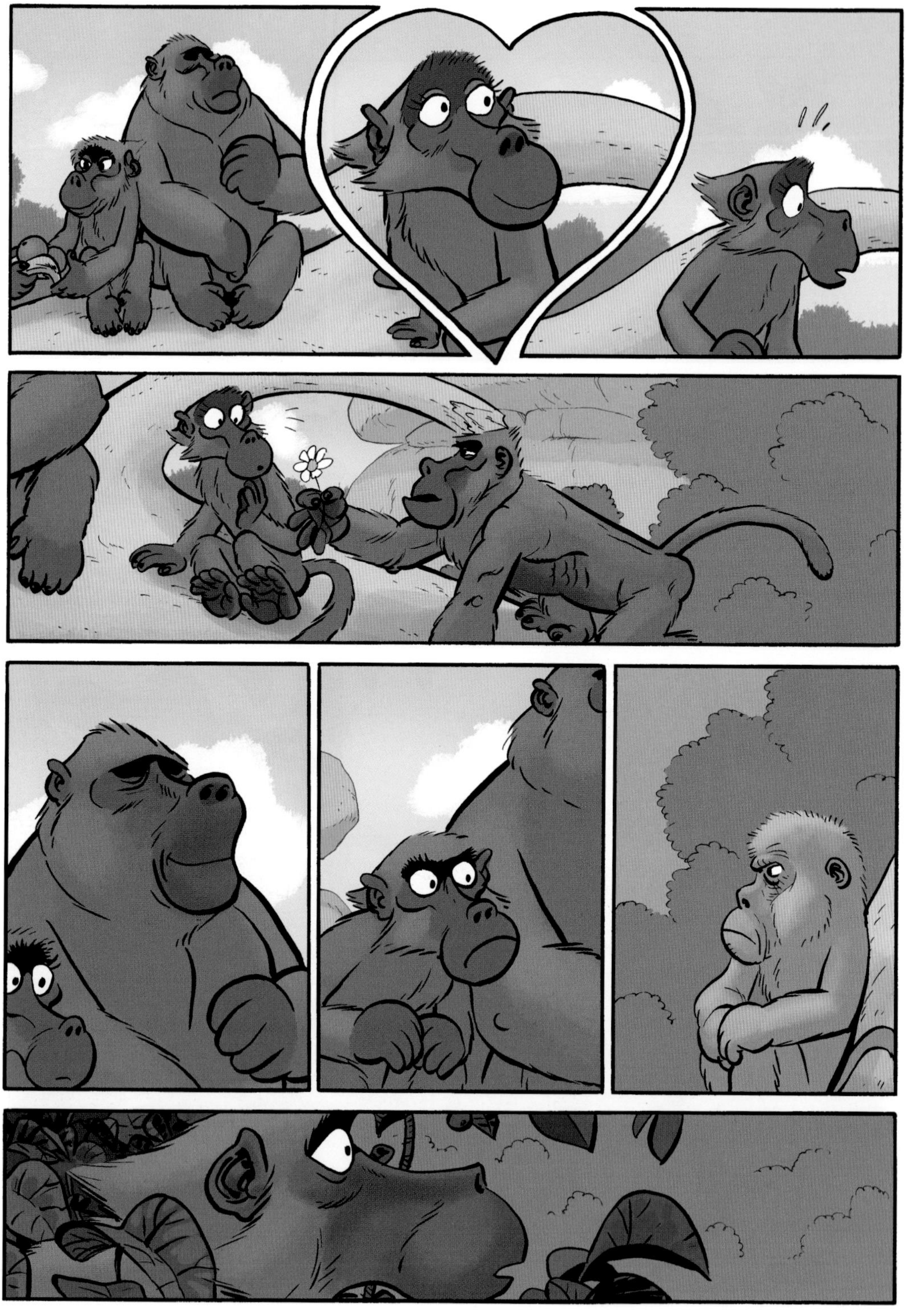

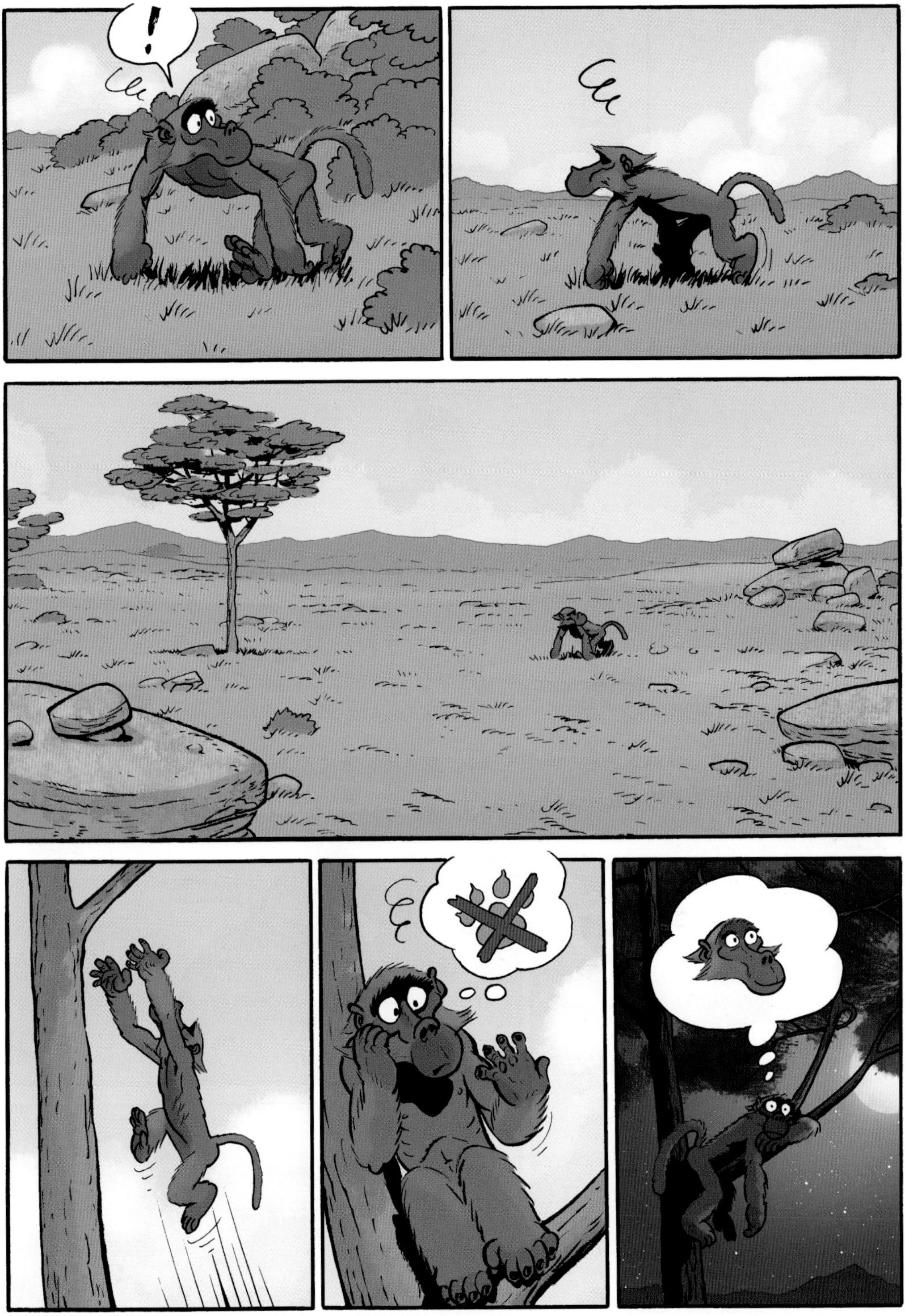
!

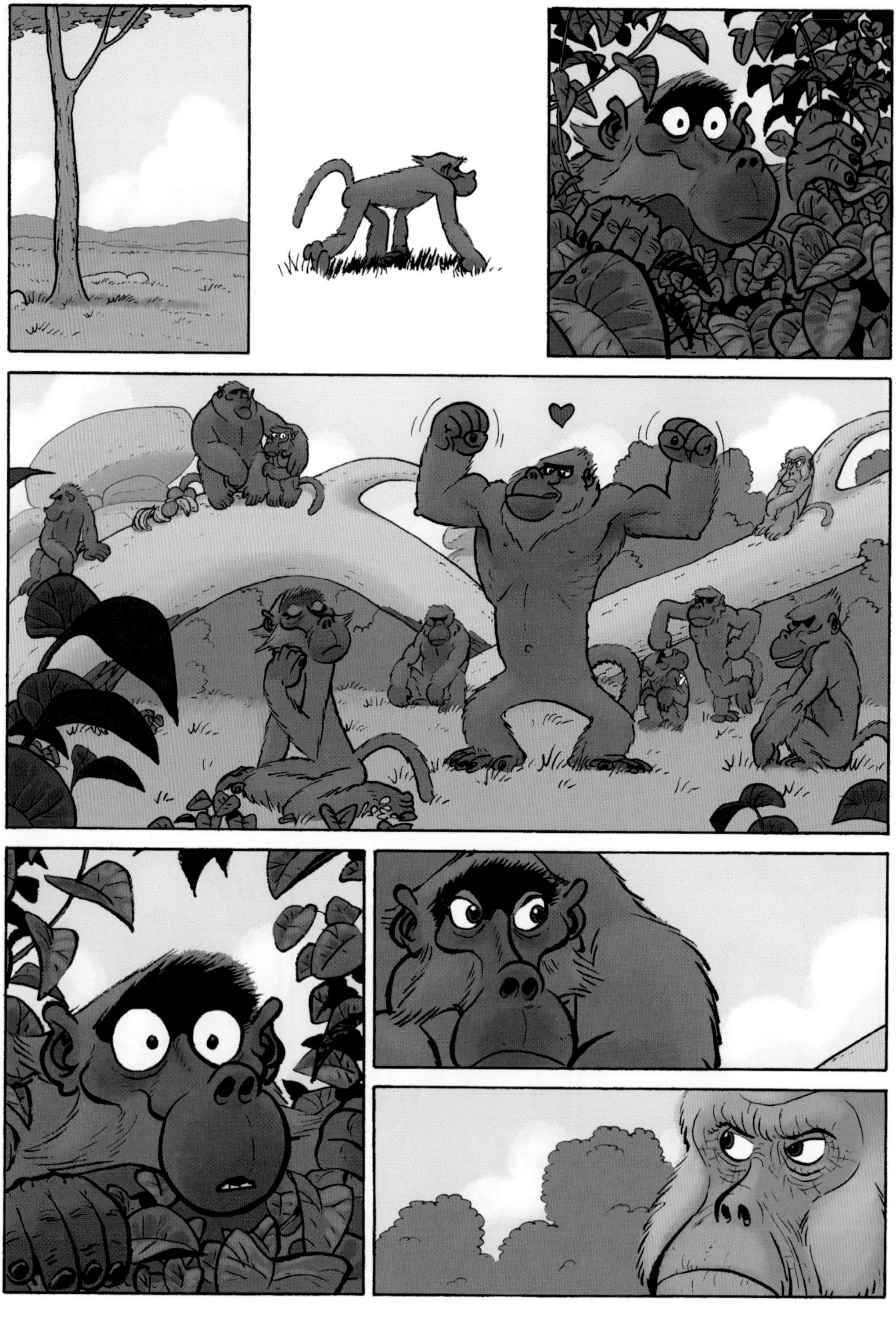

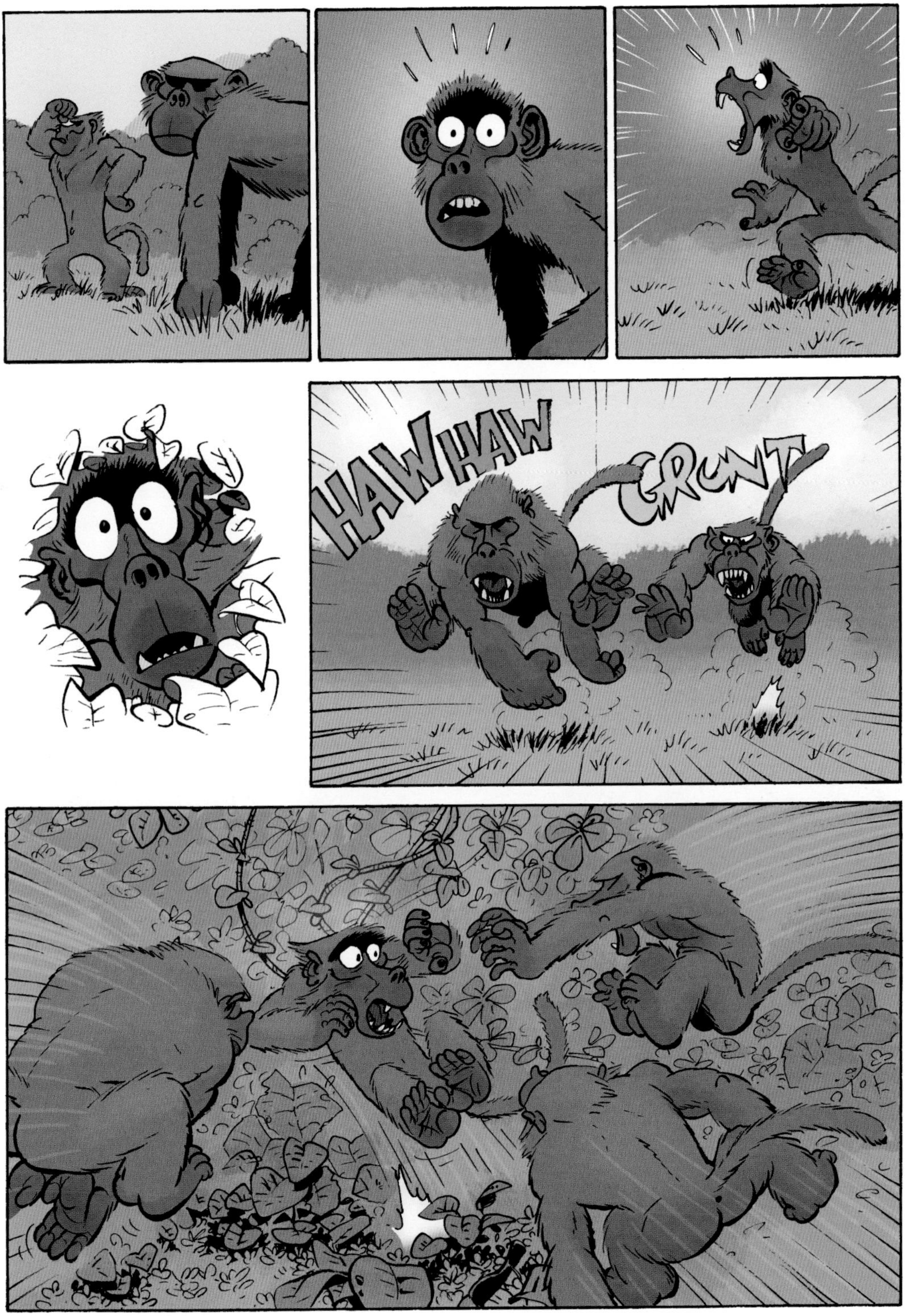
HAWHAW
GRUNT

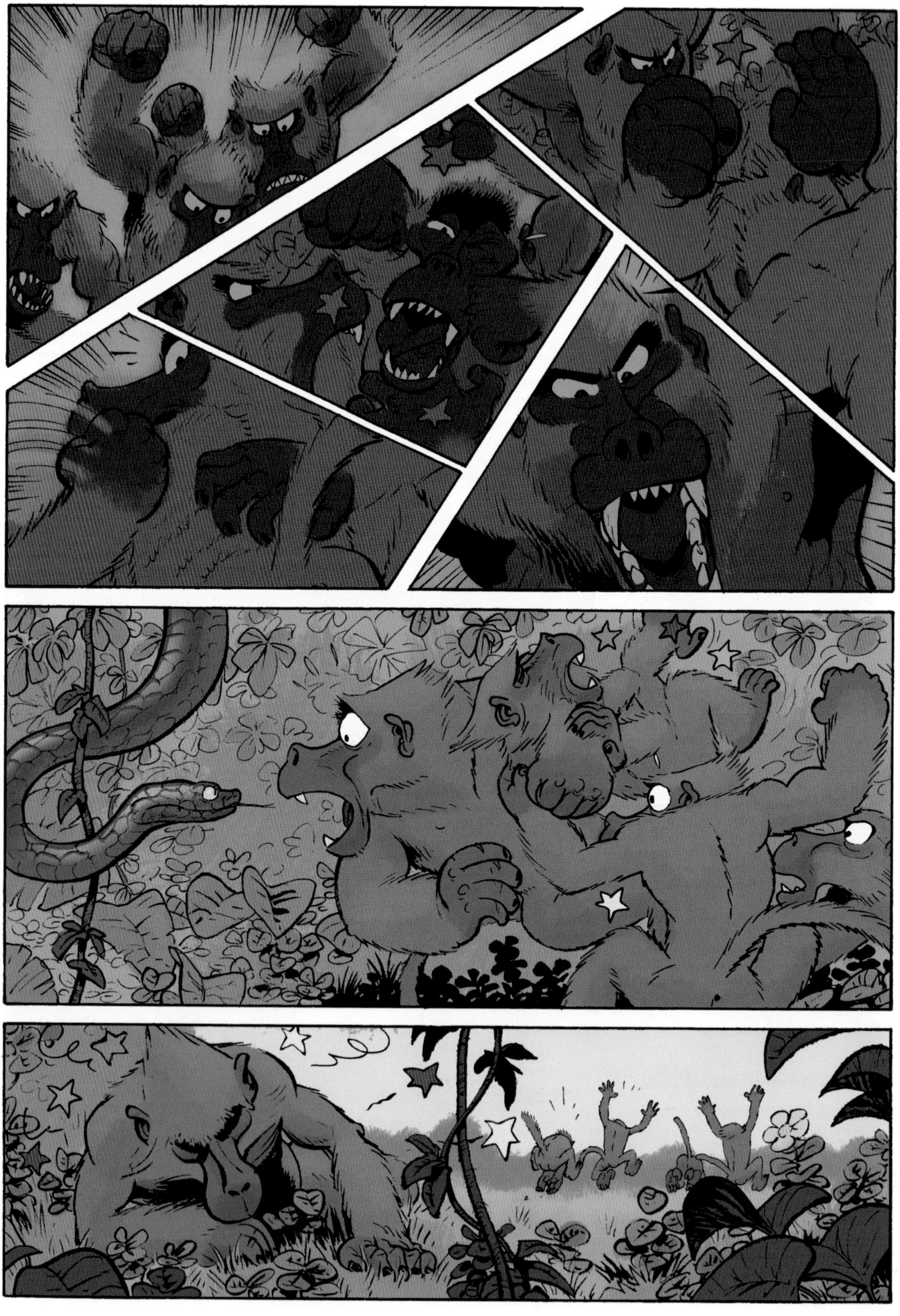

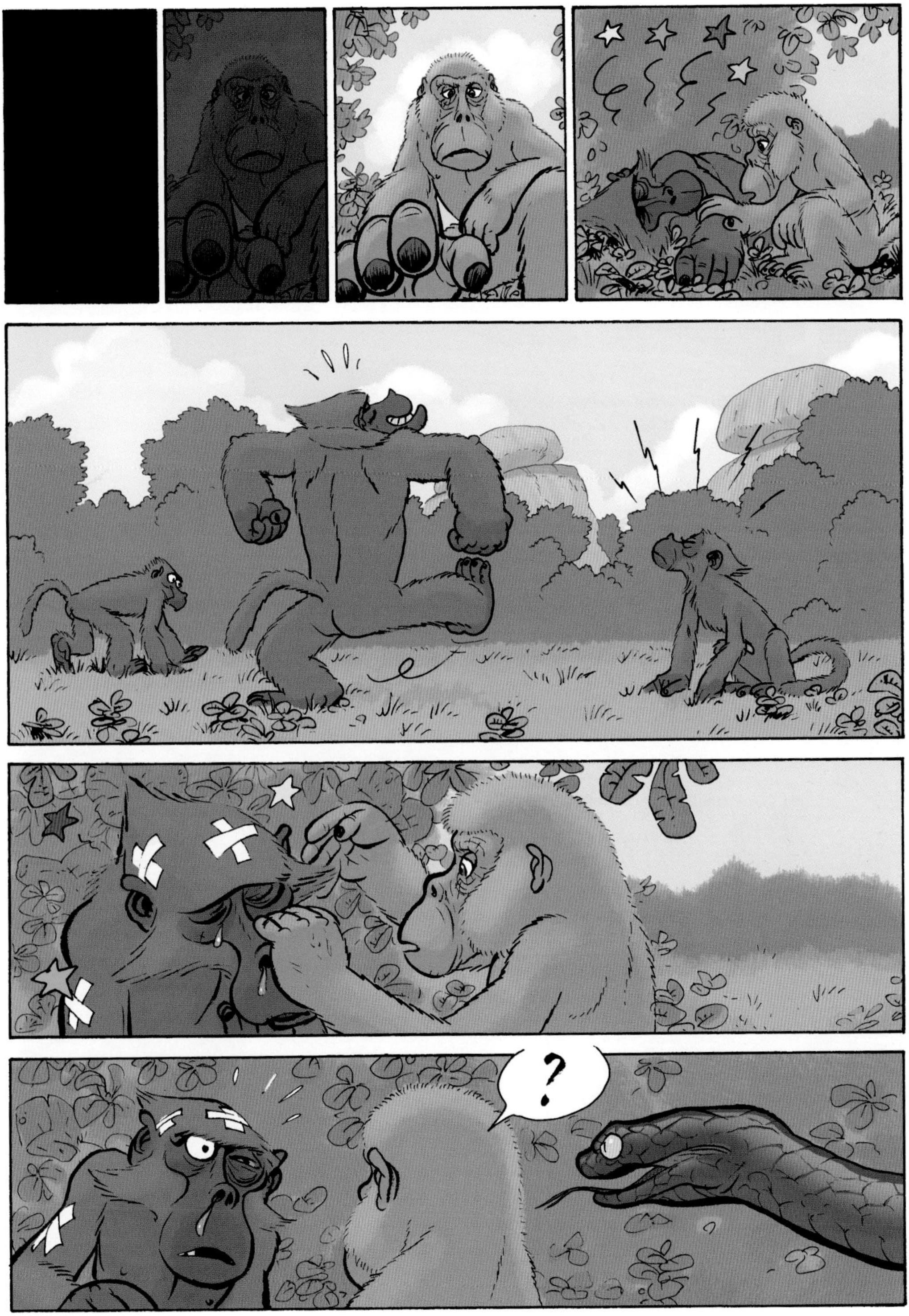
?

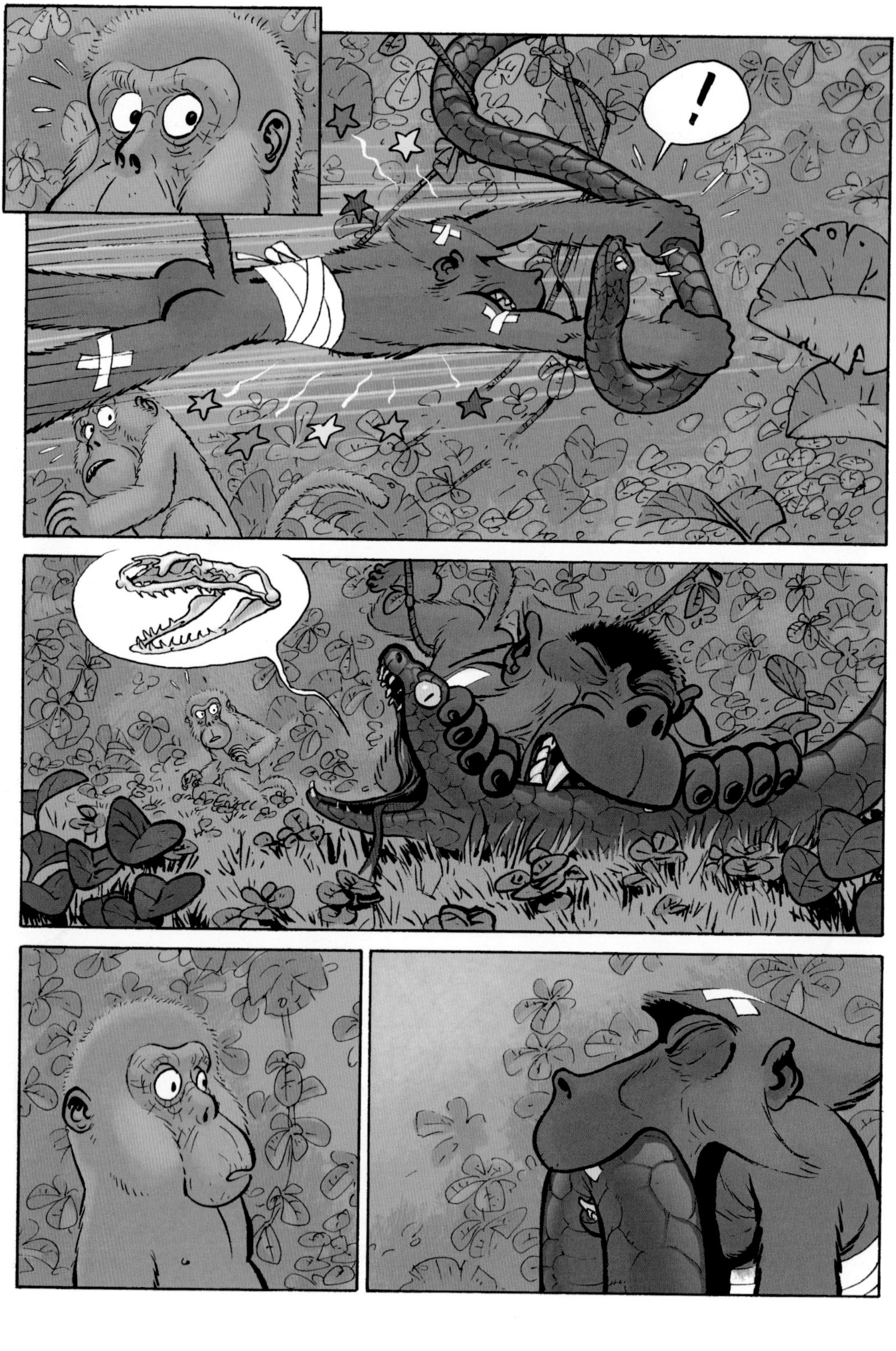
!

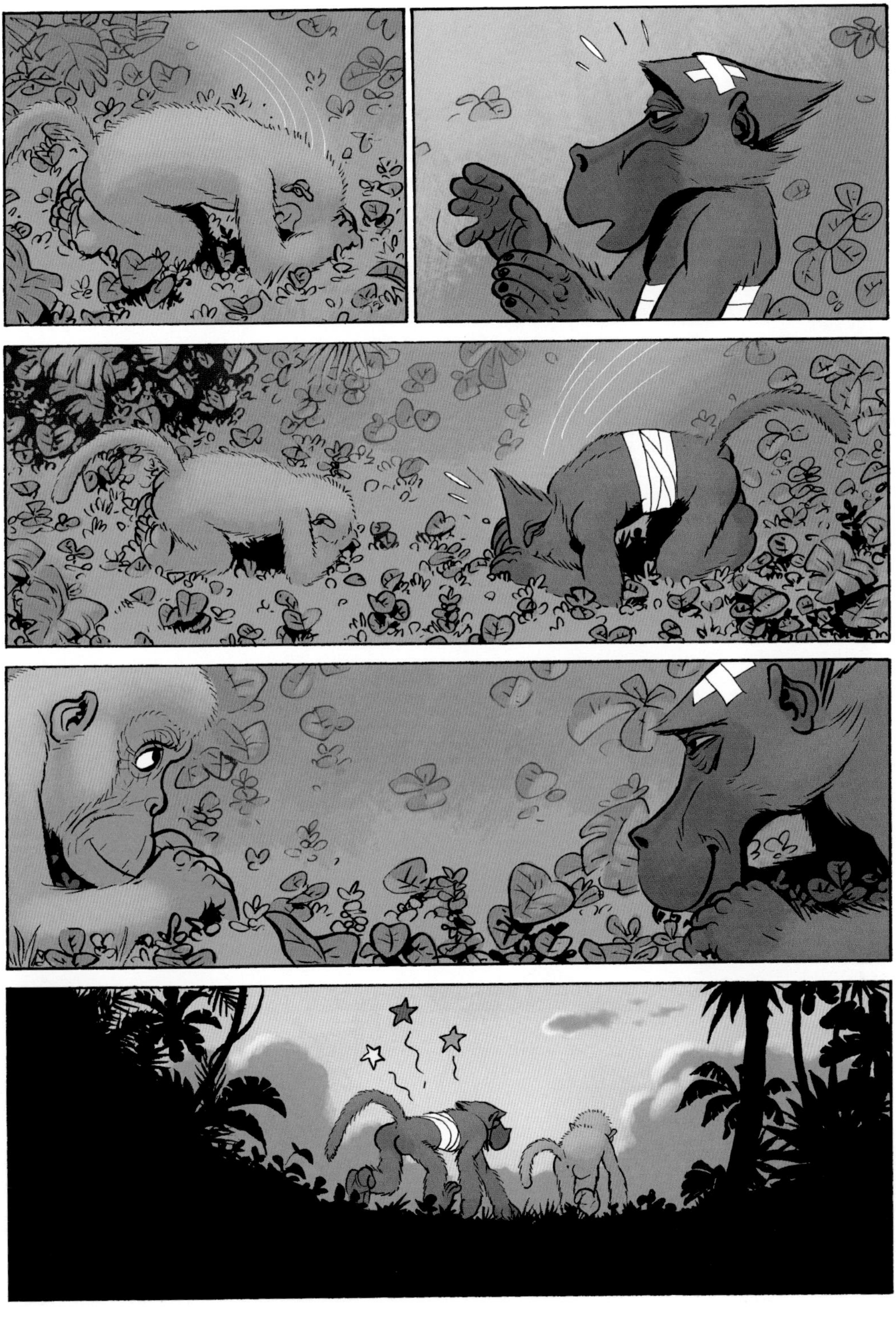

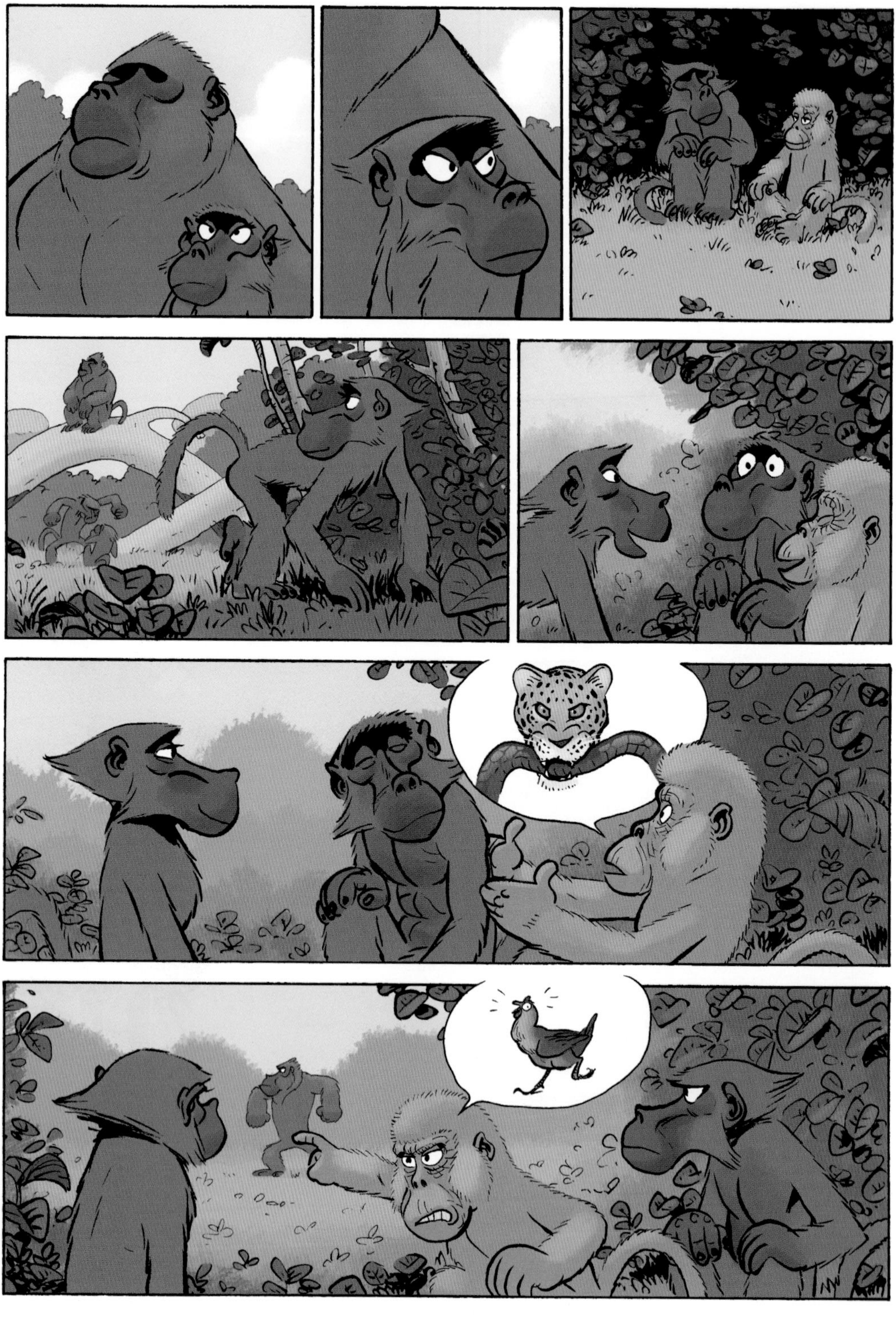

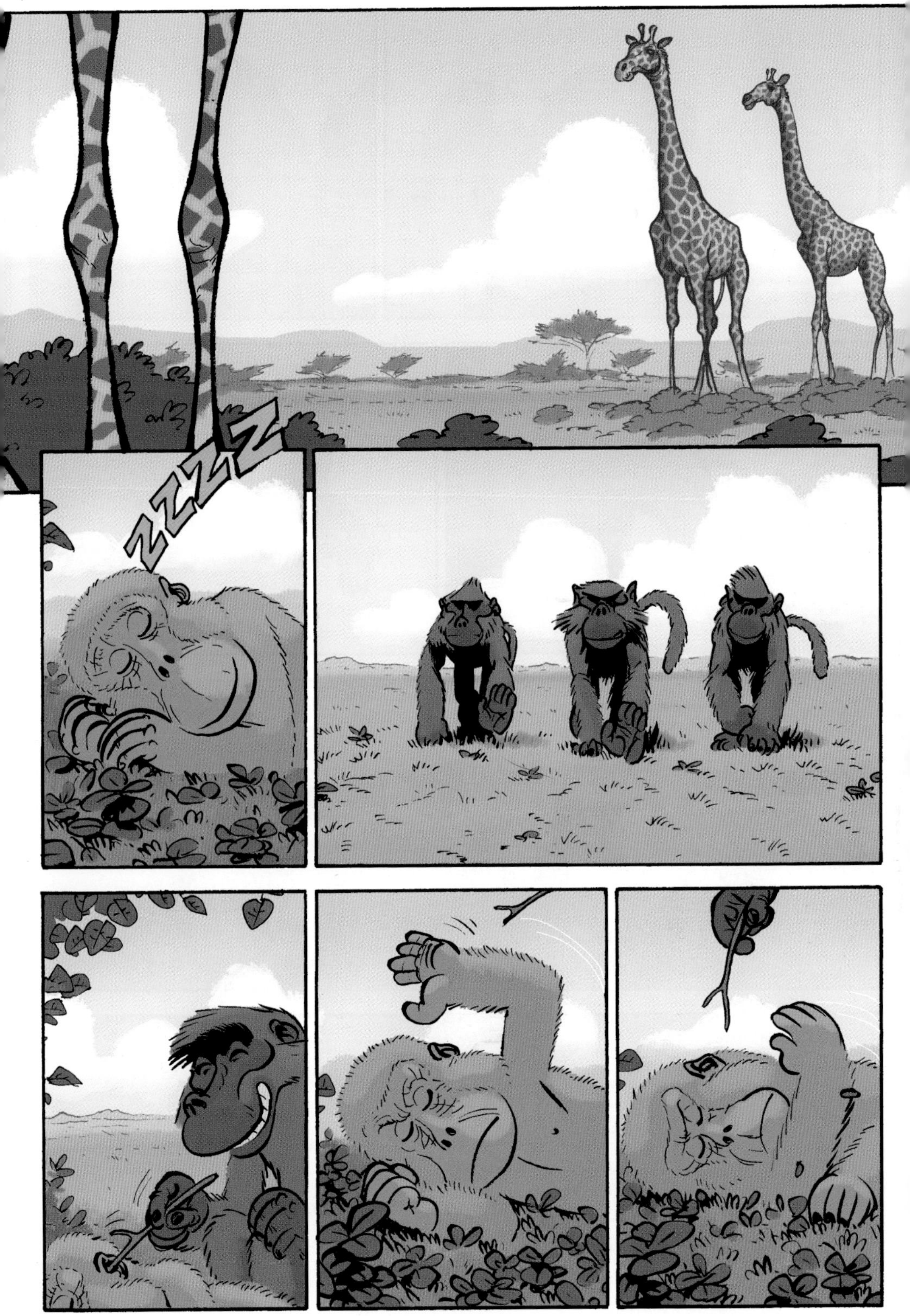
ZZZZ

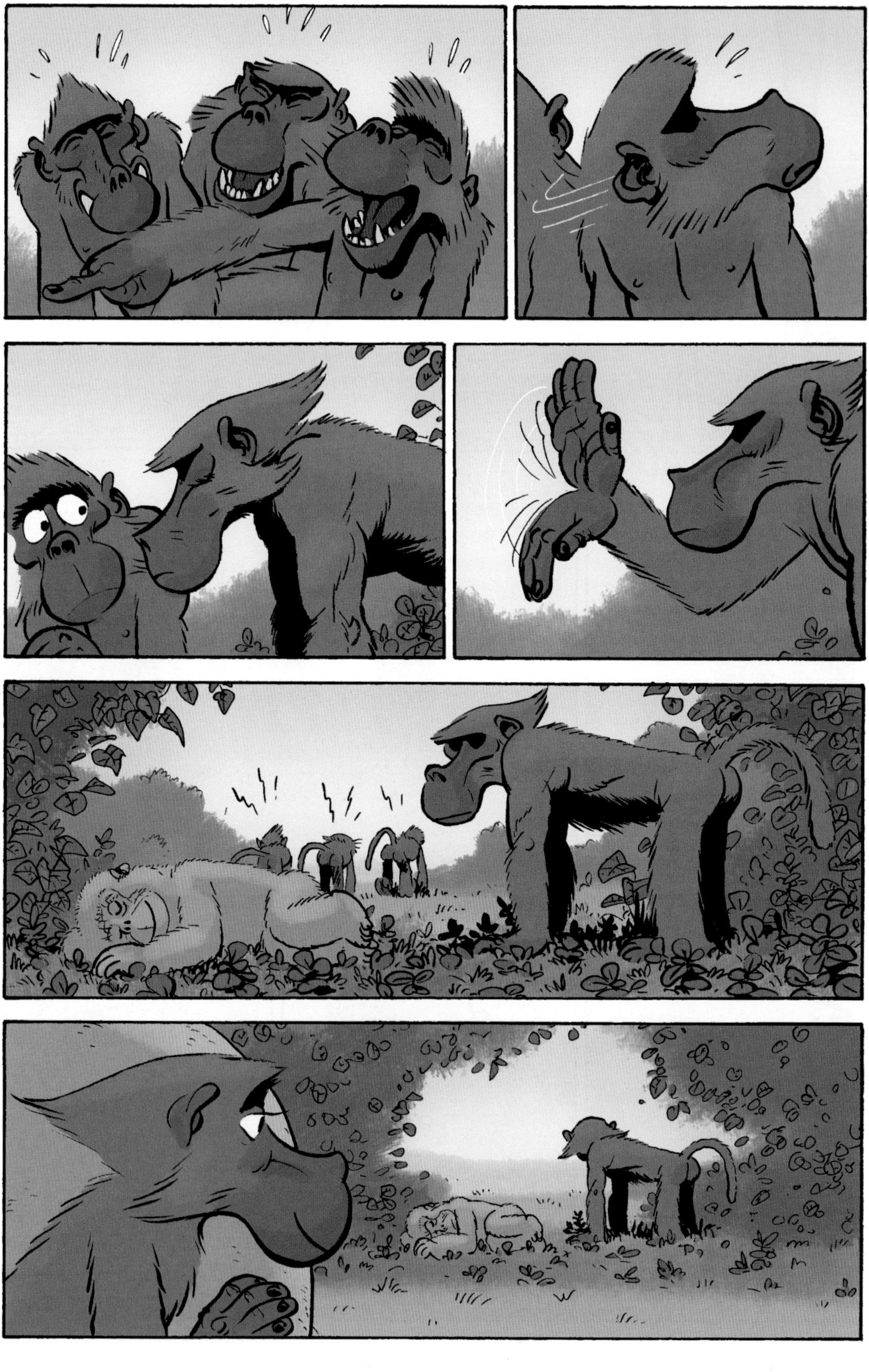

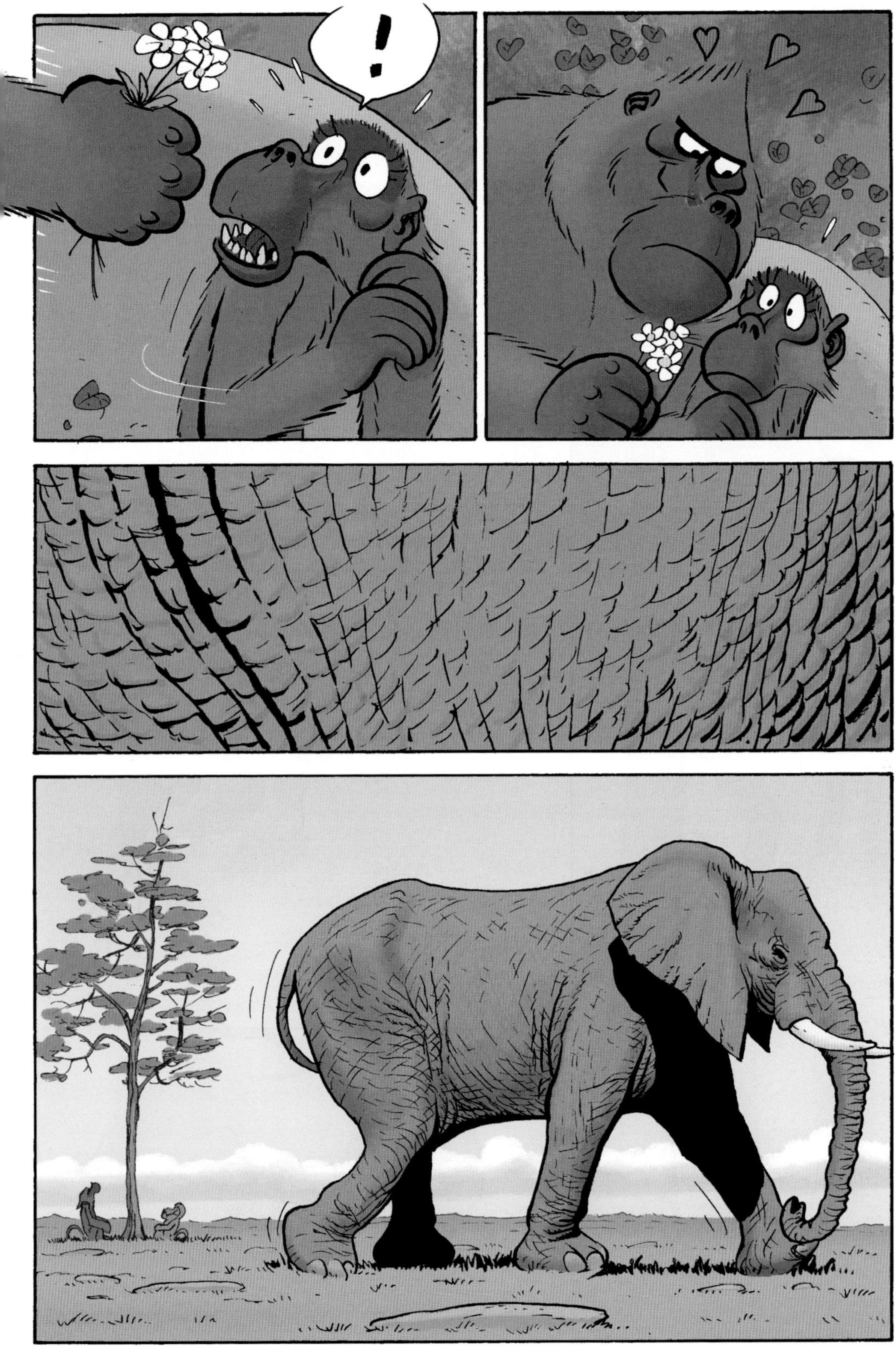
!

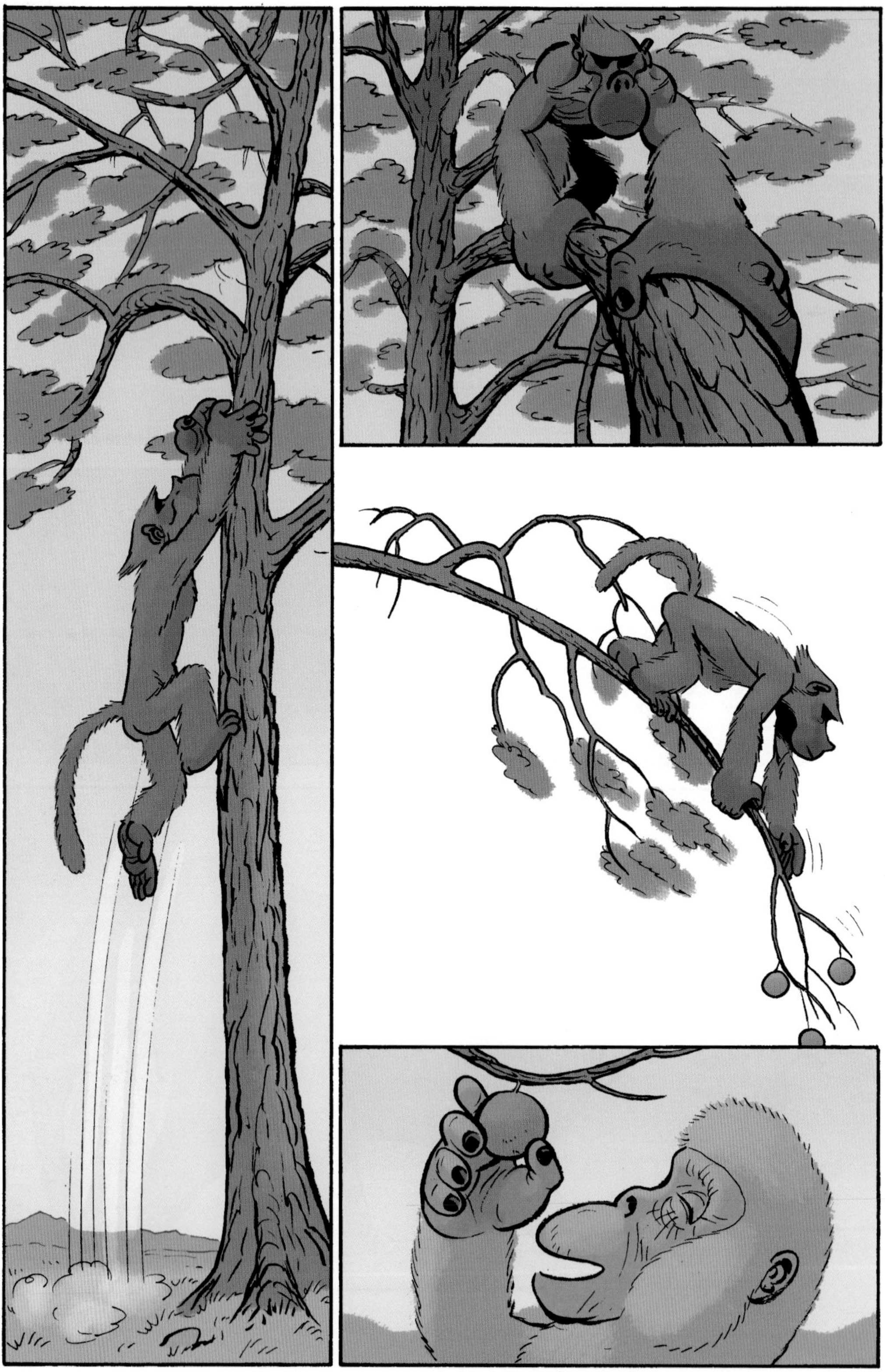

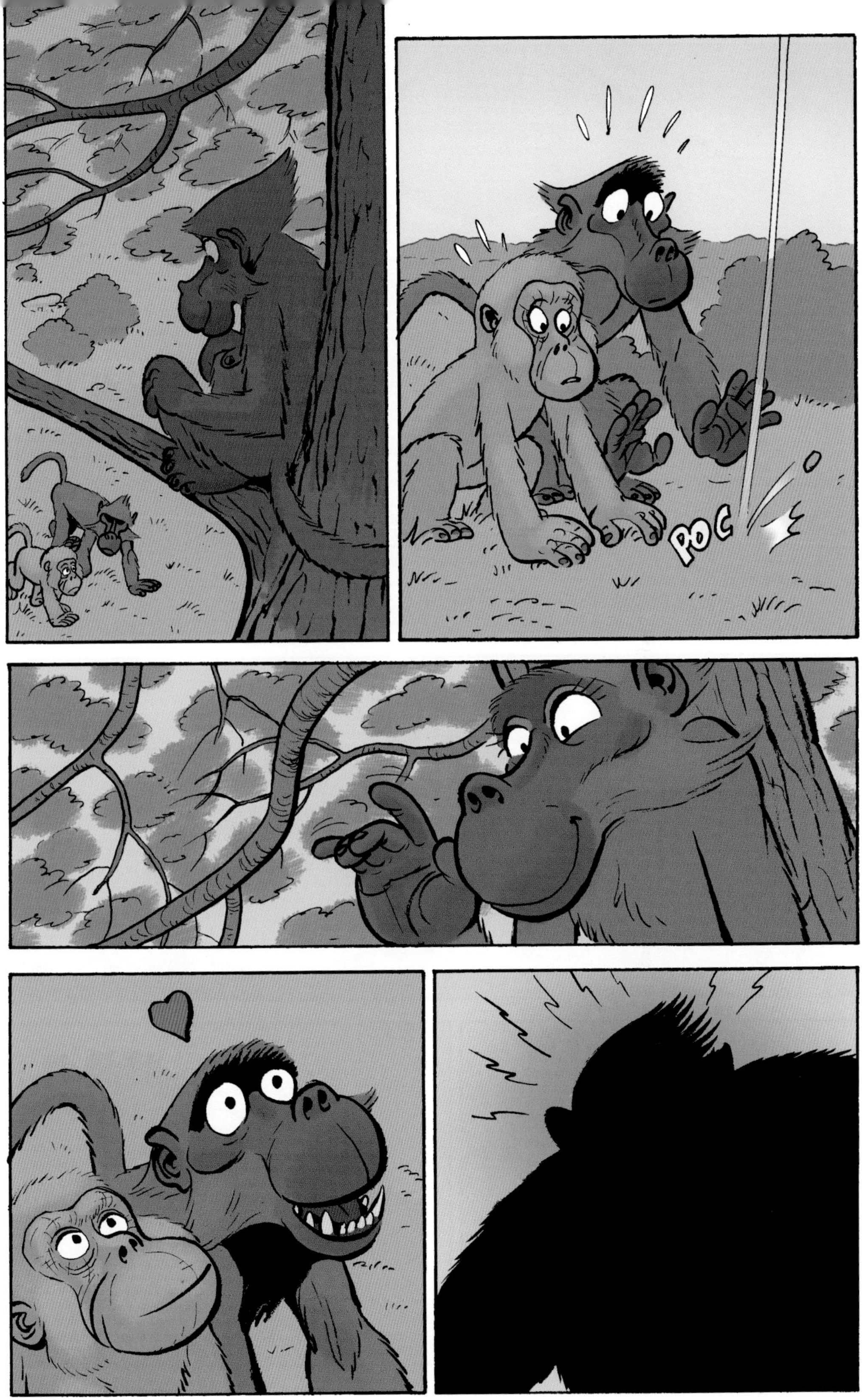
POC

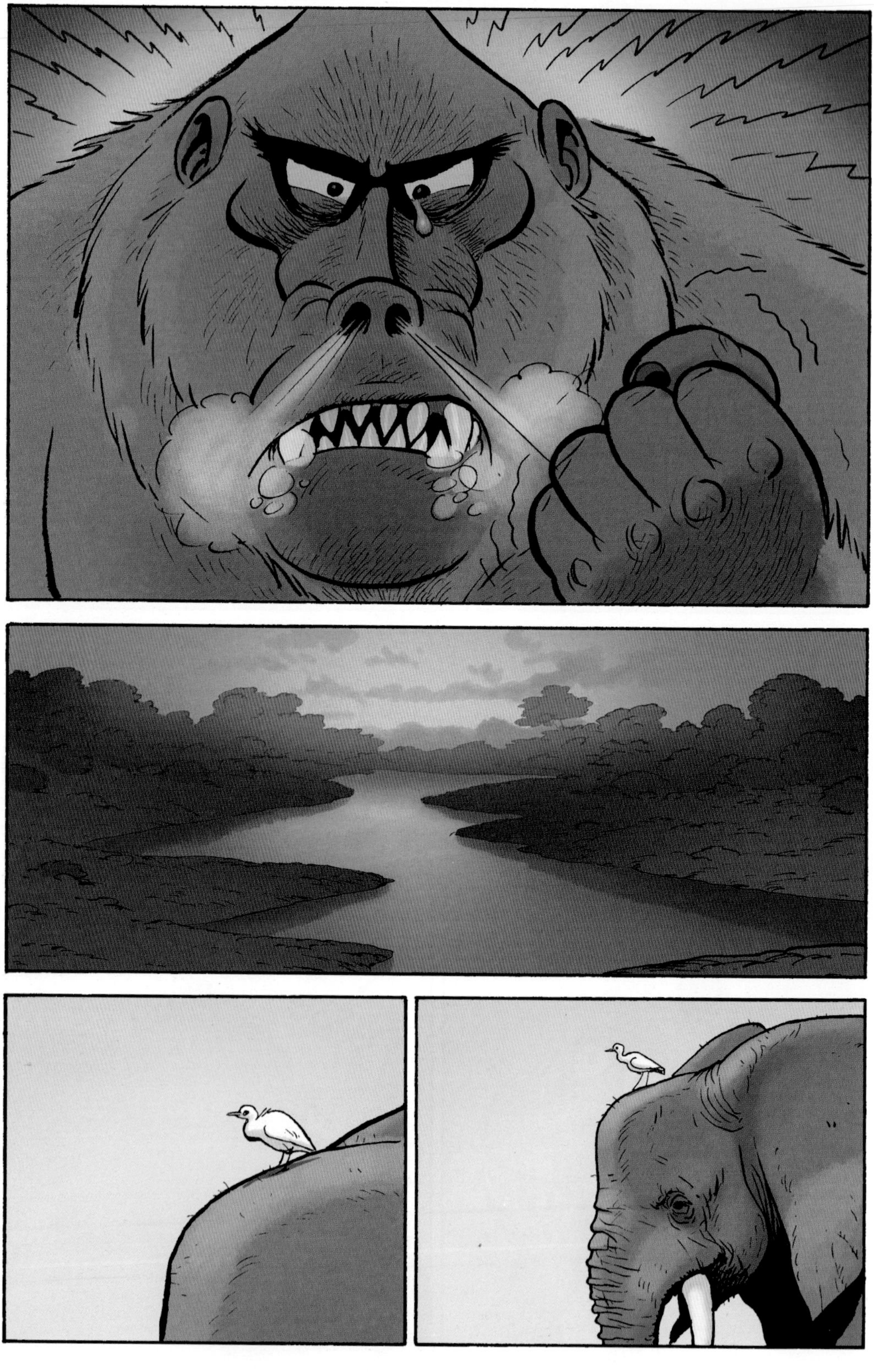

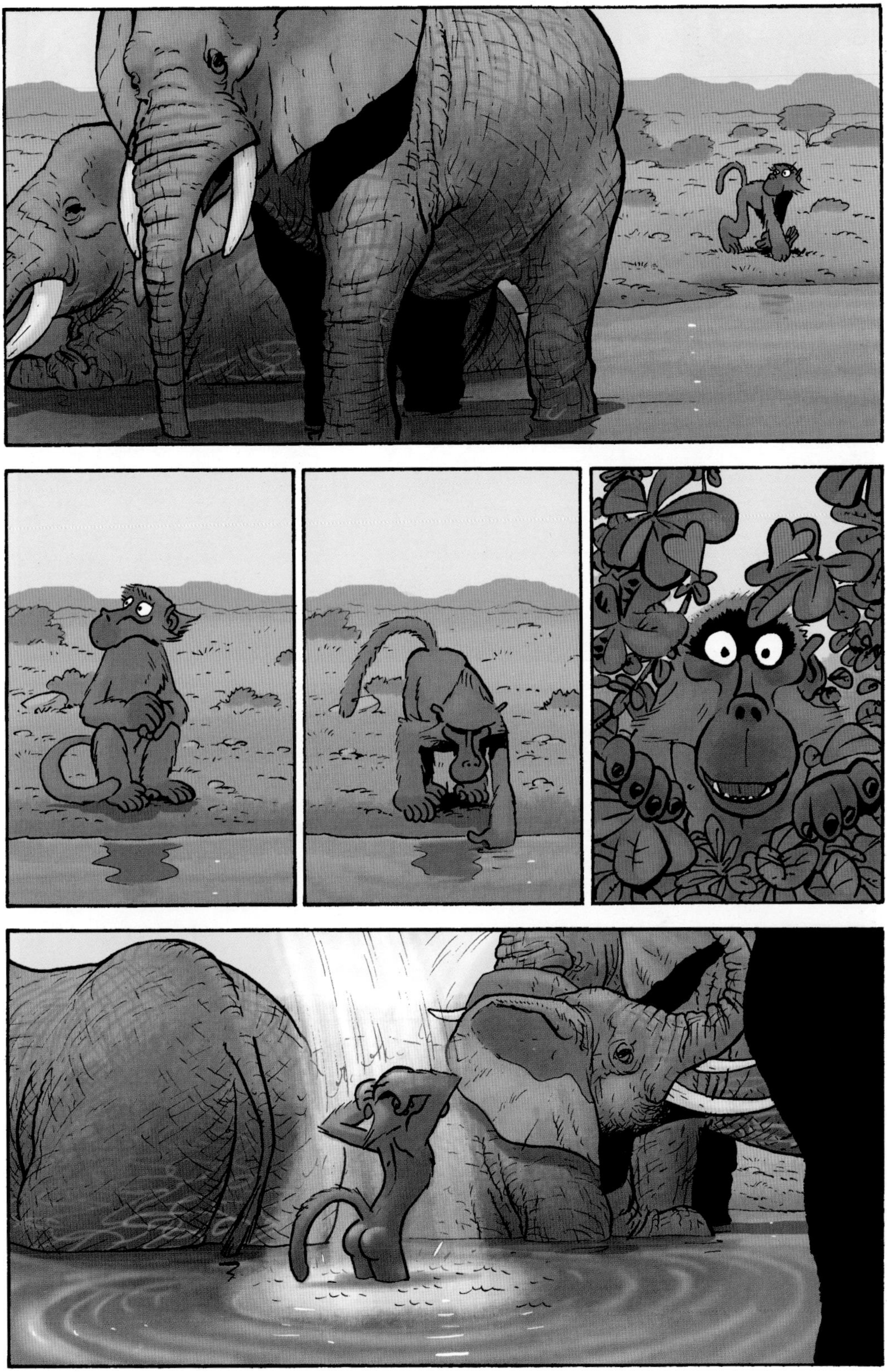

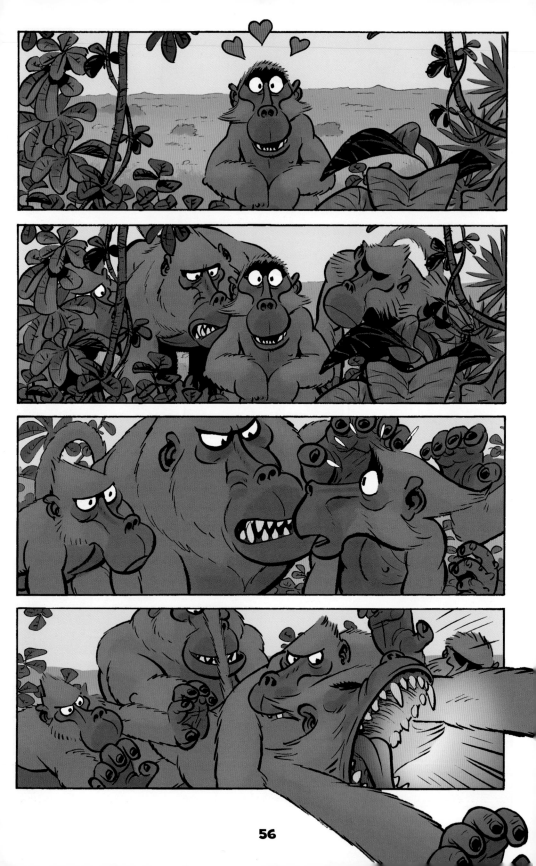

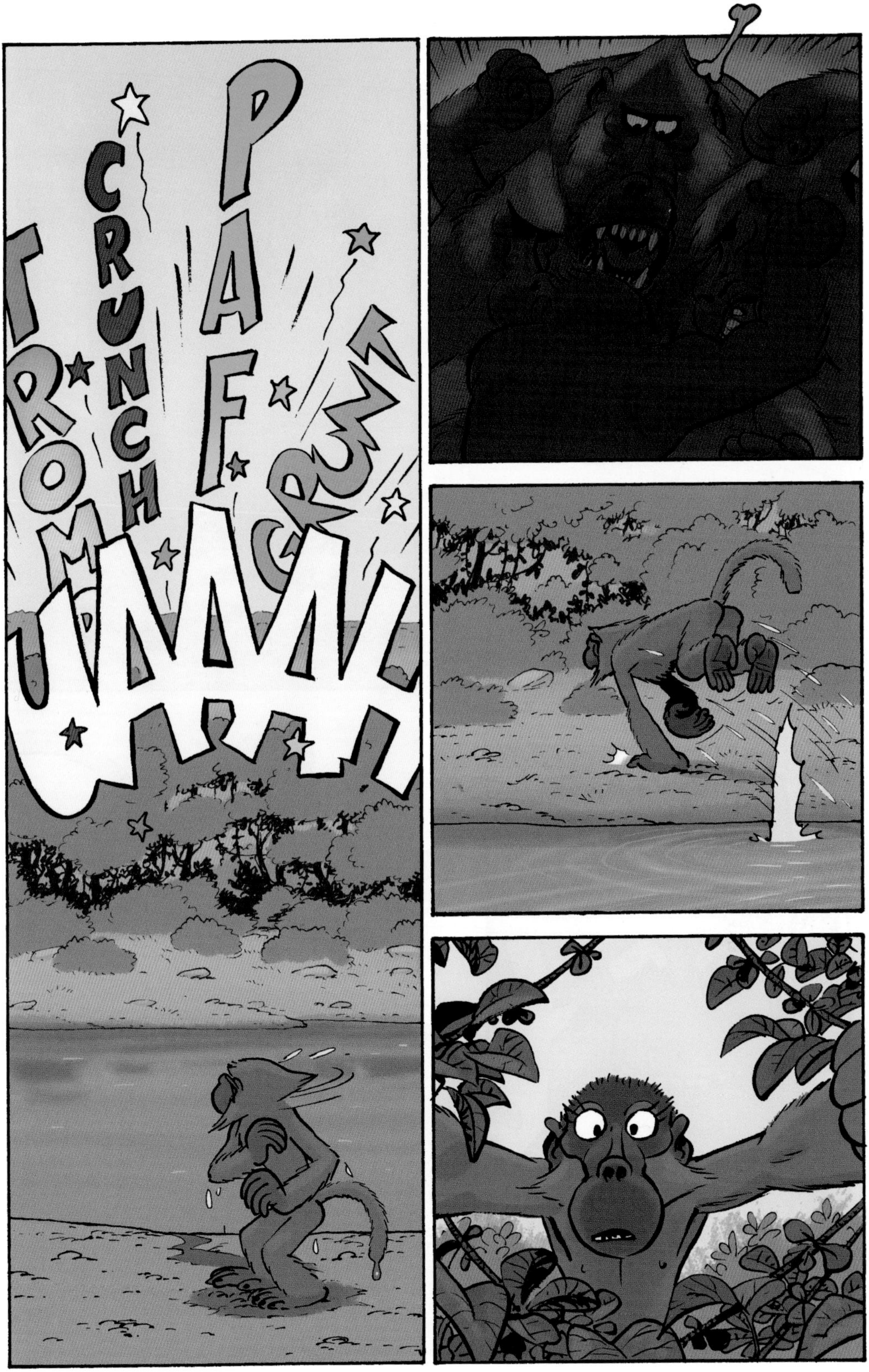
TROM
CRUNCH
PAF

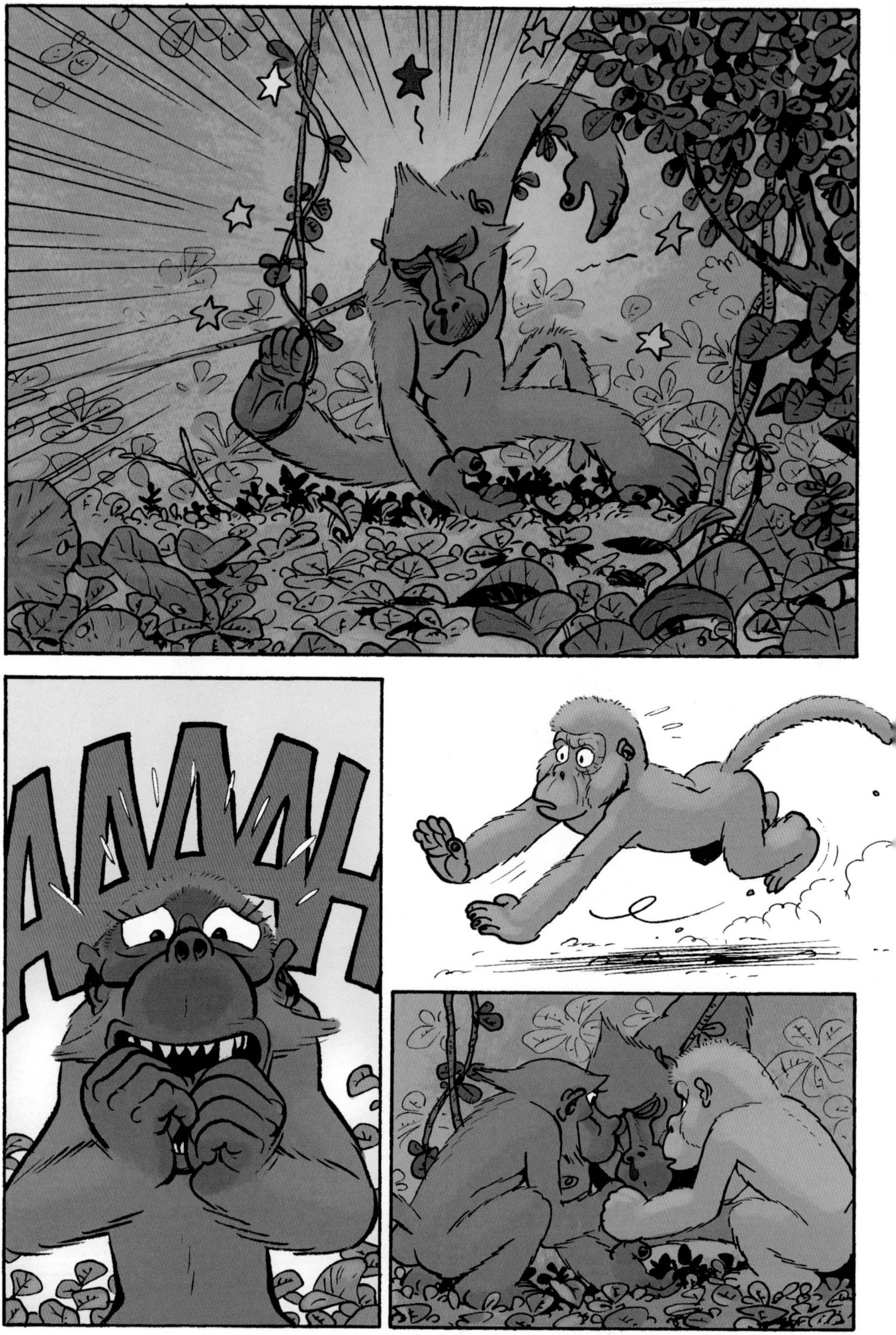

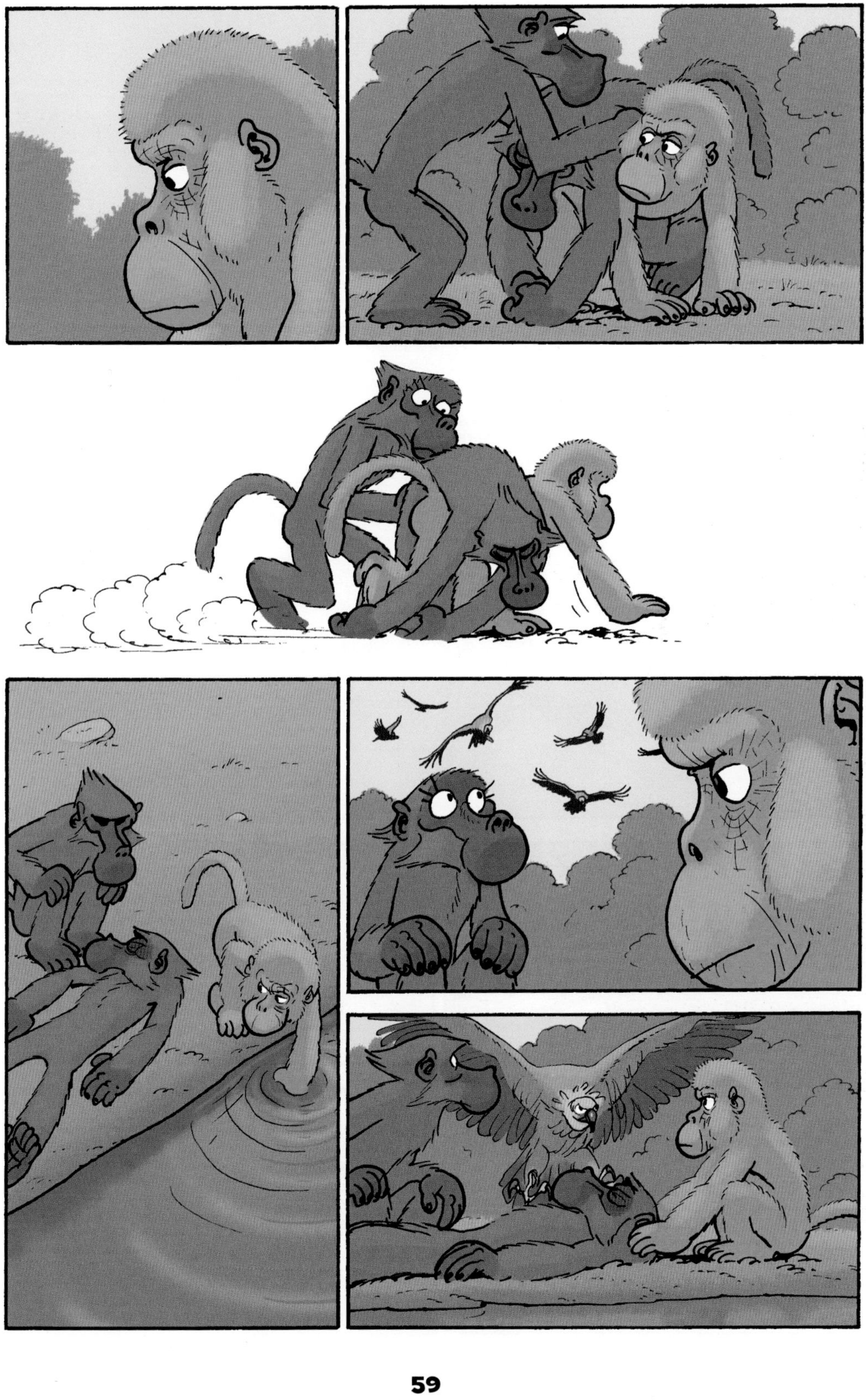

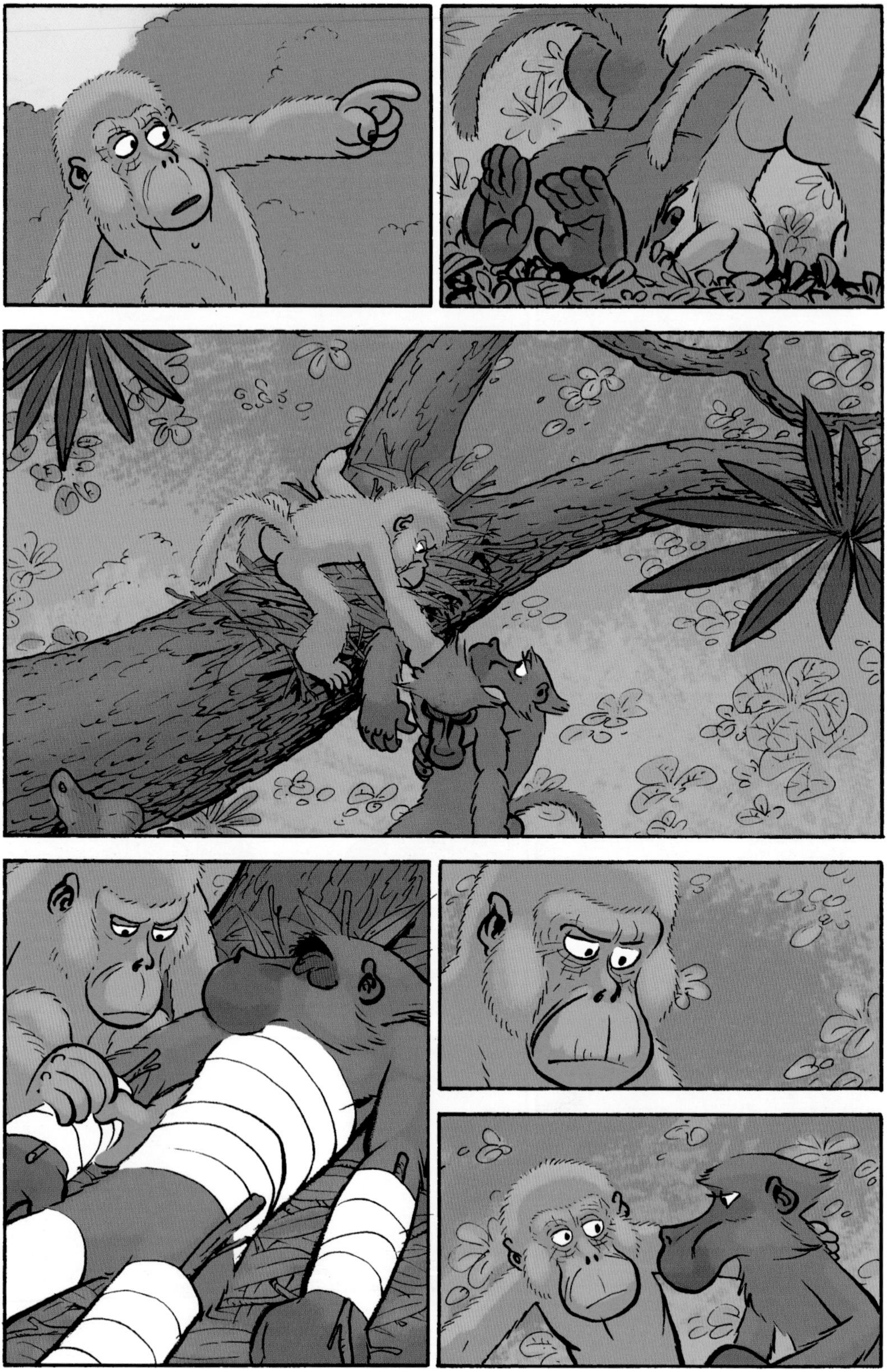

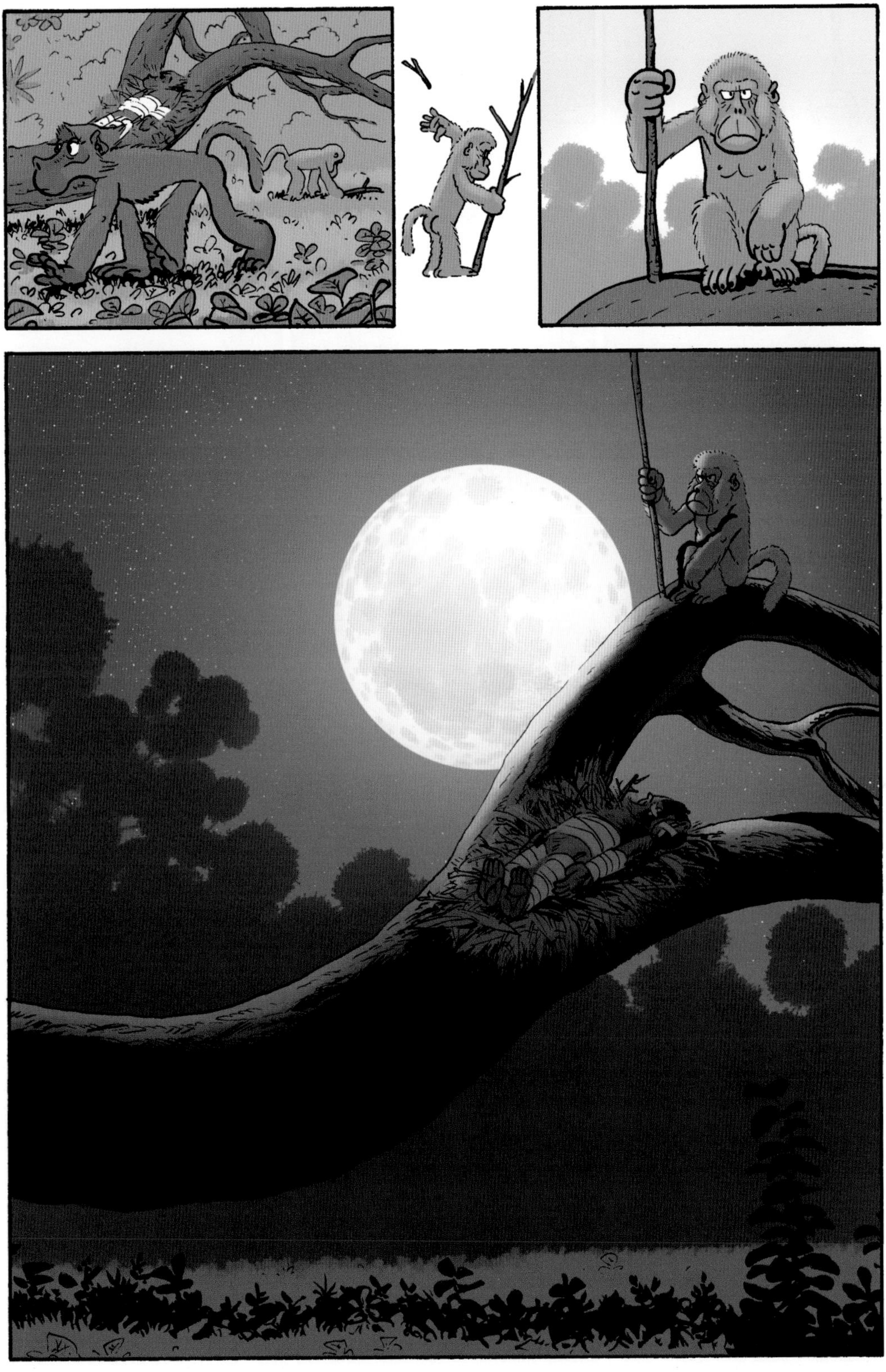

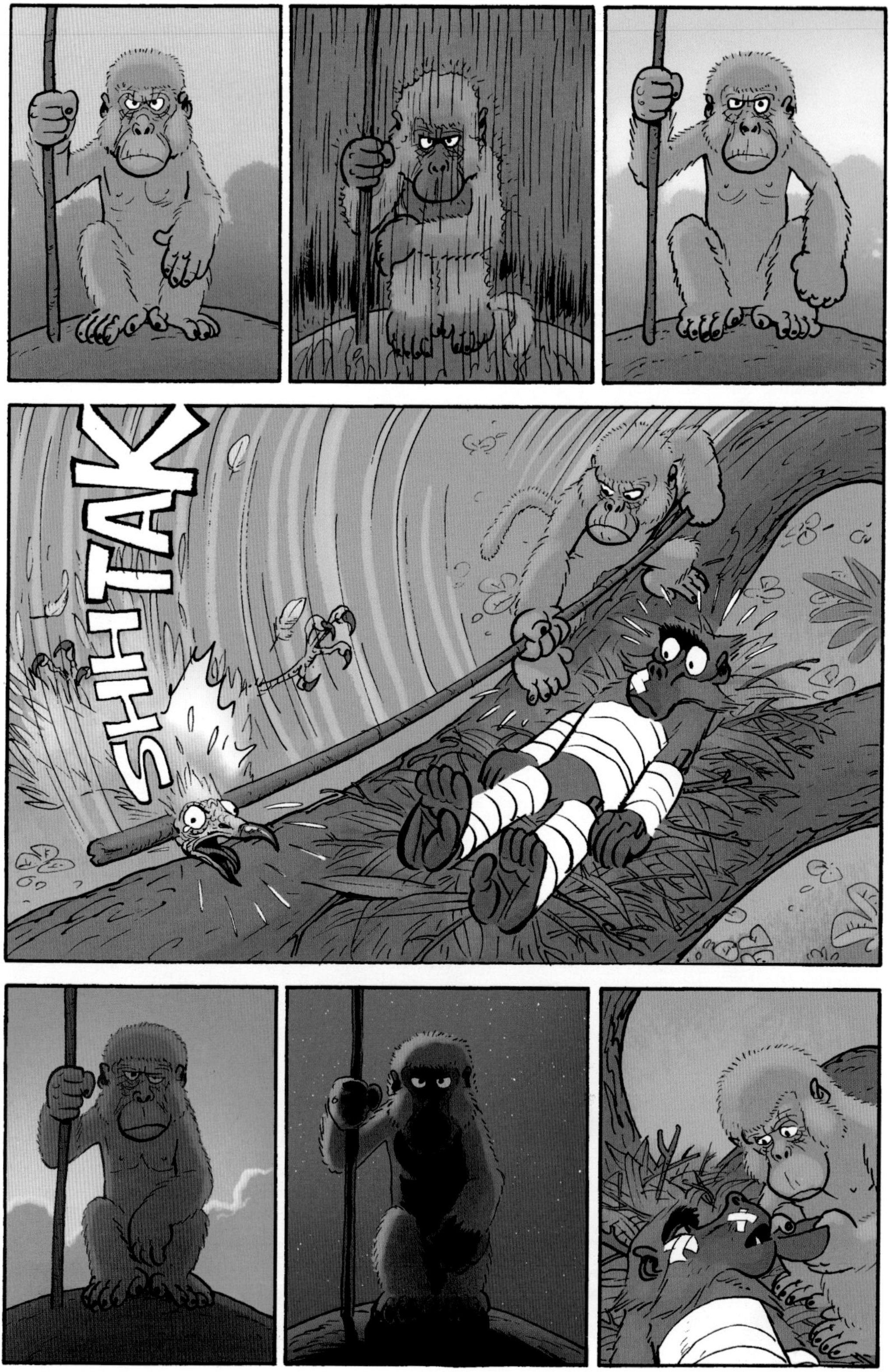
SHHTAK

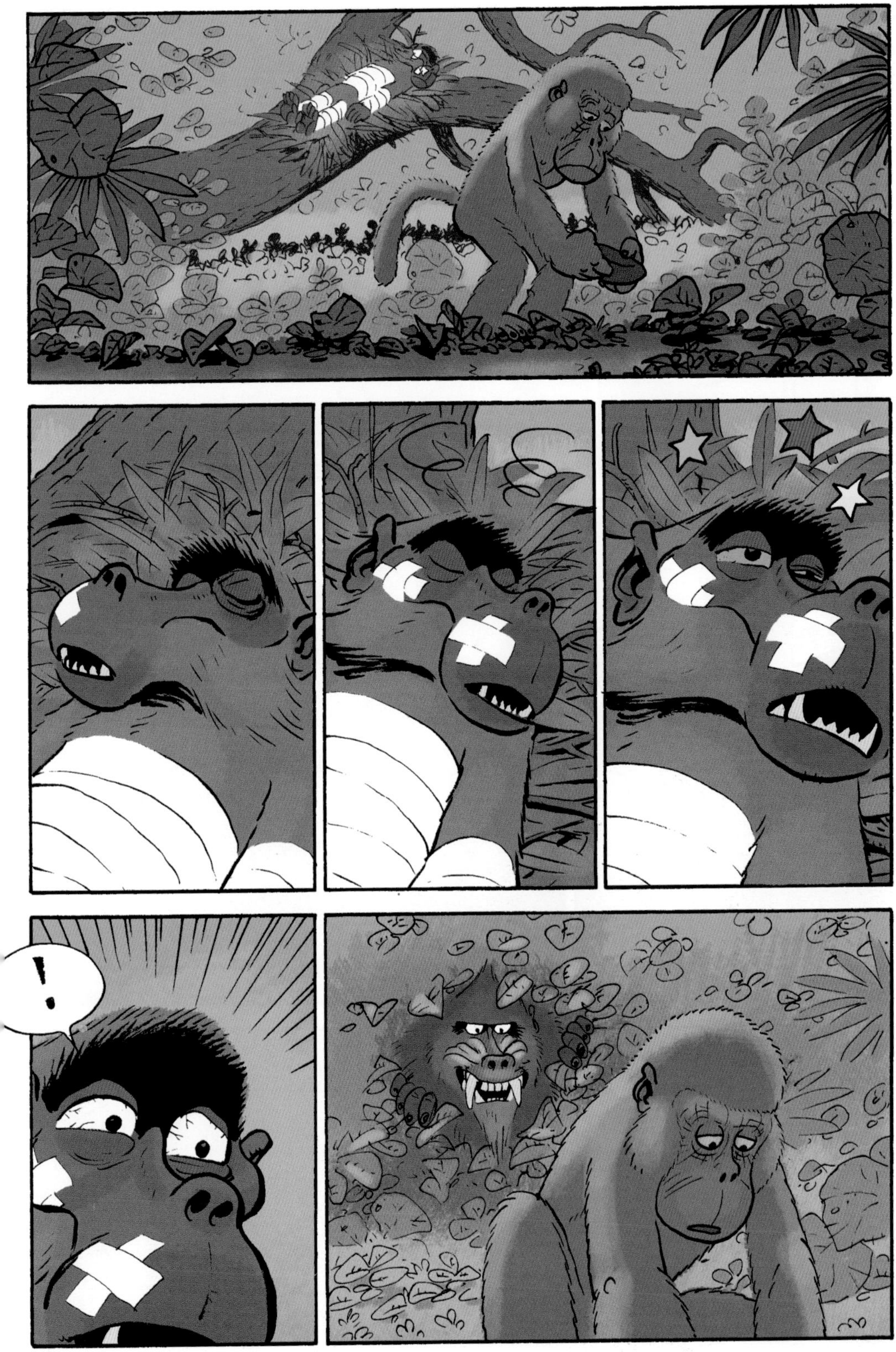
!

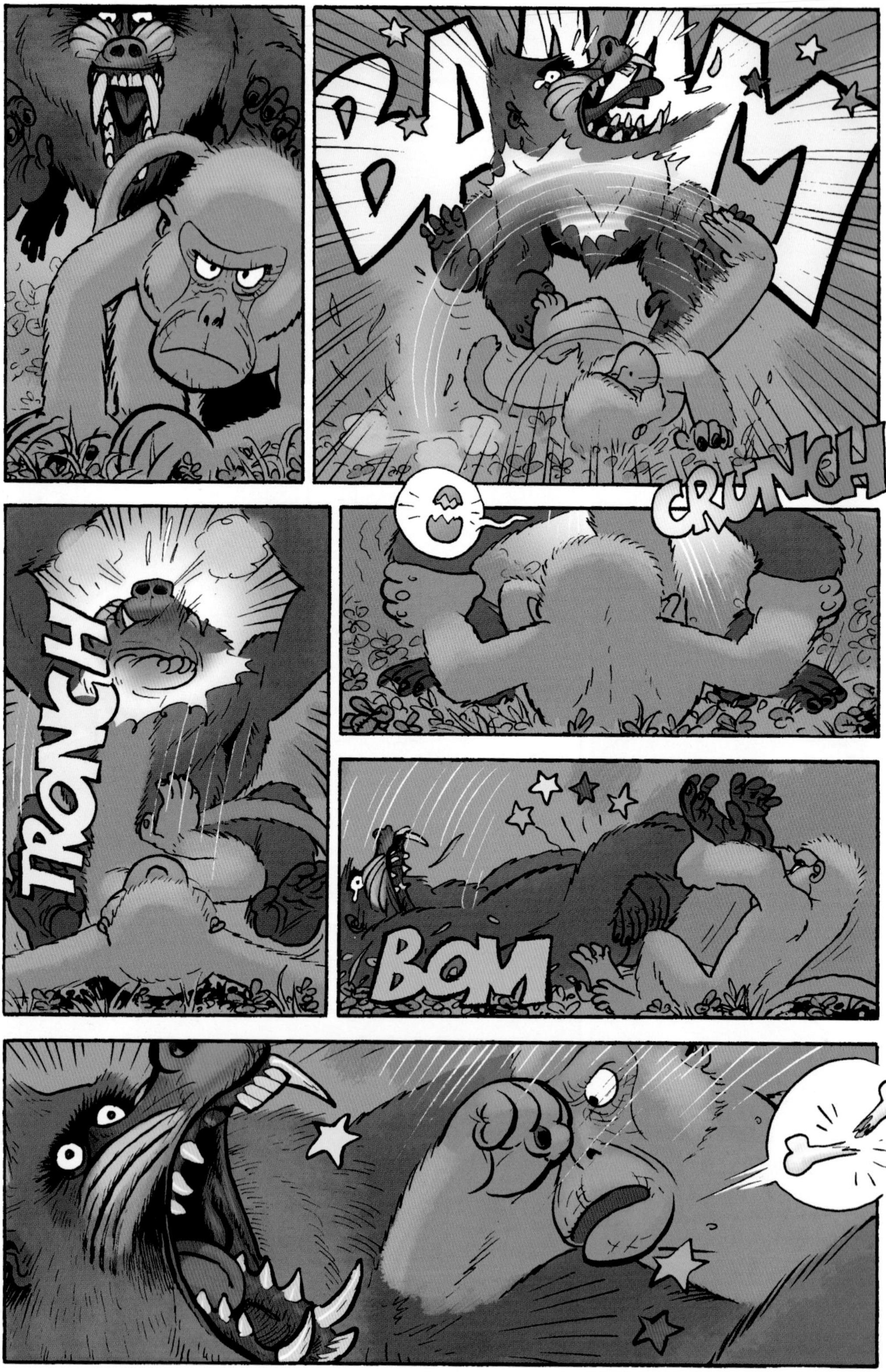
BAM
CRUNCH
TRONCH
BOM

CRACK

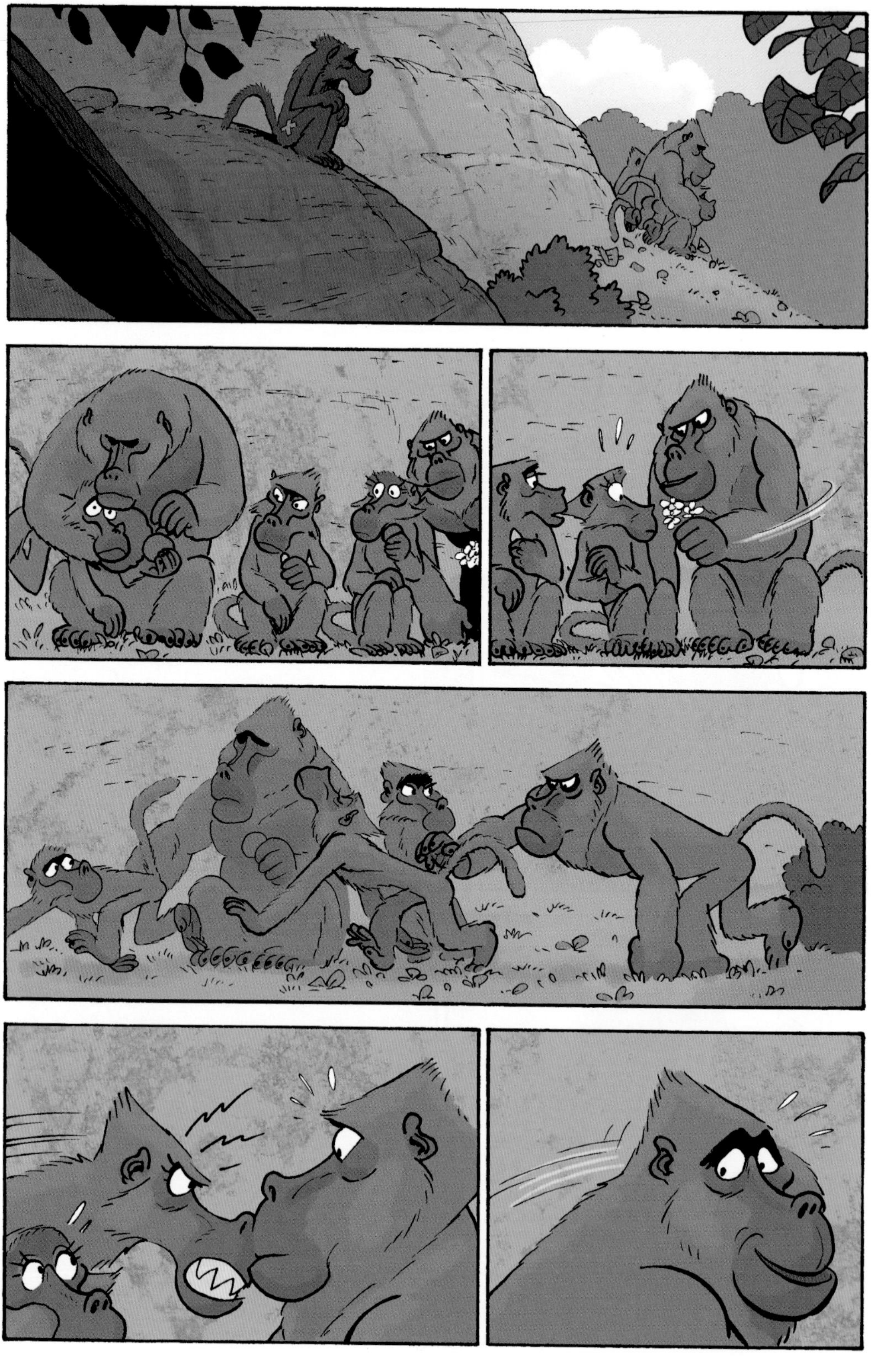

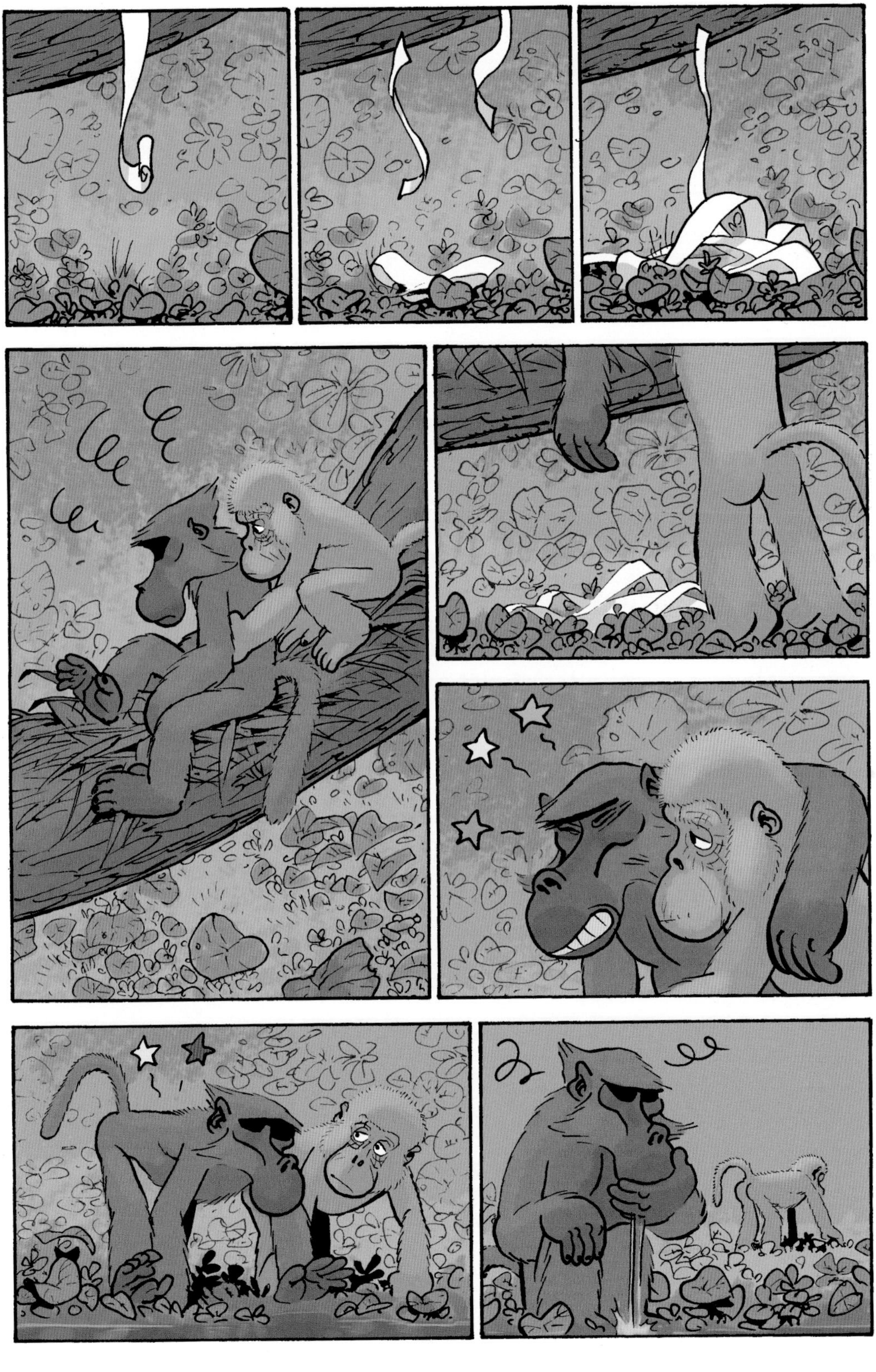

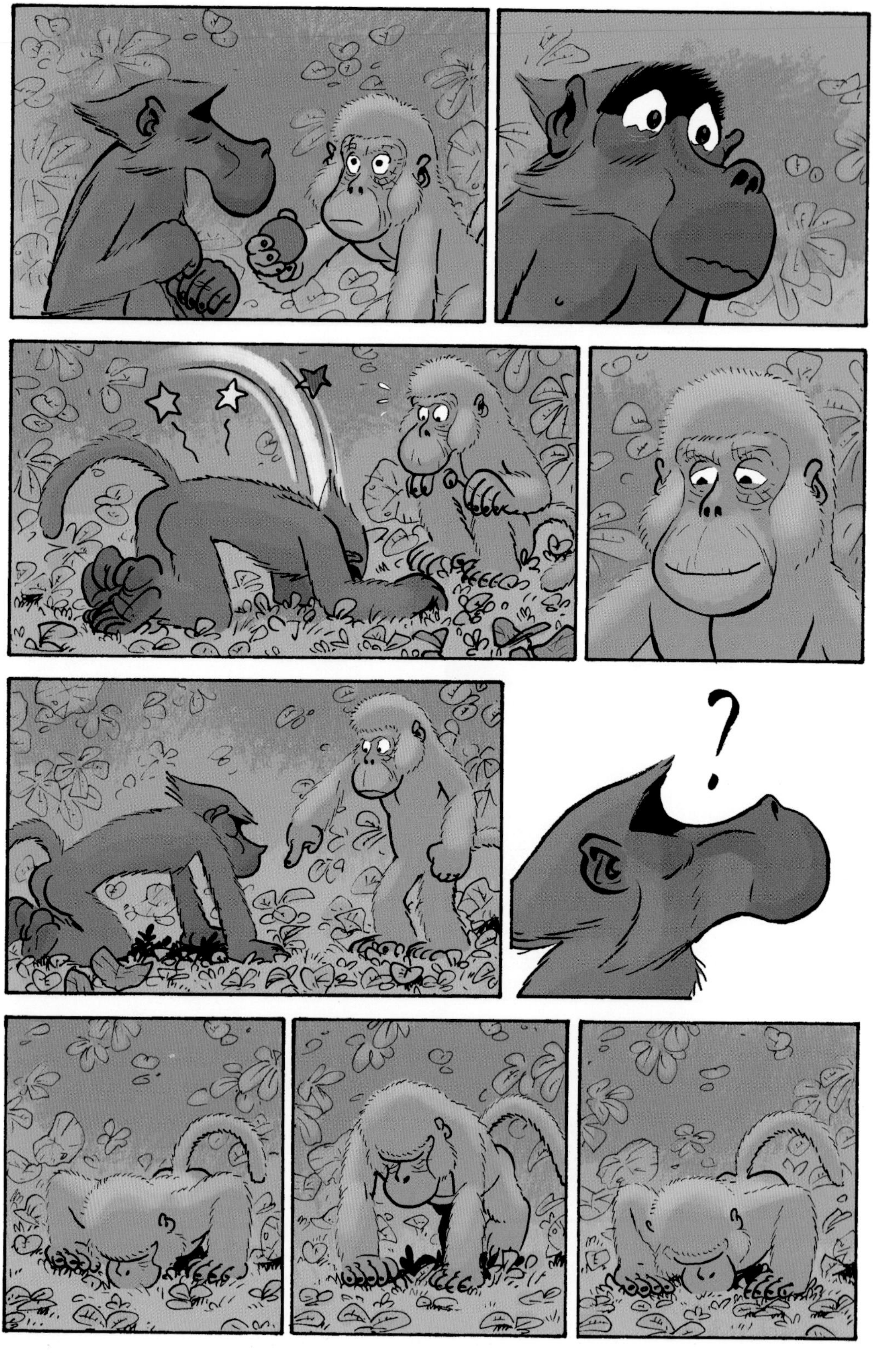
?

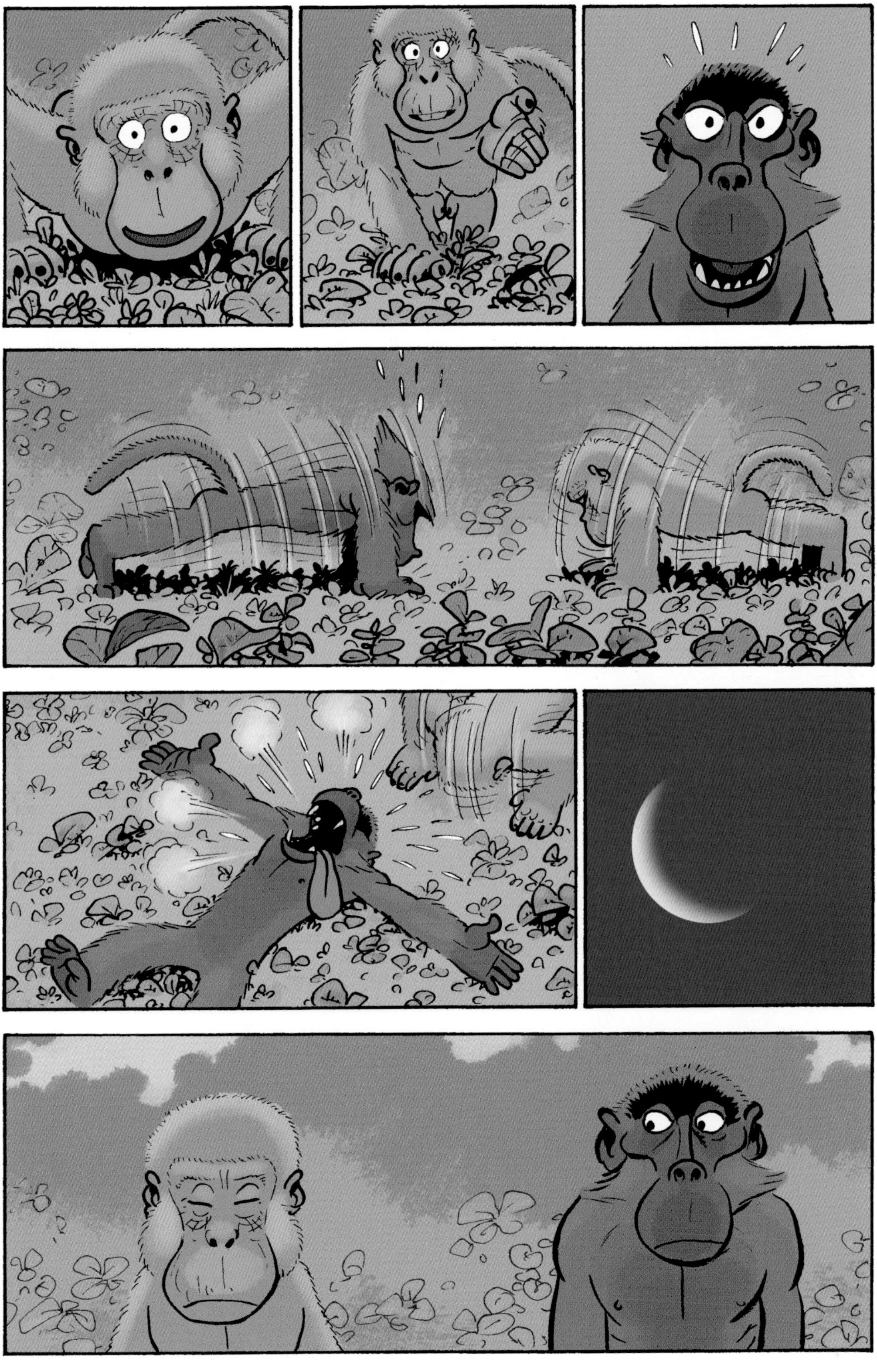

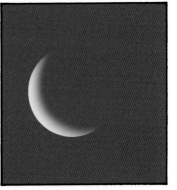

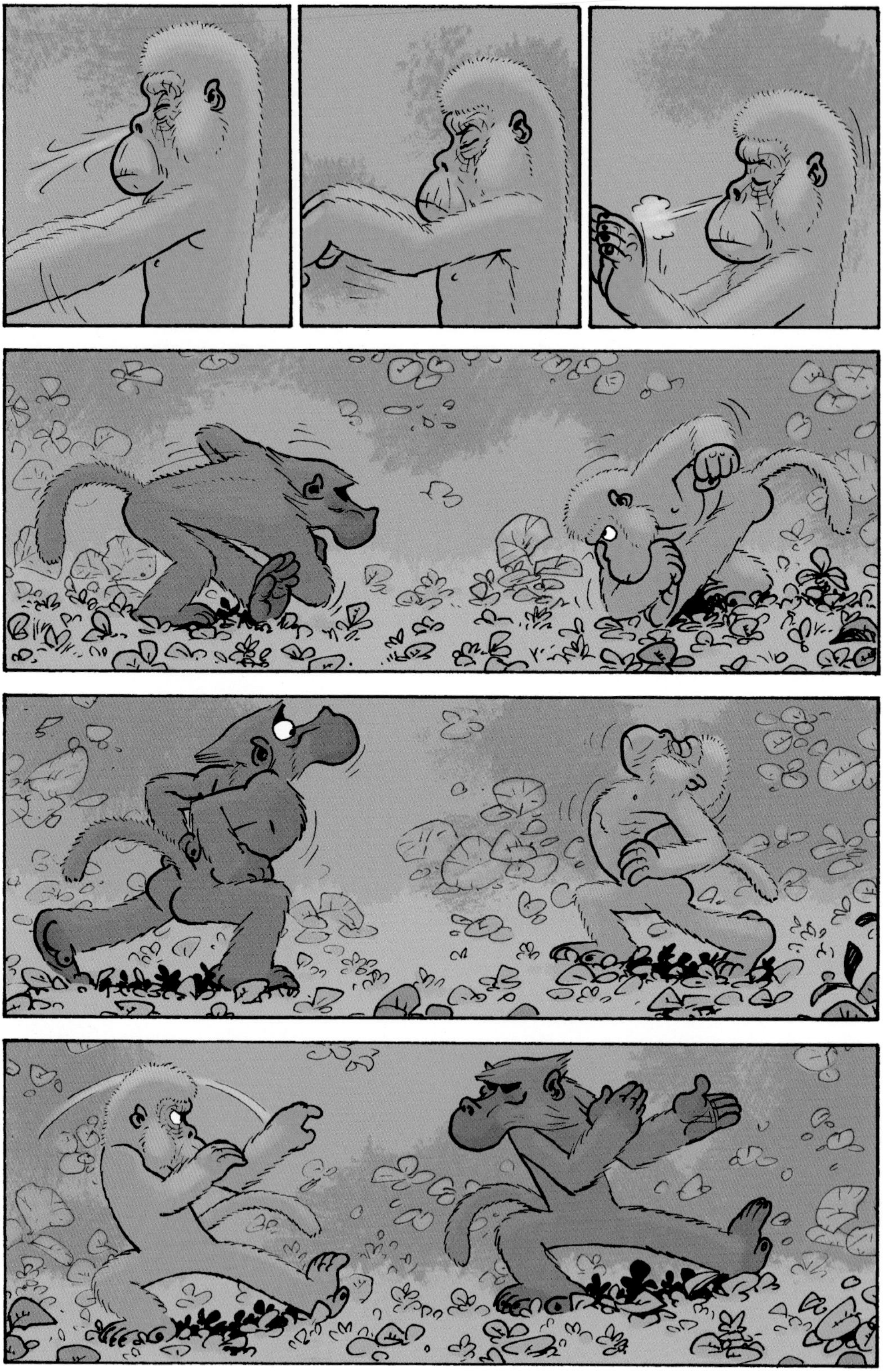

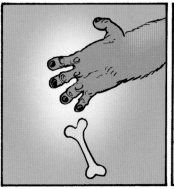

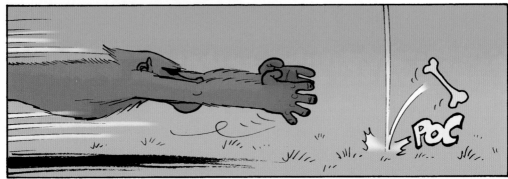

POC

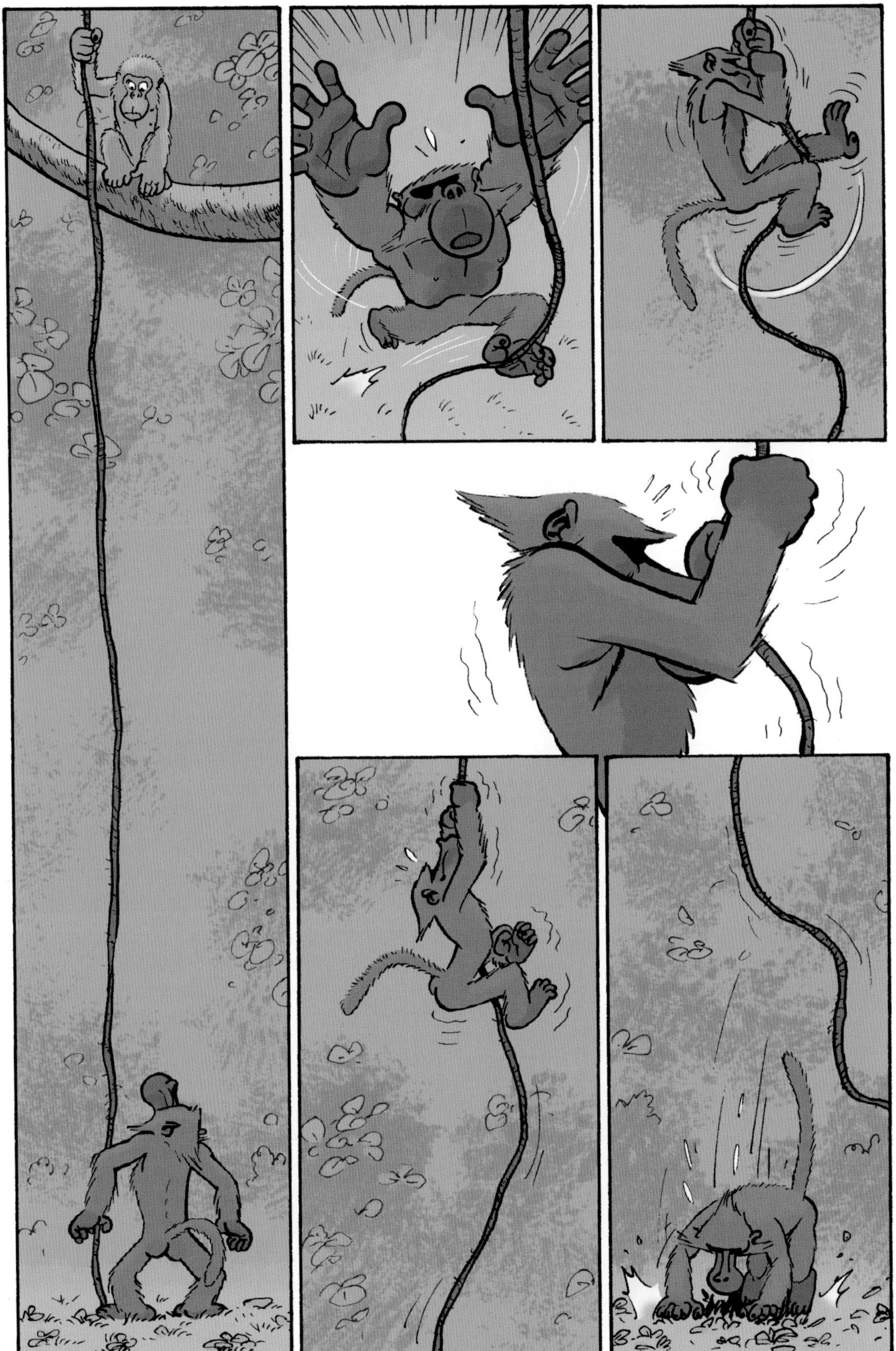

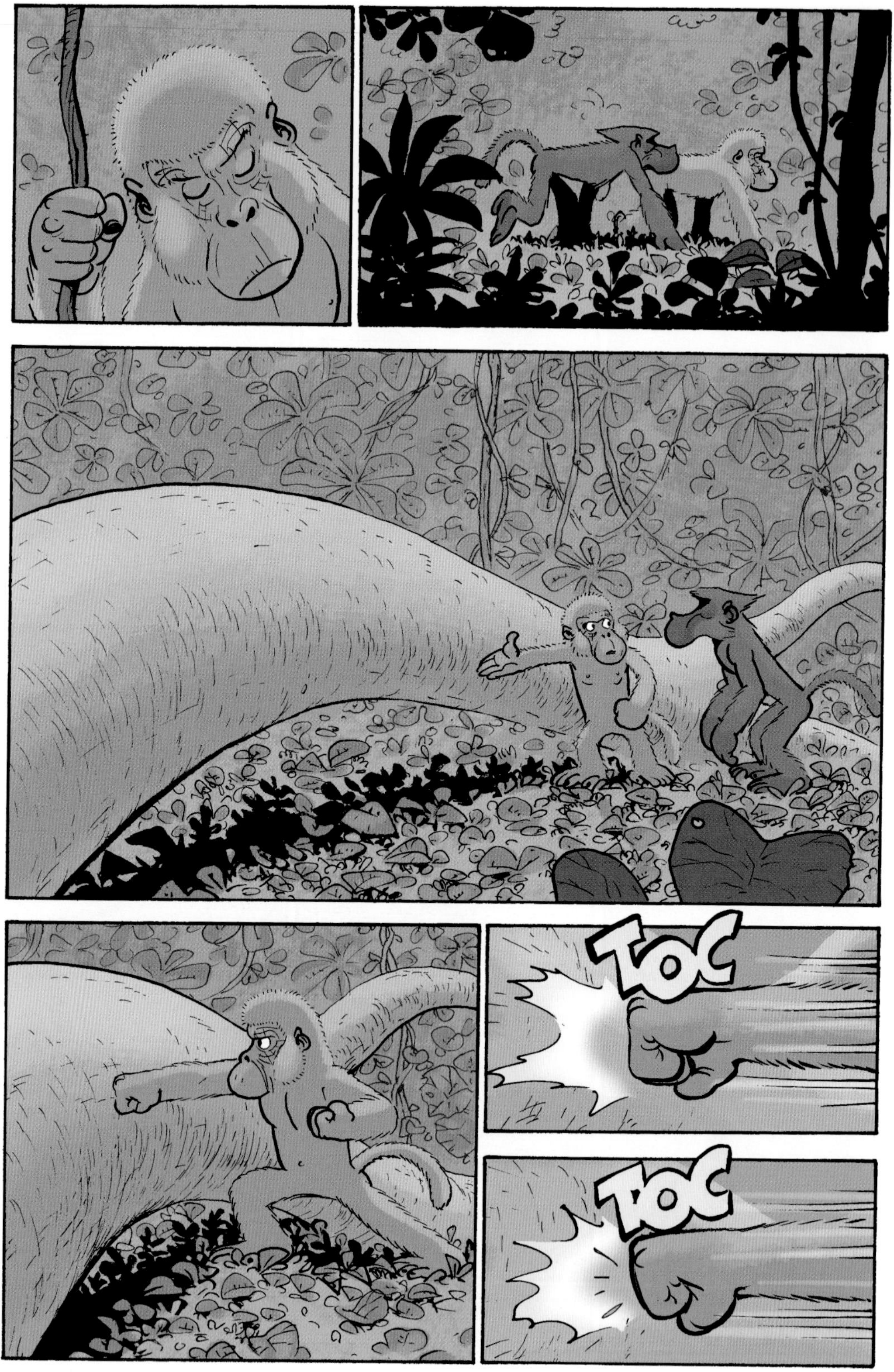
TOC
TOC

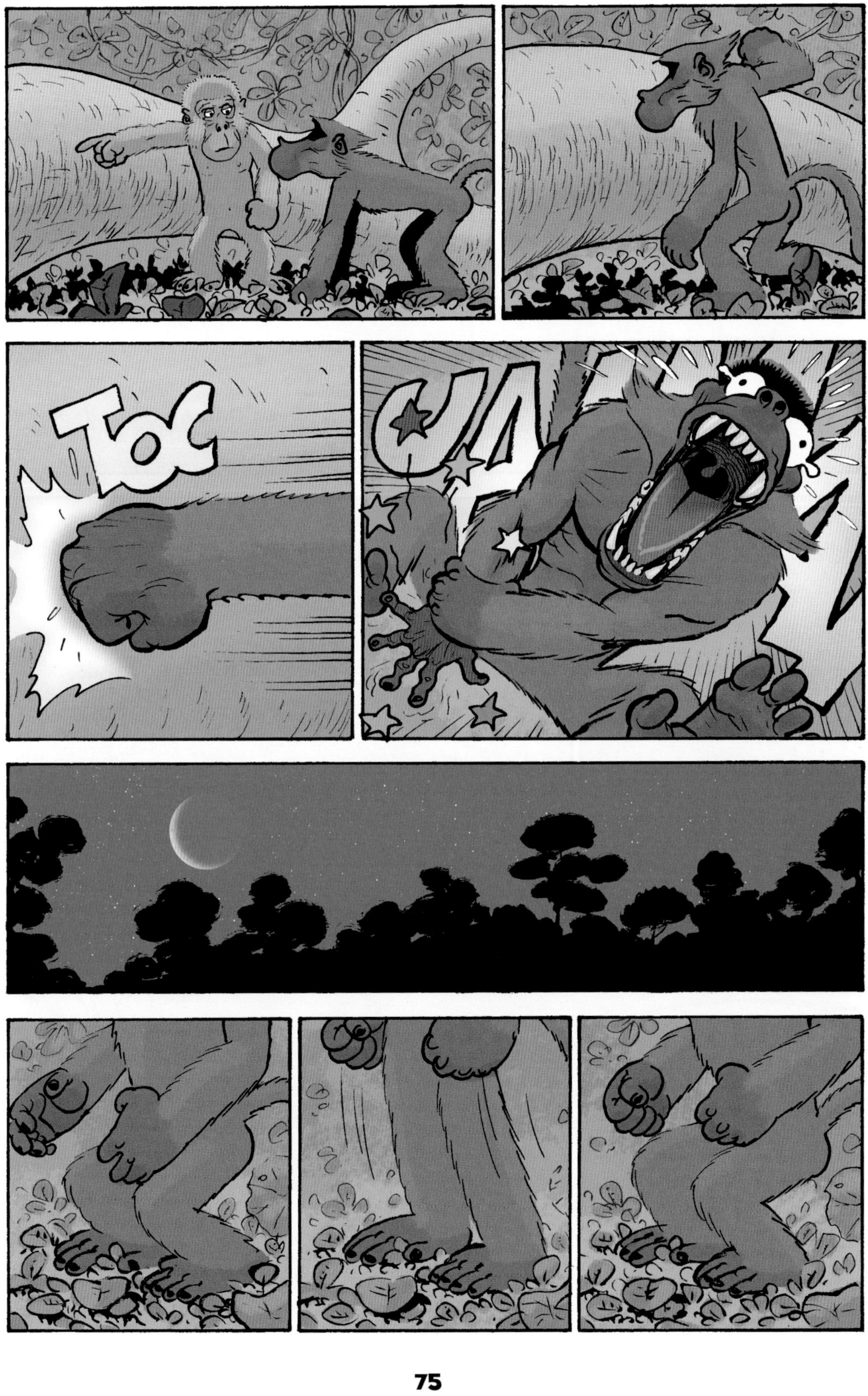
TOC

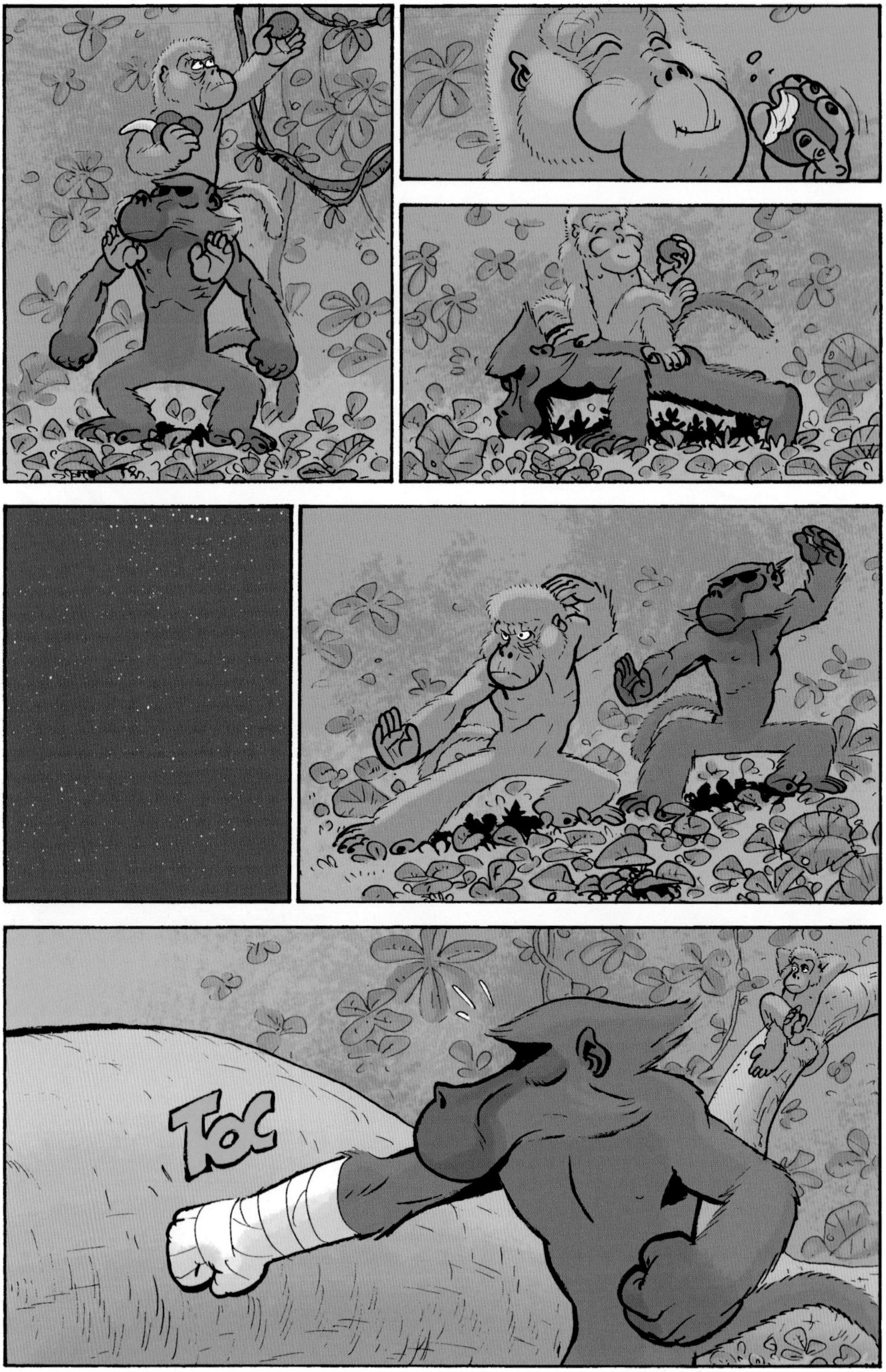
TOC

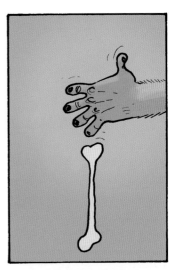

POC

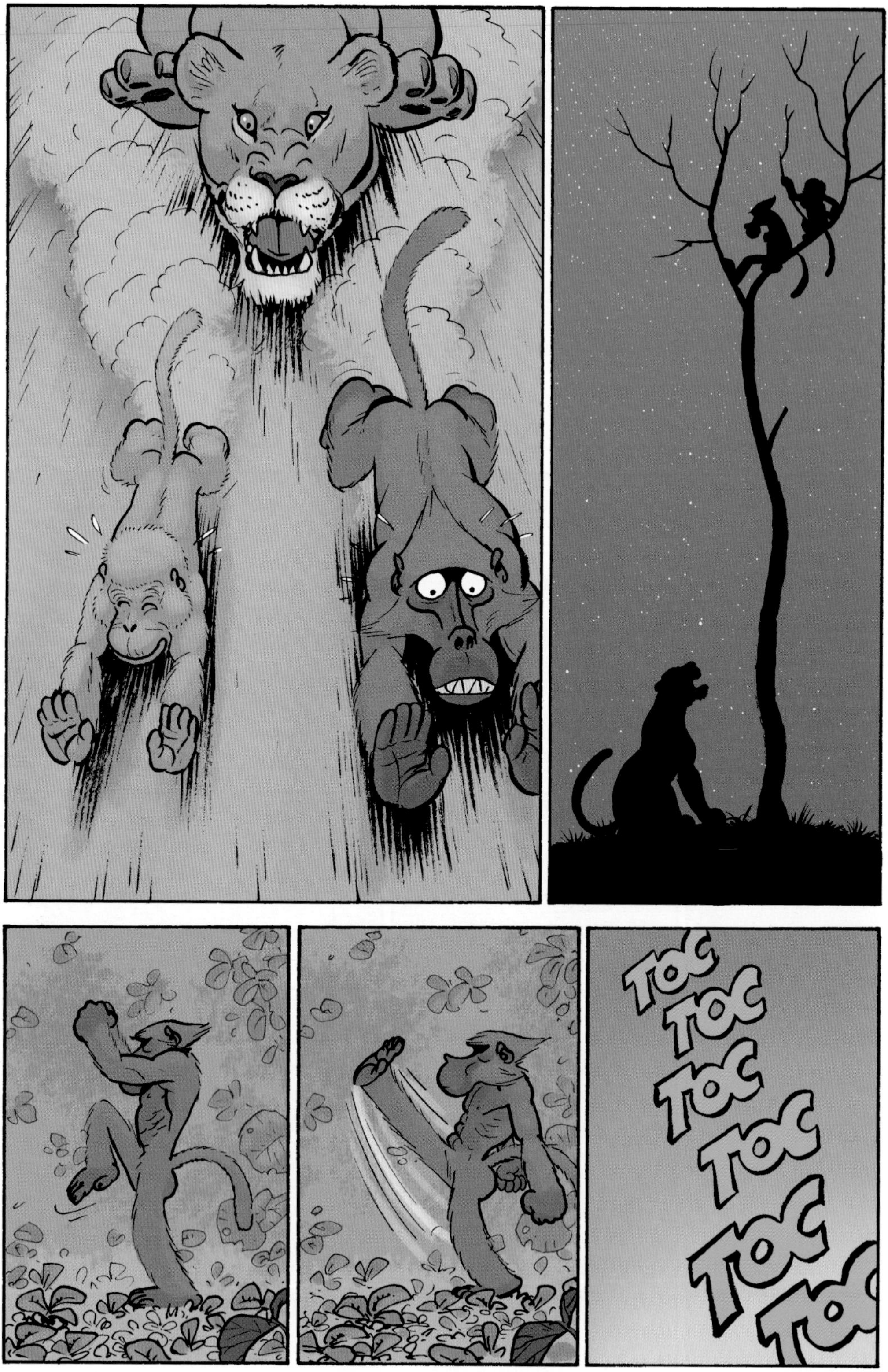
TOC
TOC
TOC
TOC
TOC
TOC

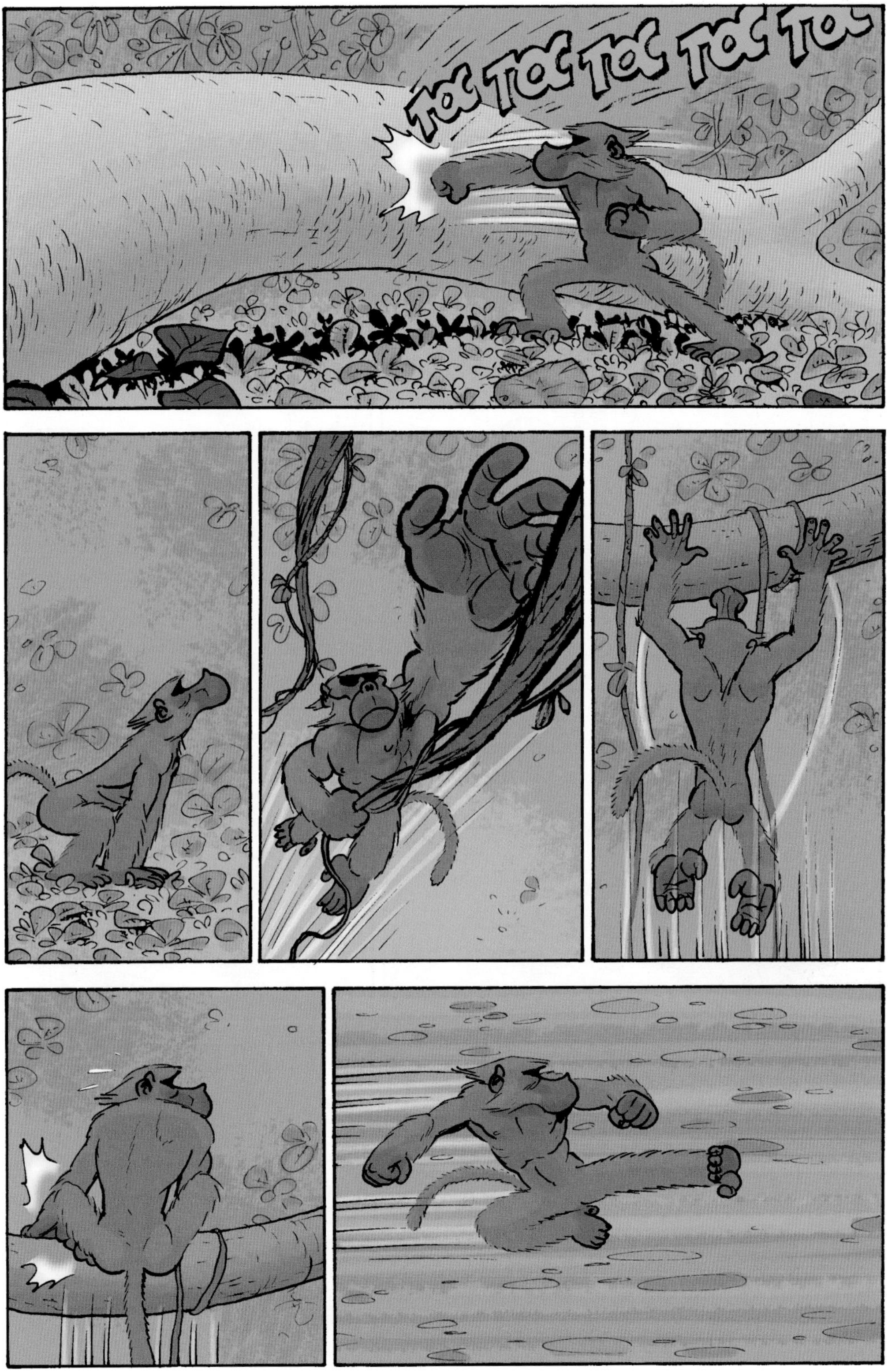
TOC TOC TOC TOC TOC

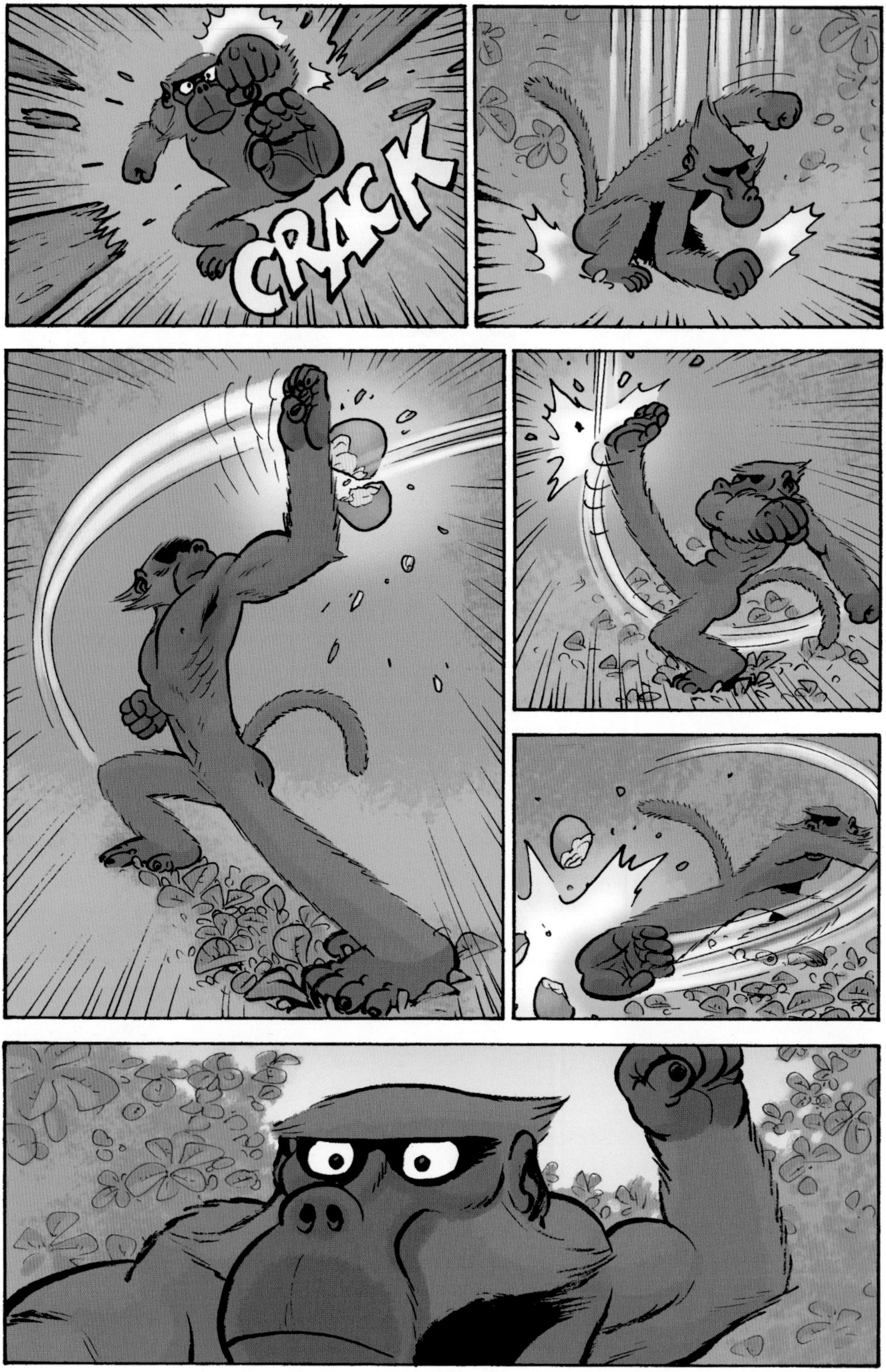
CRACK

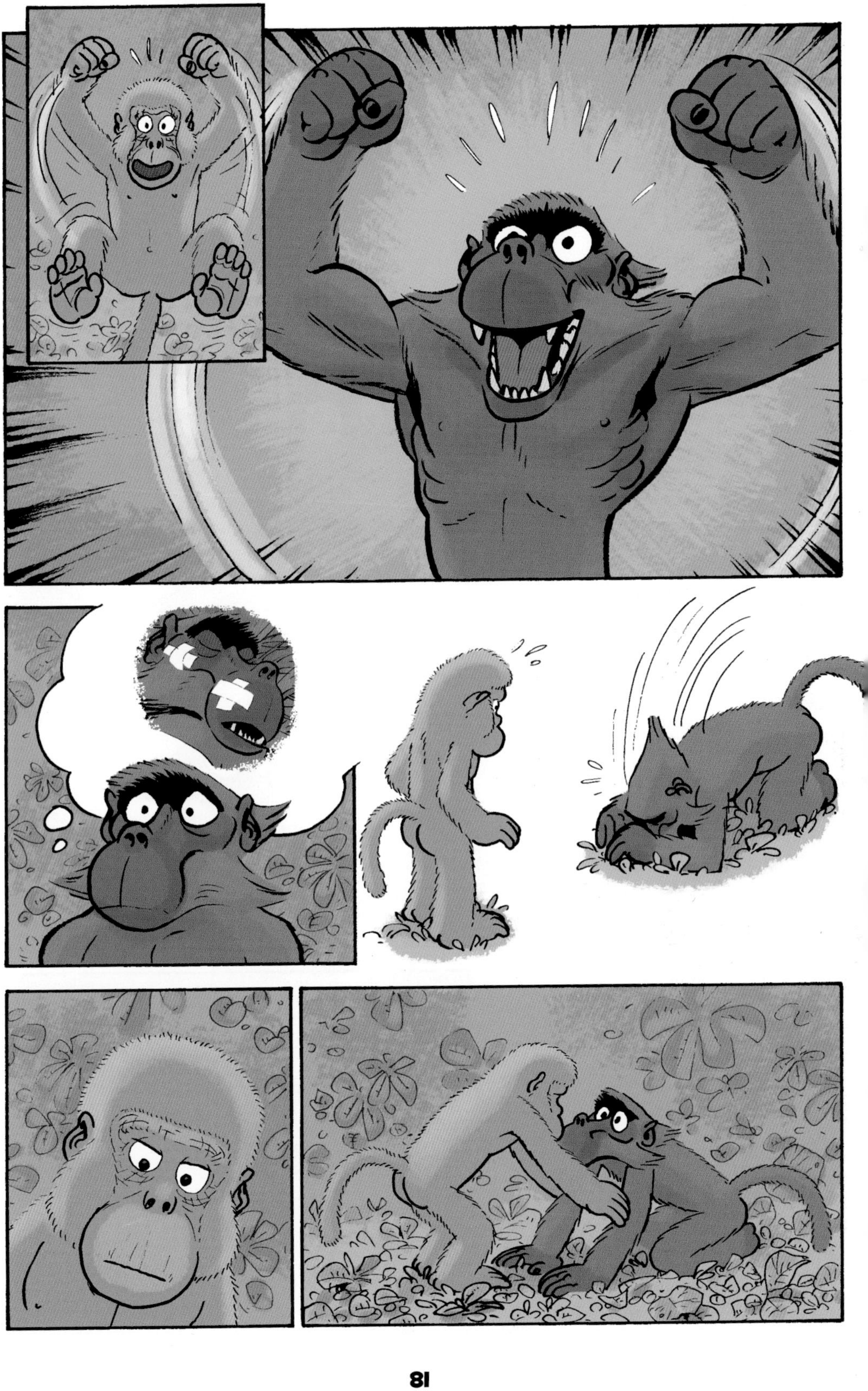

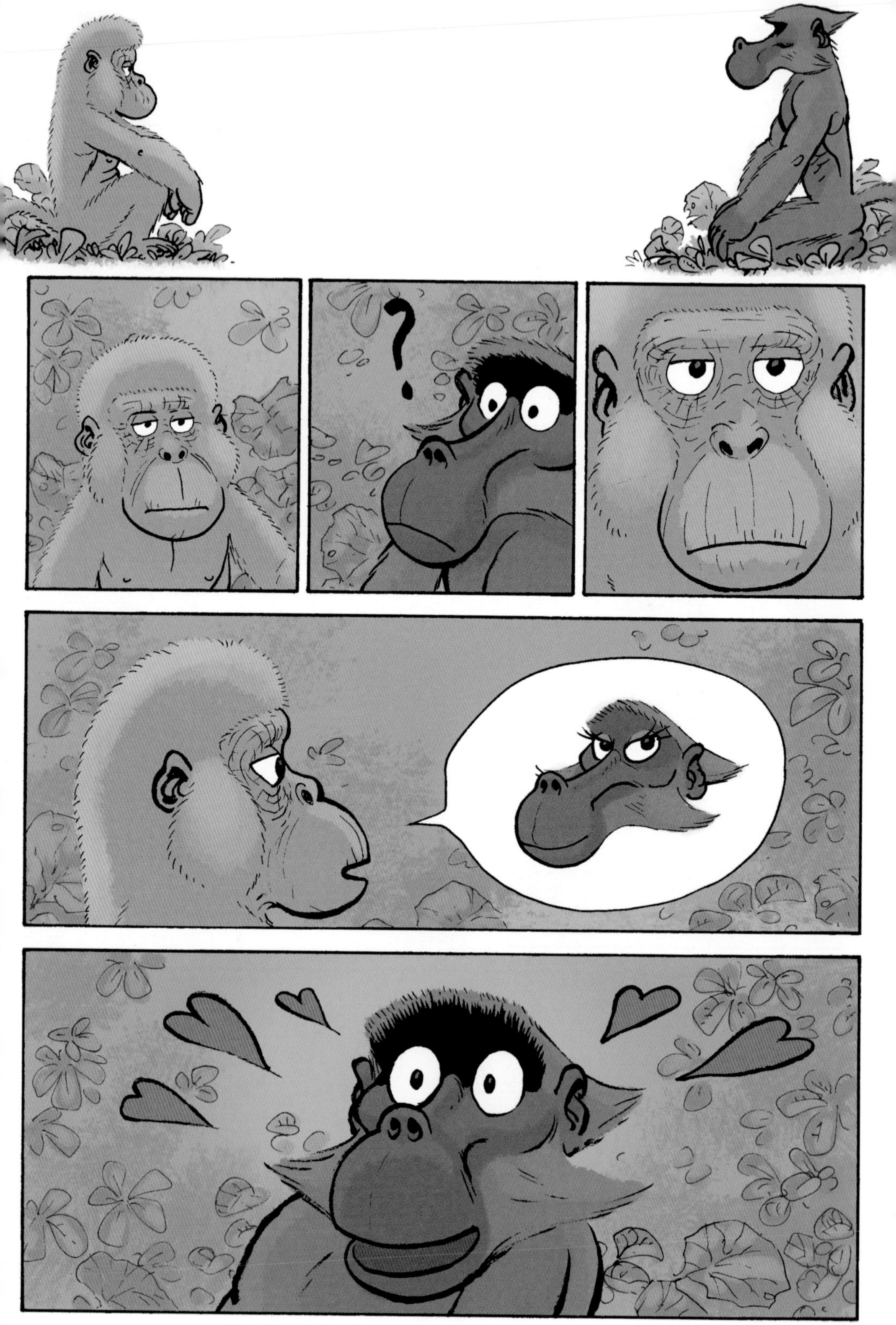
?

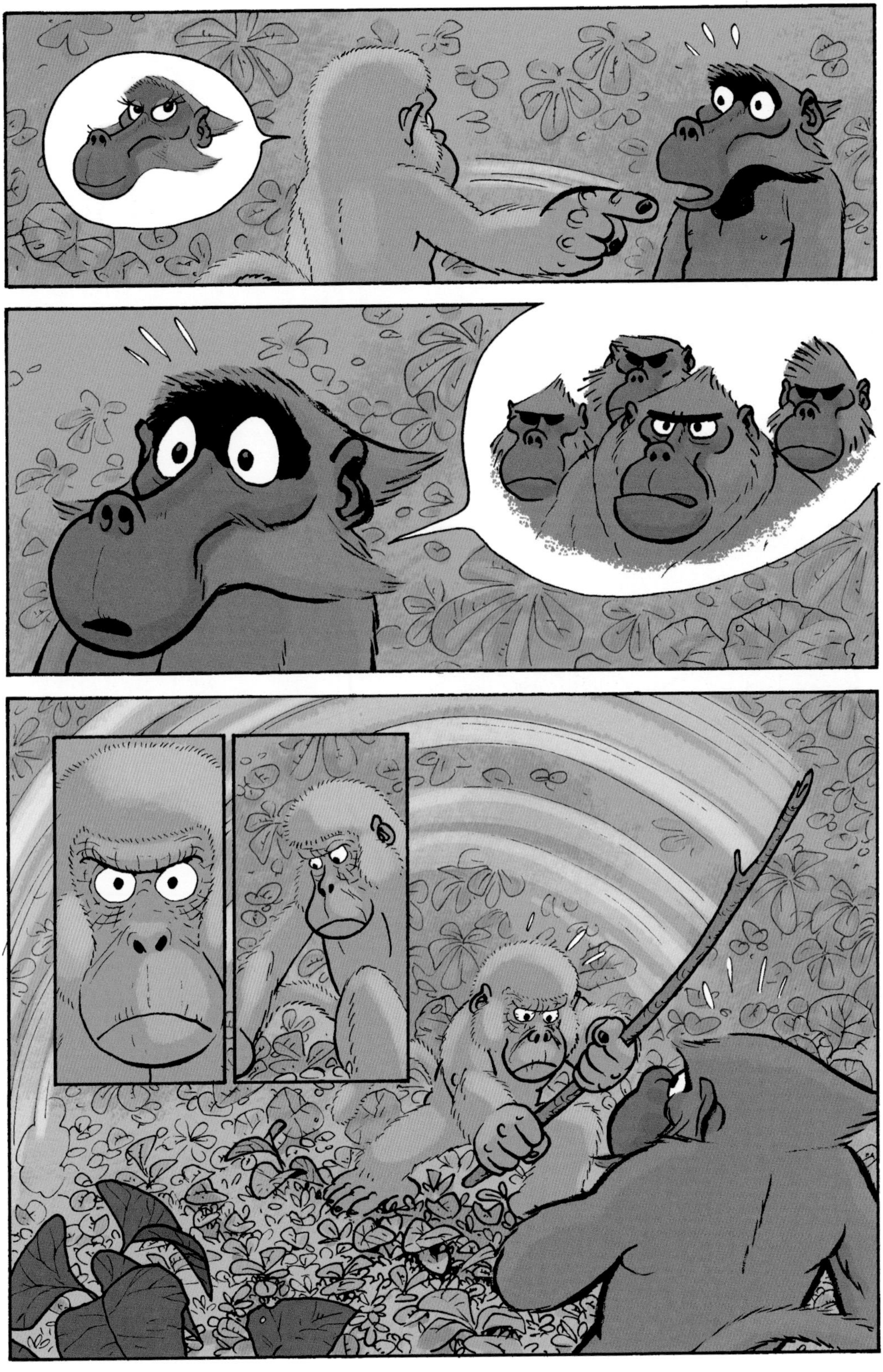

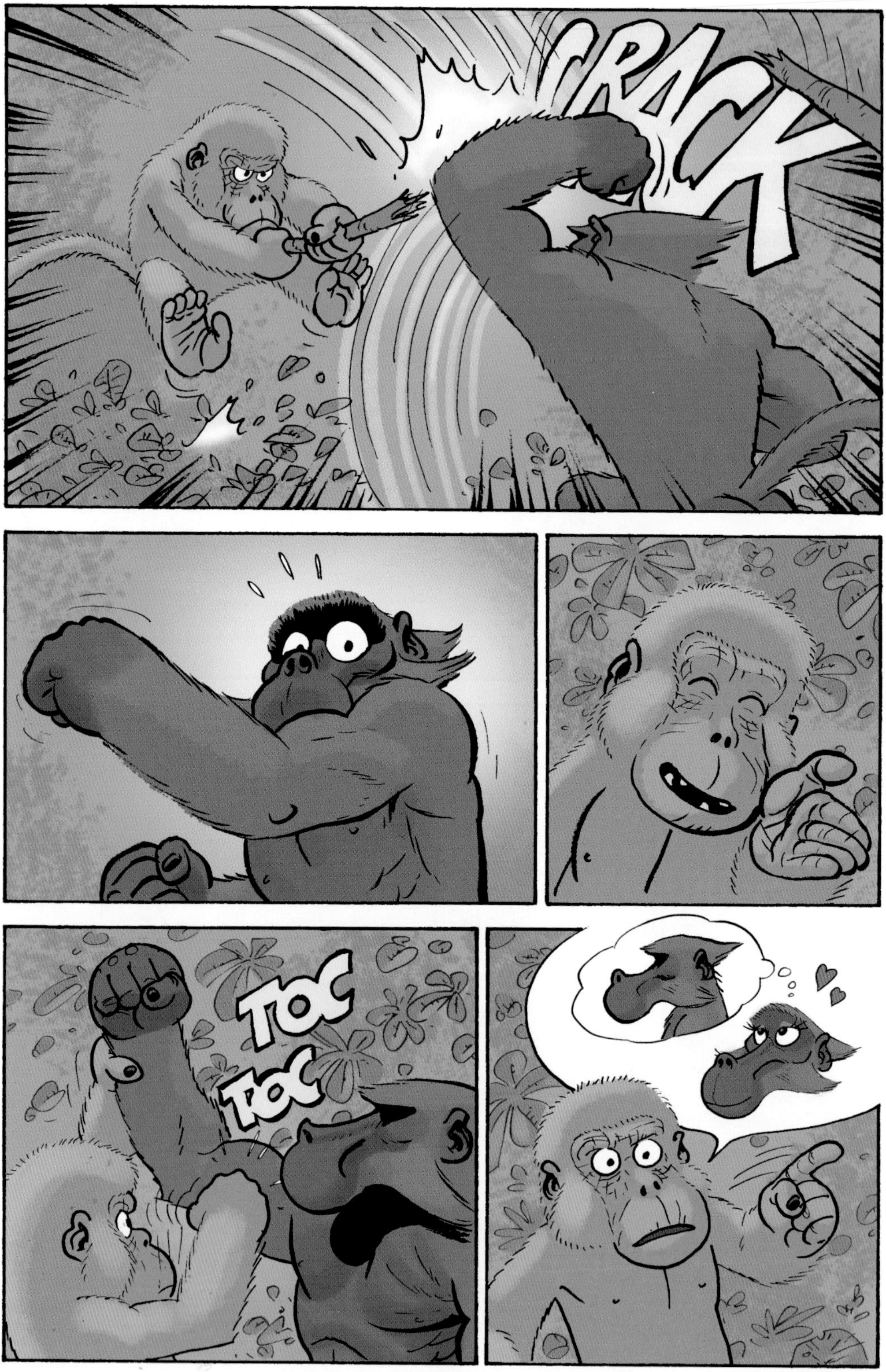
CRACK
TOC
TOC

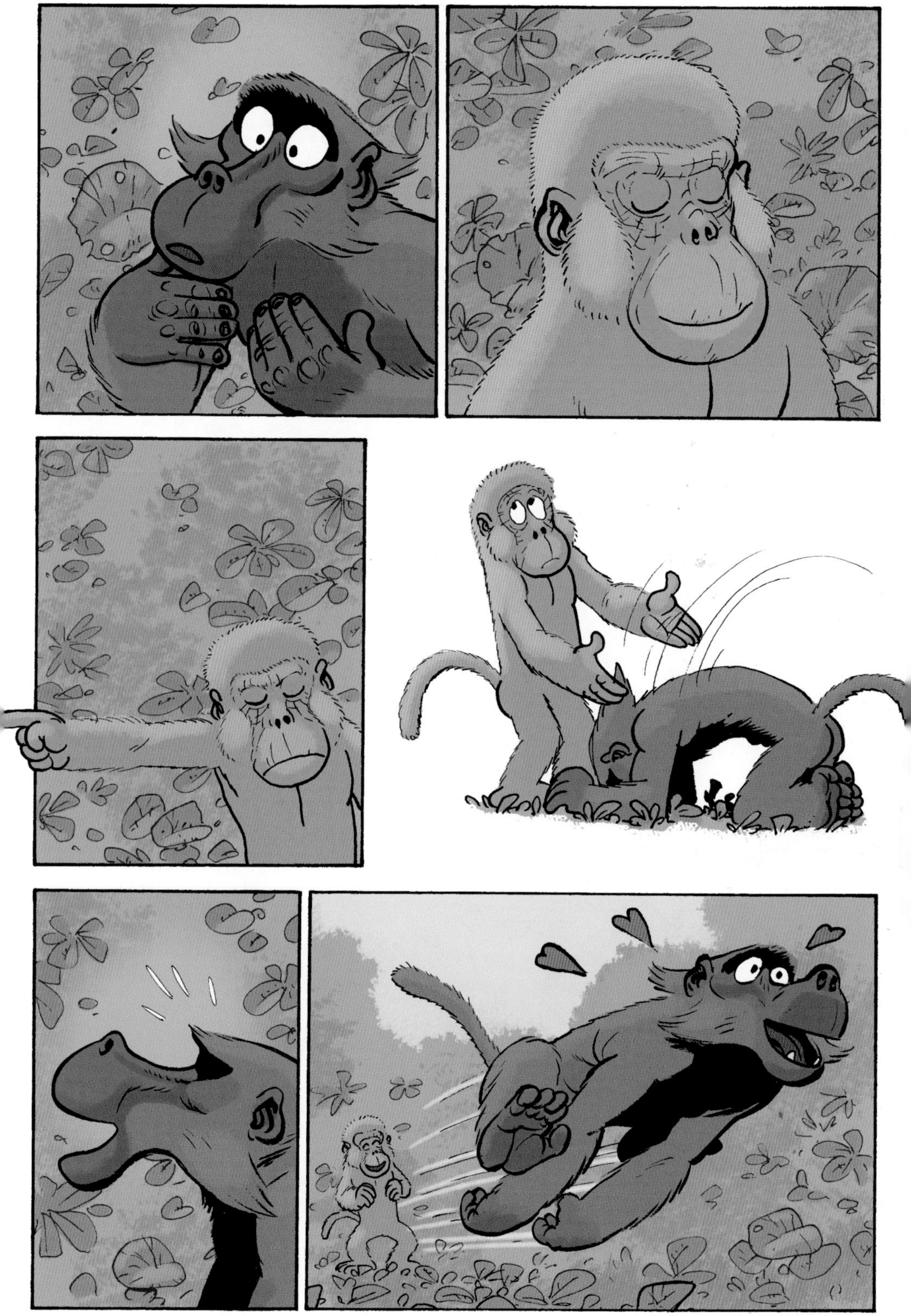

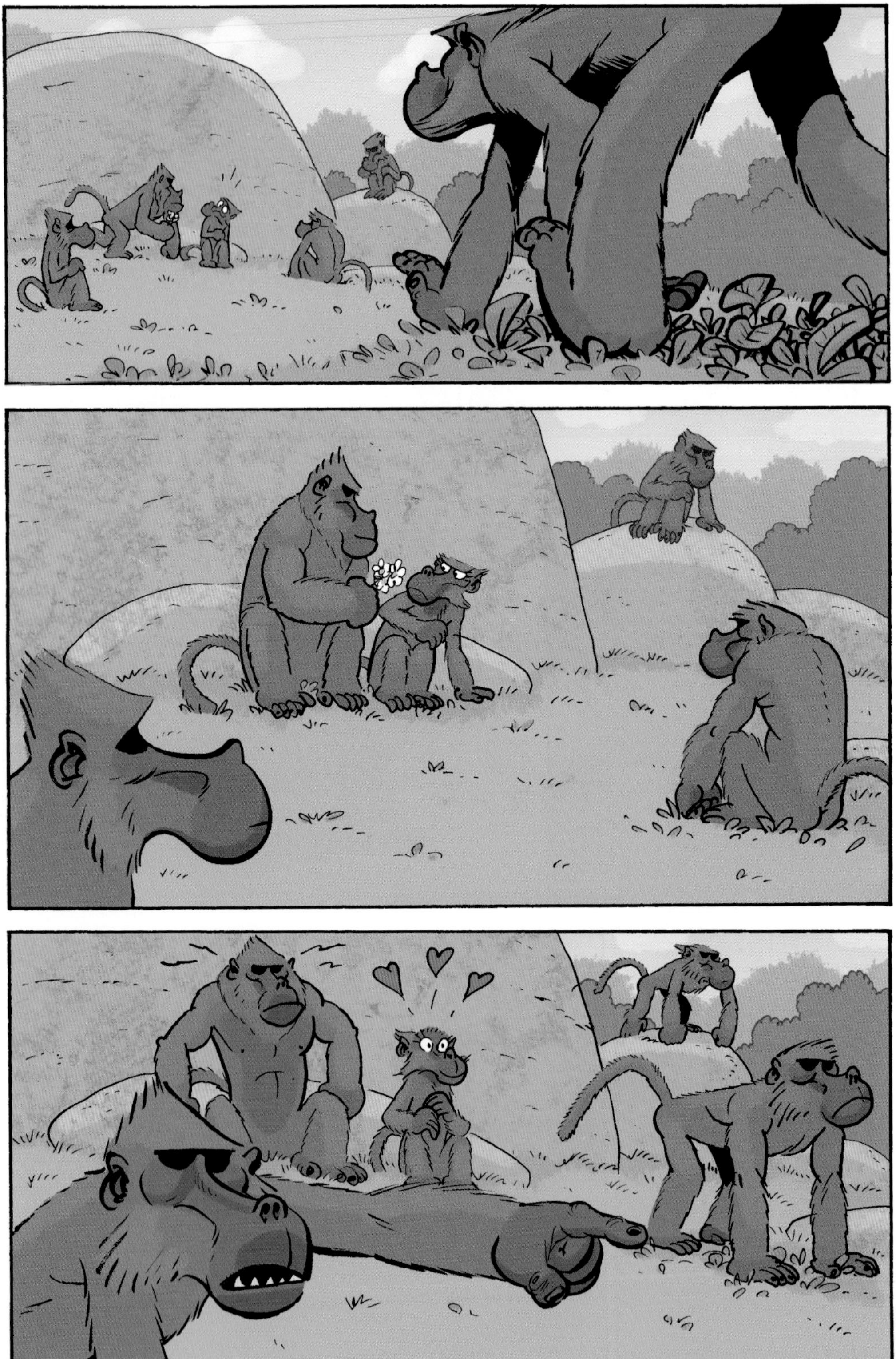

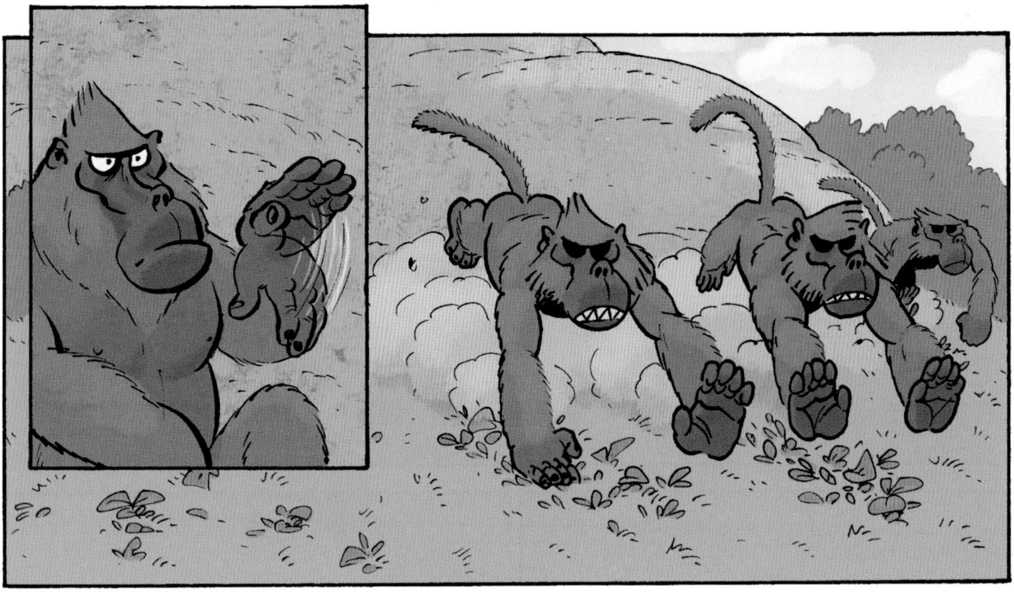

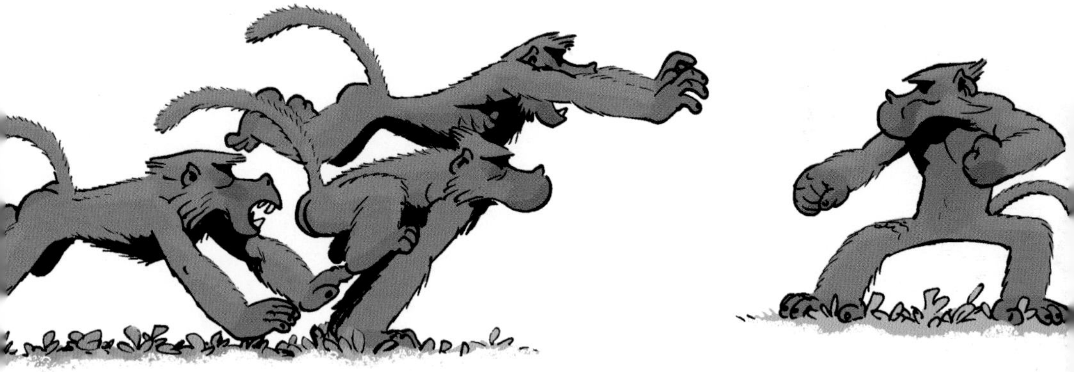

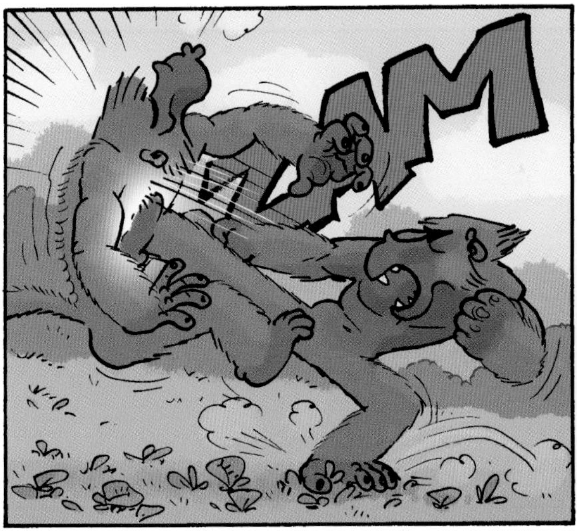

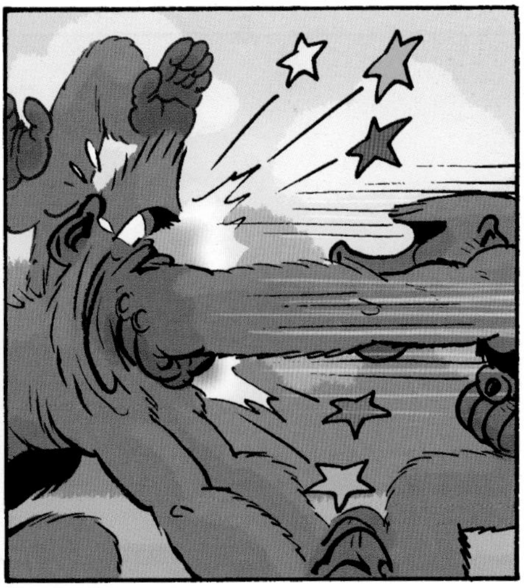

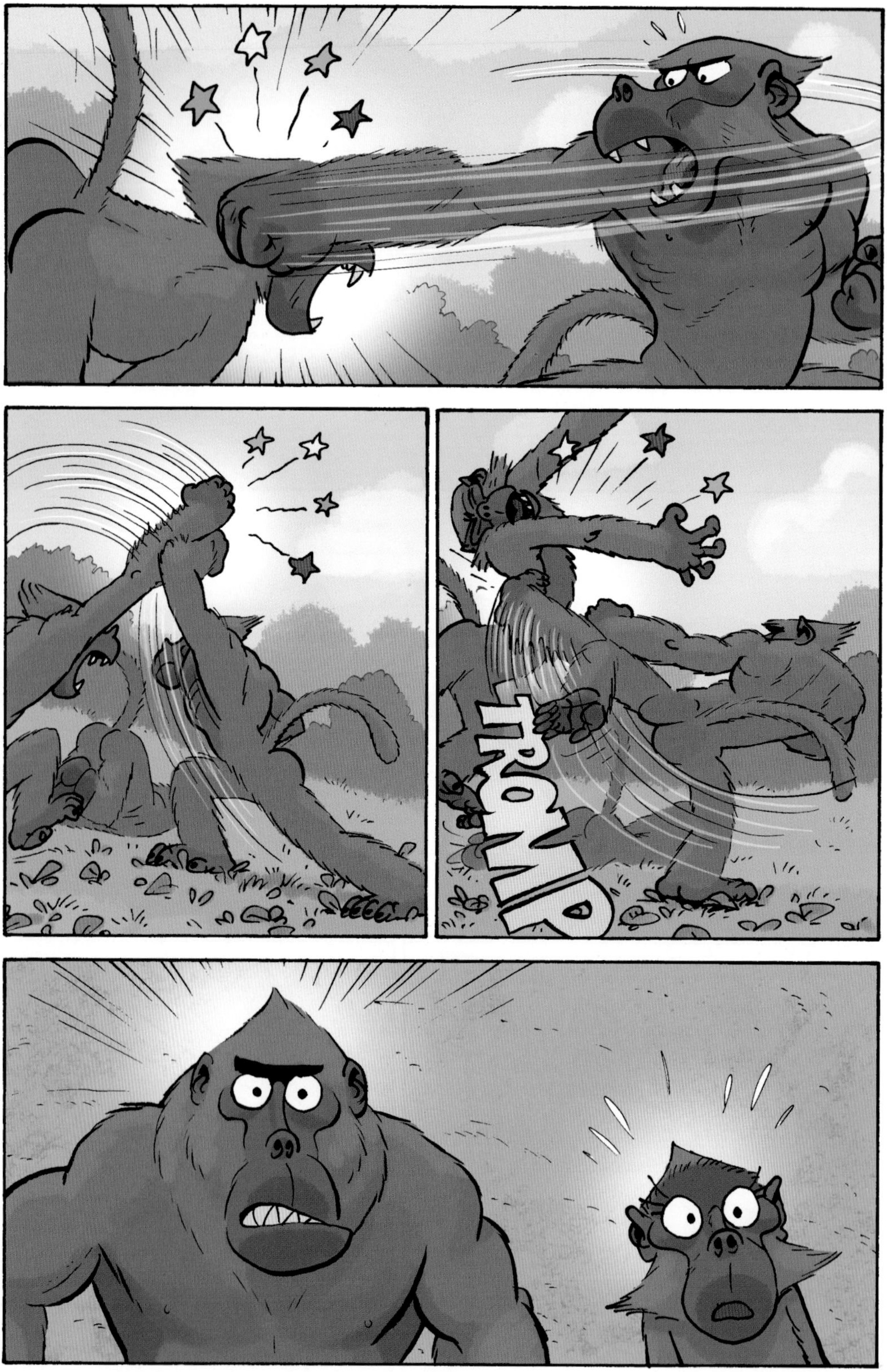
TROMP

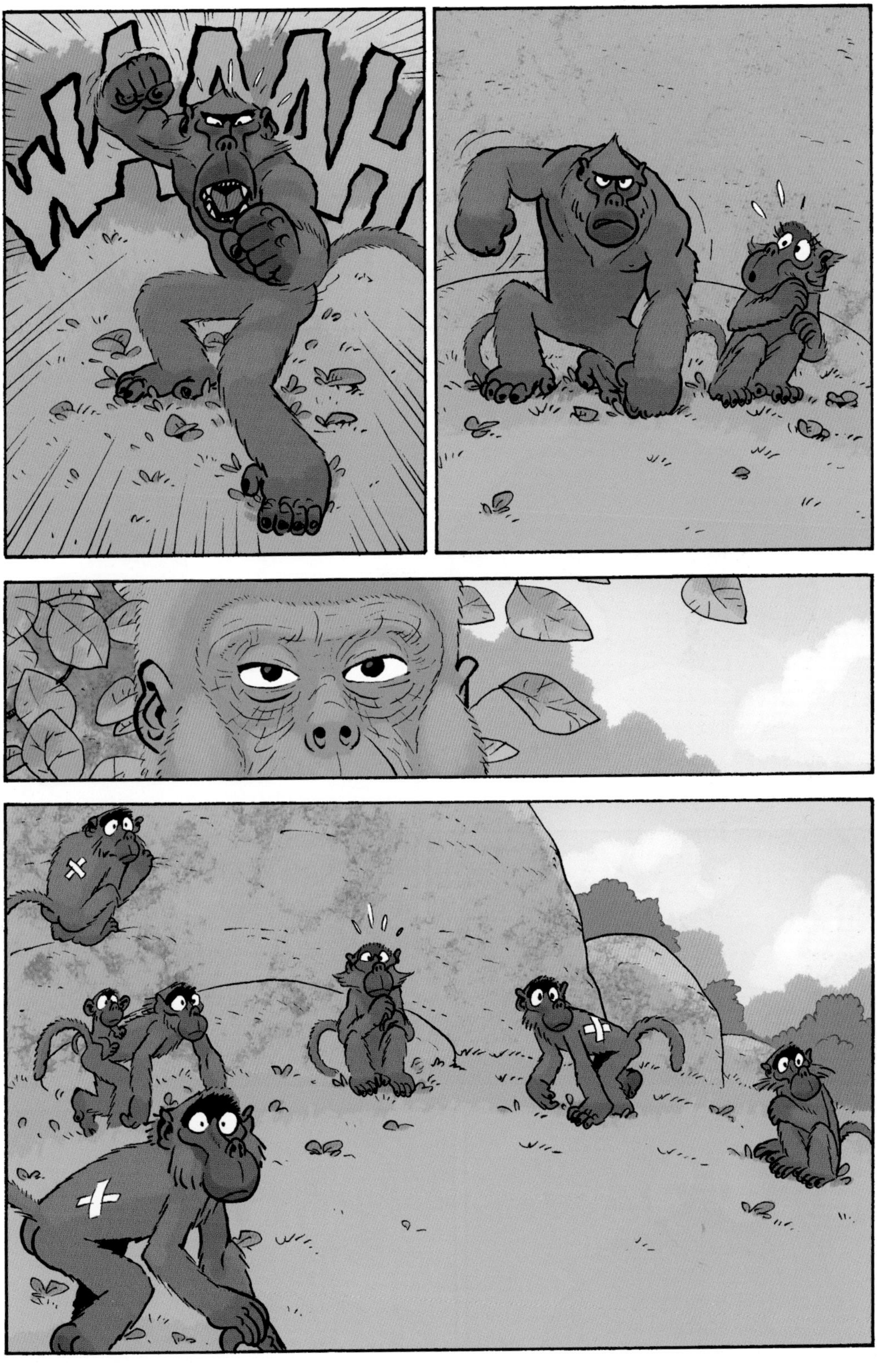

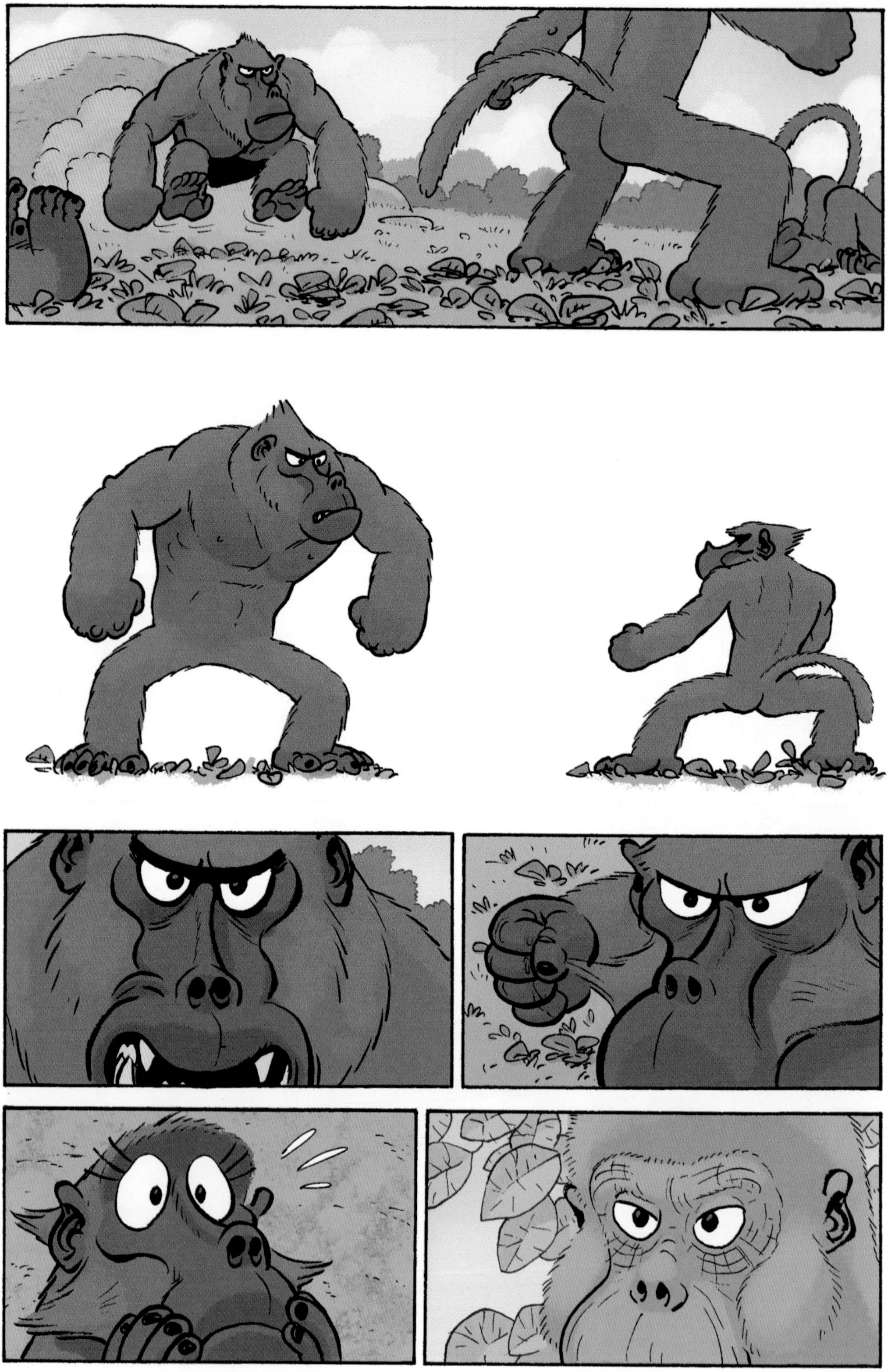

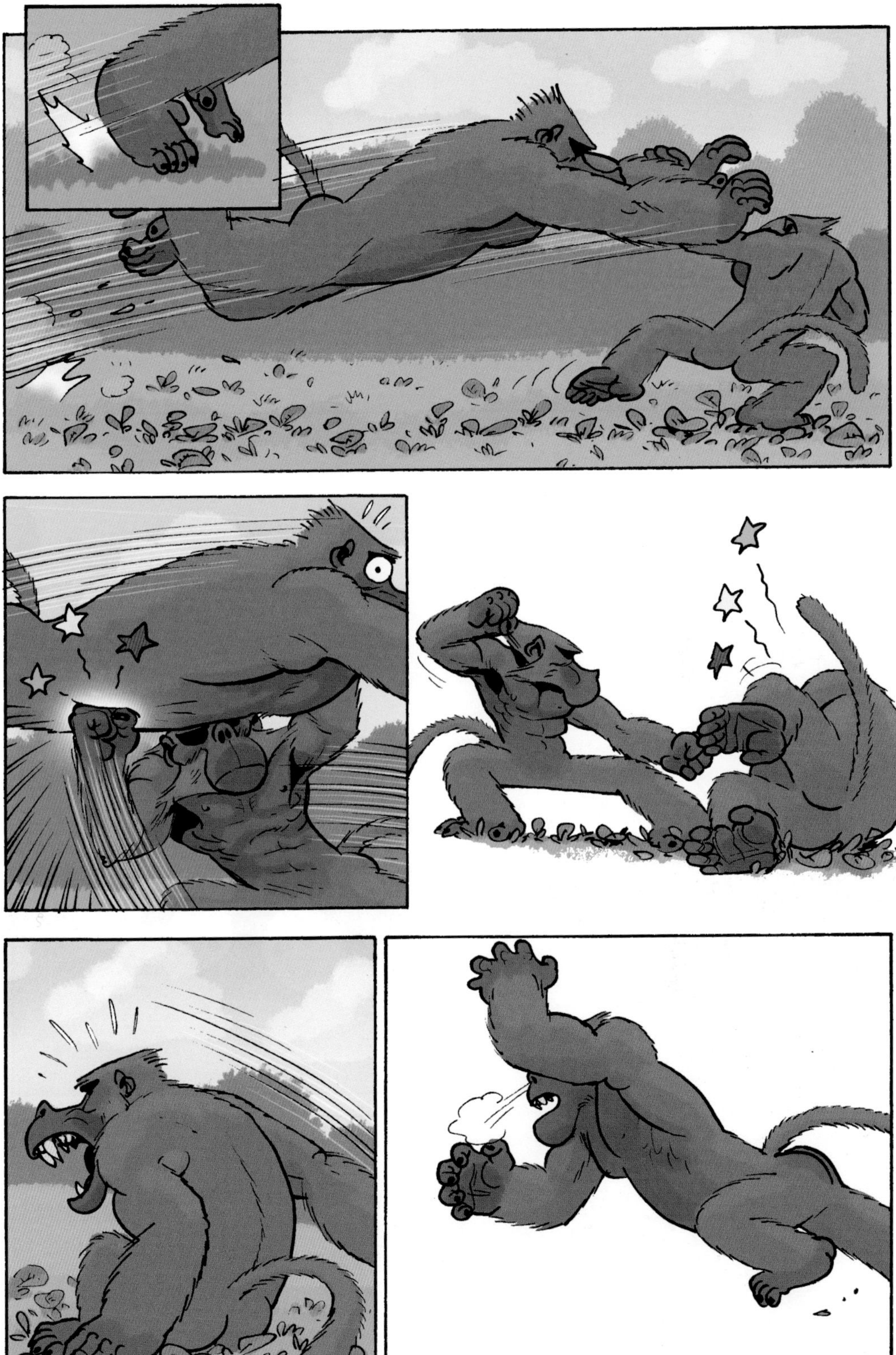

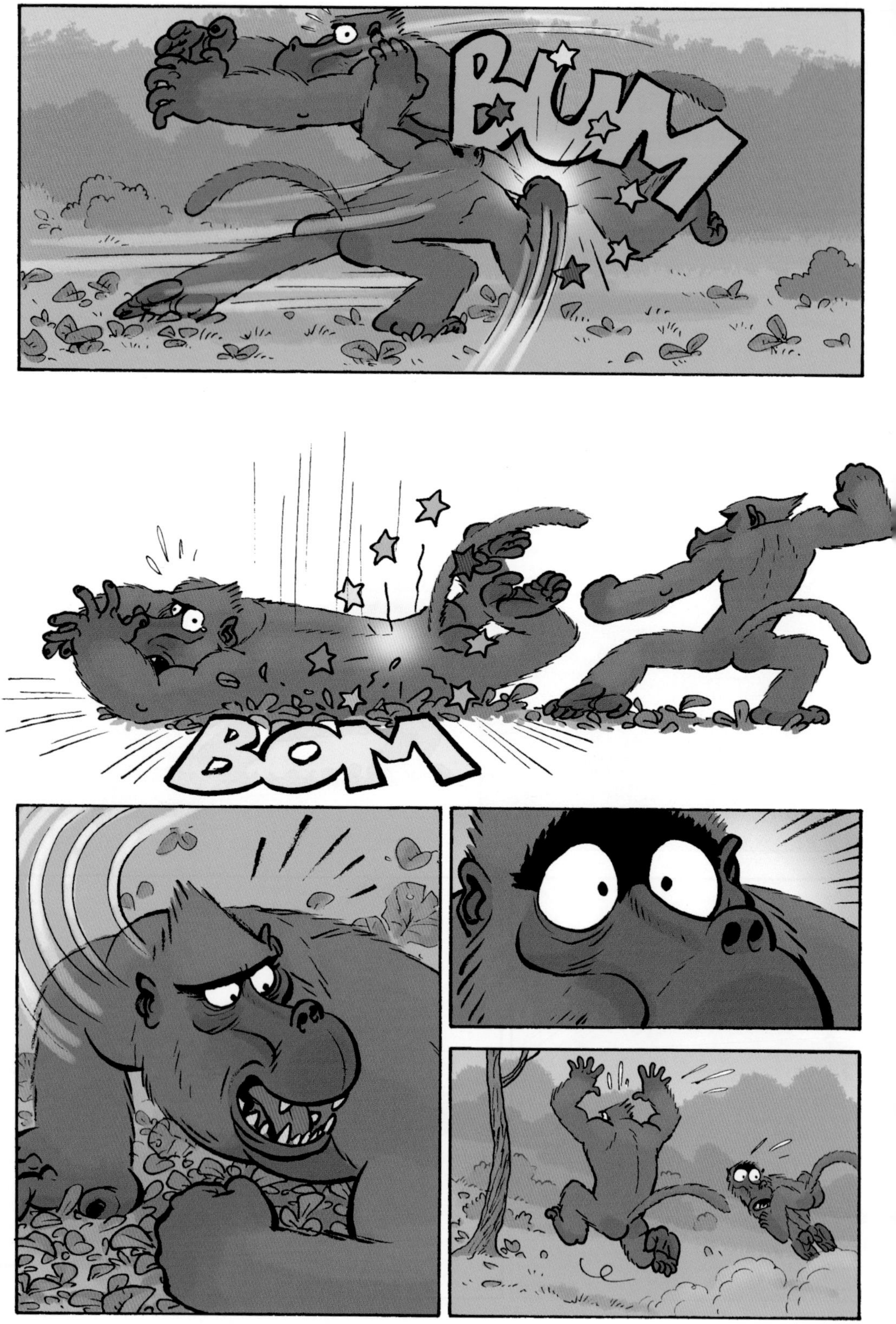
BUM
BOM

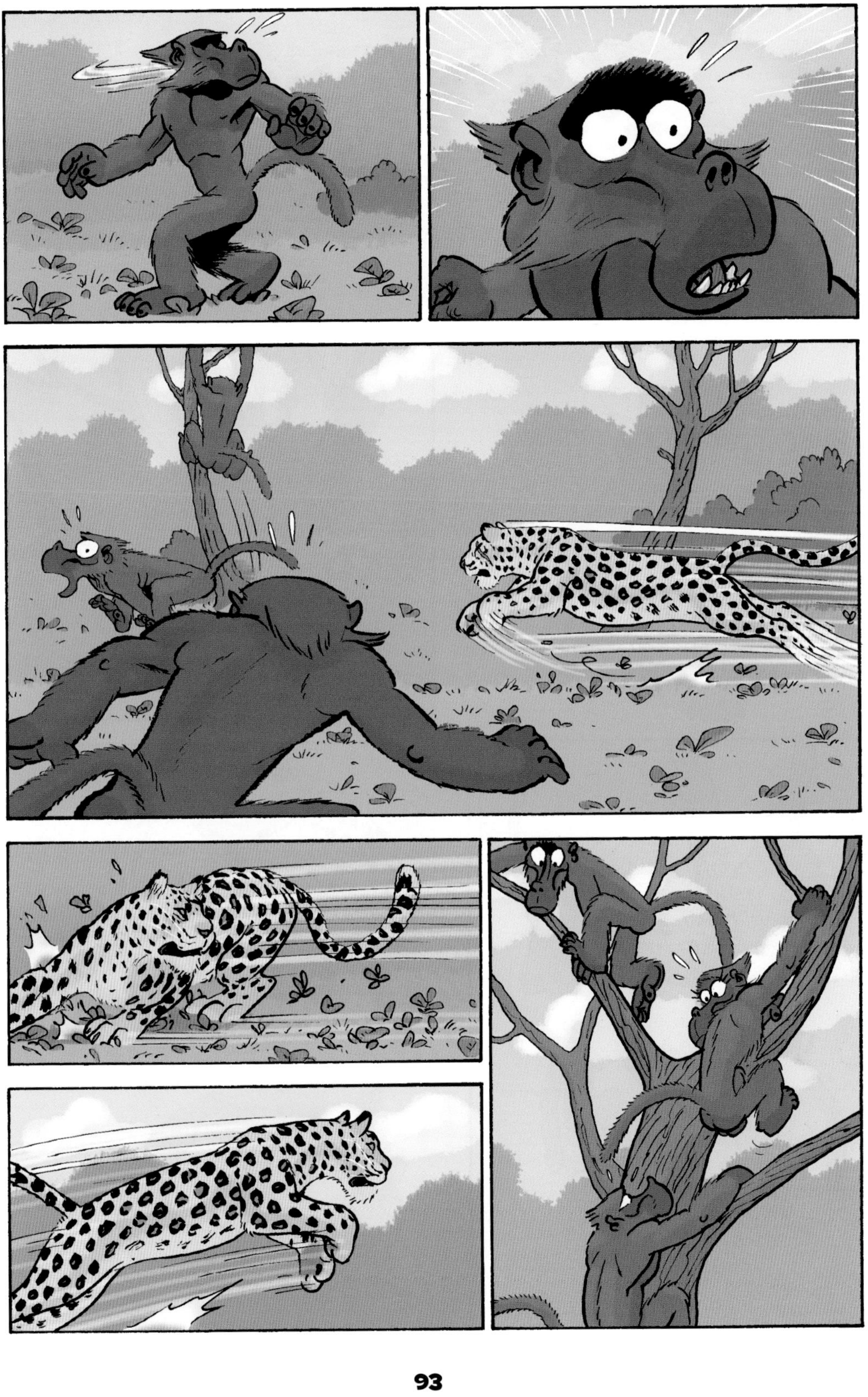

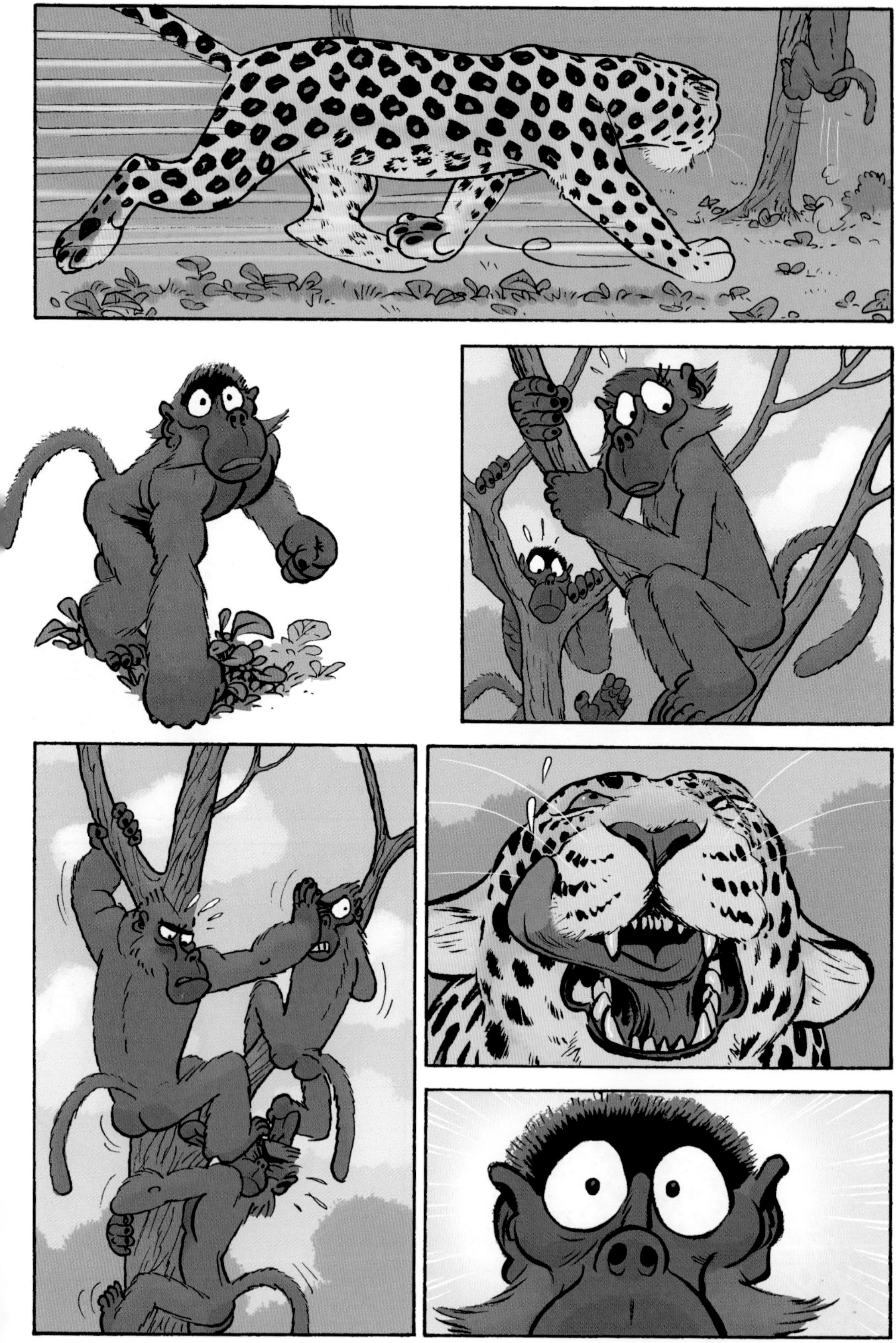

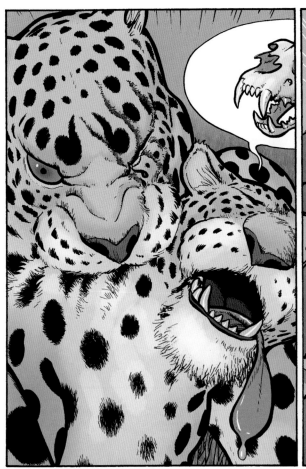

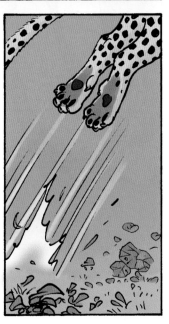

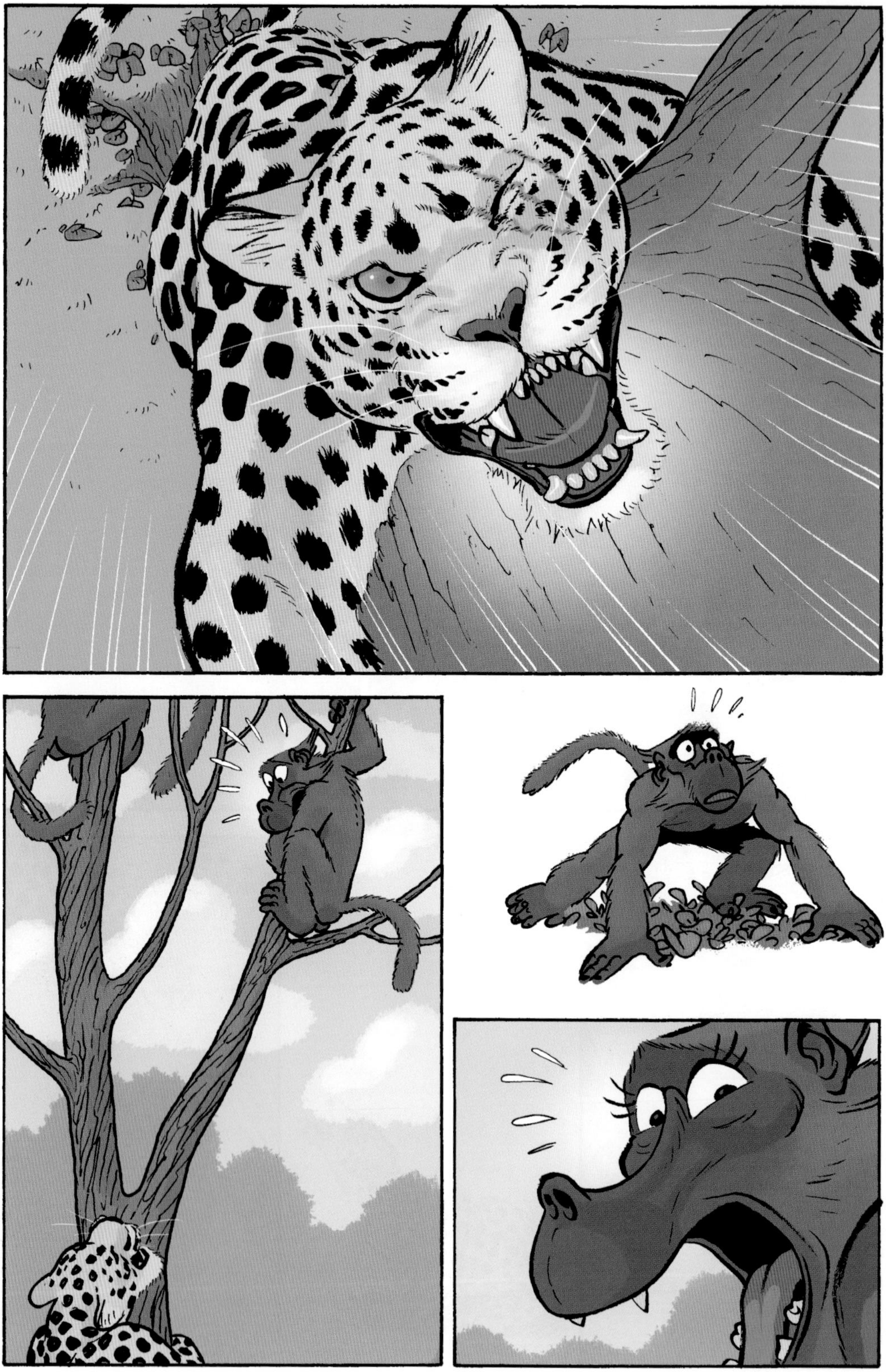

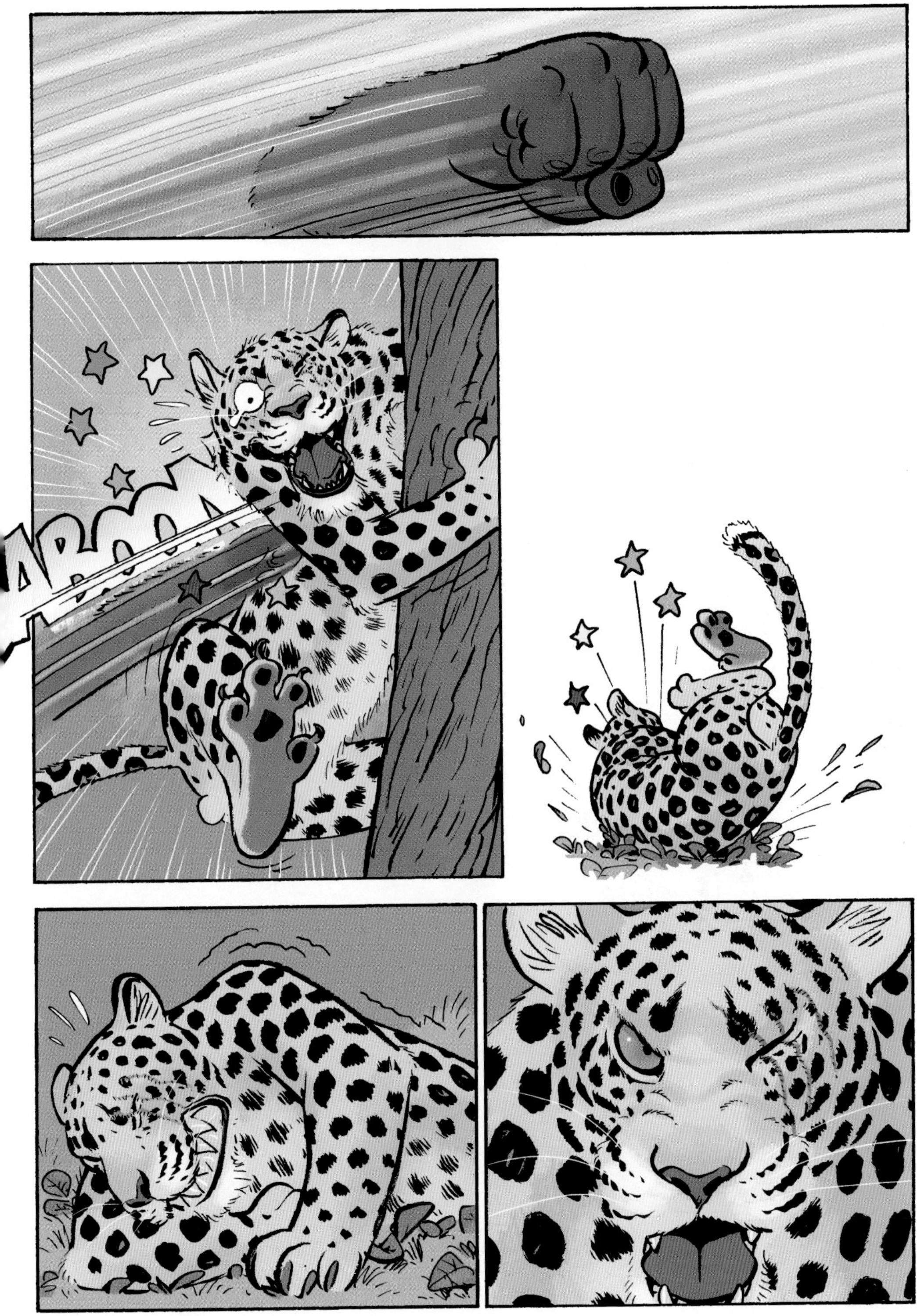

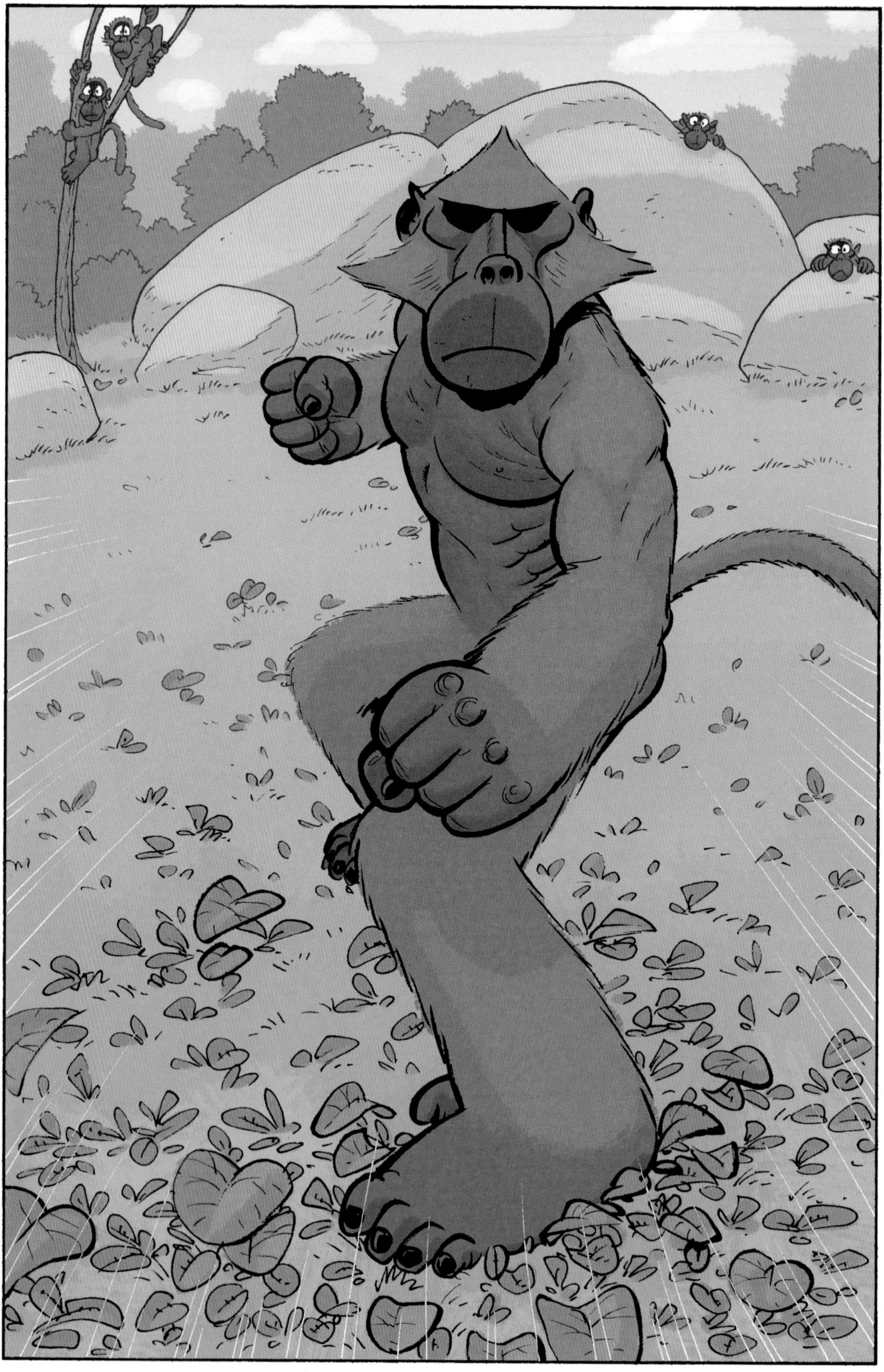

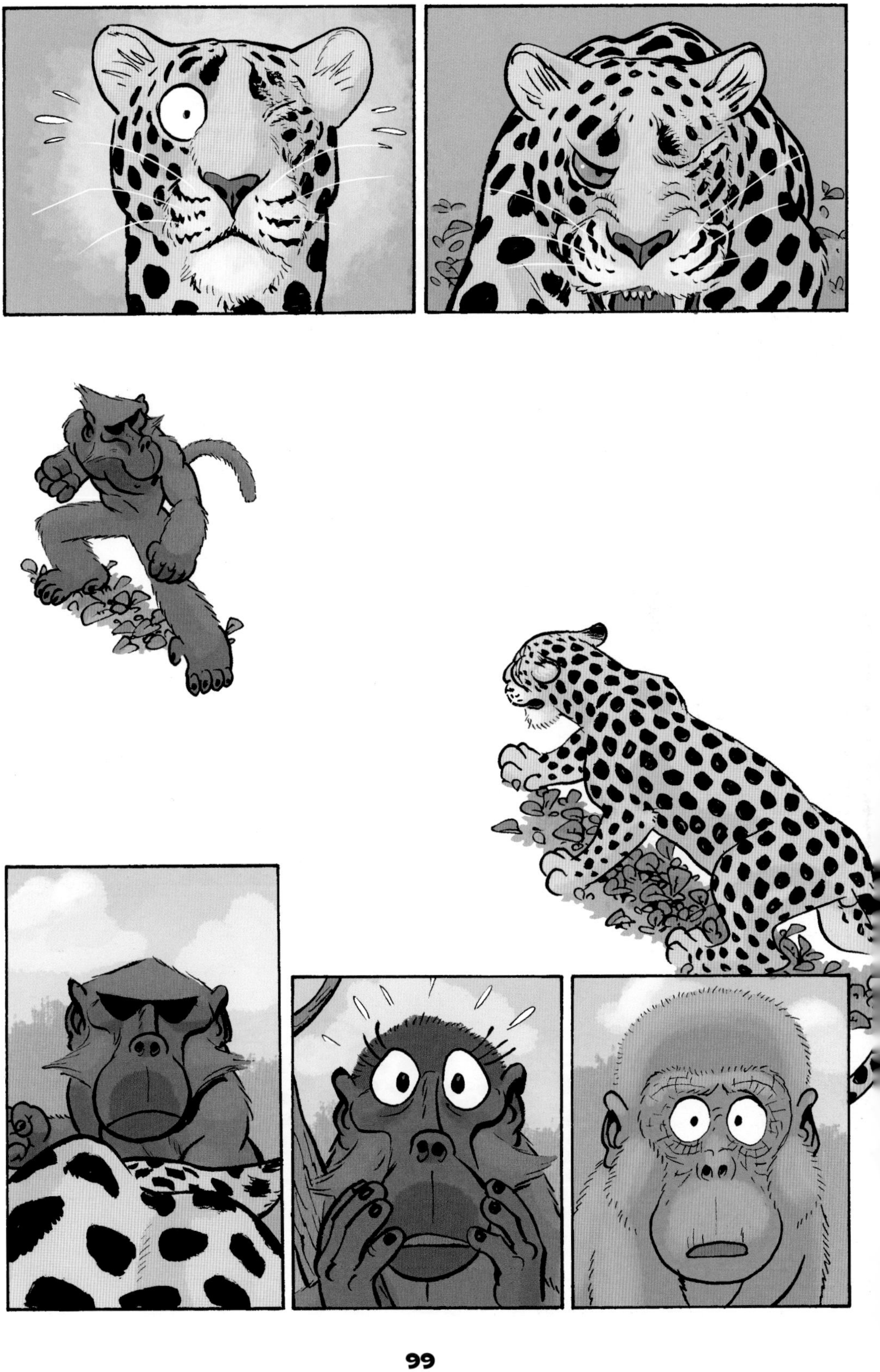

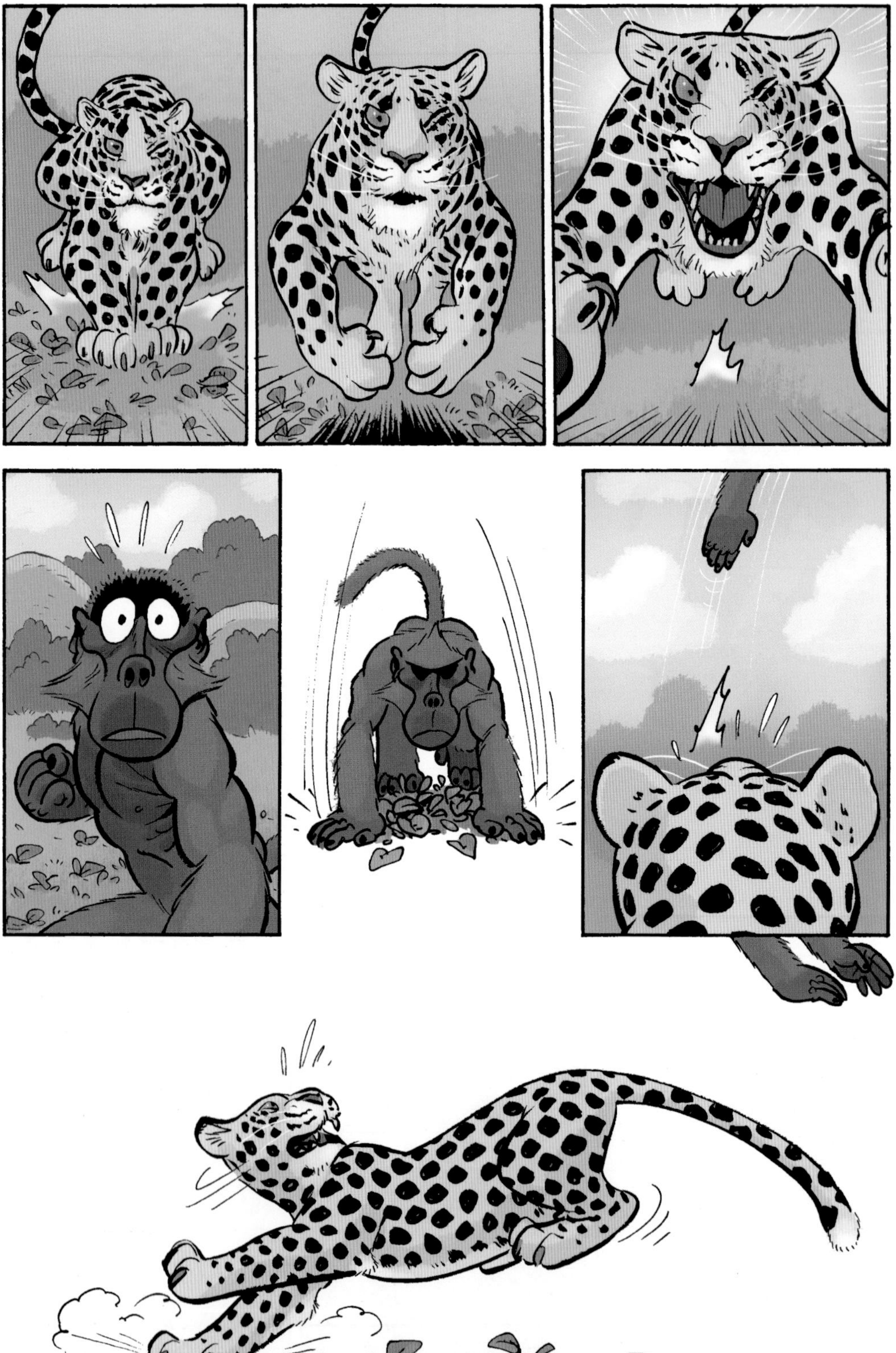

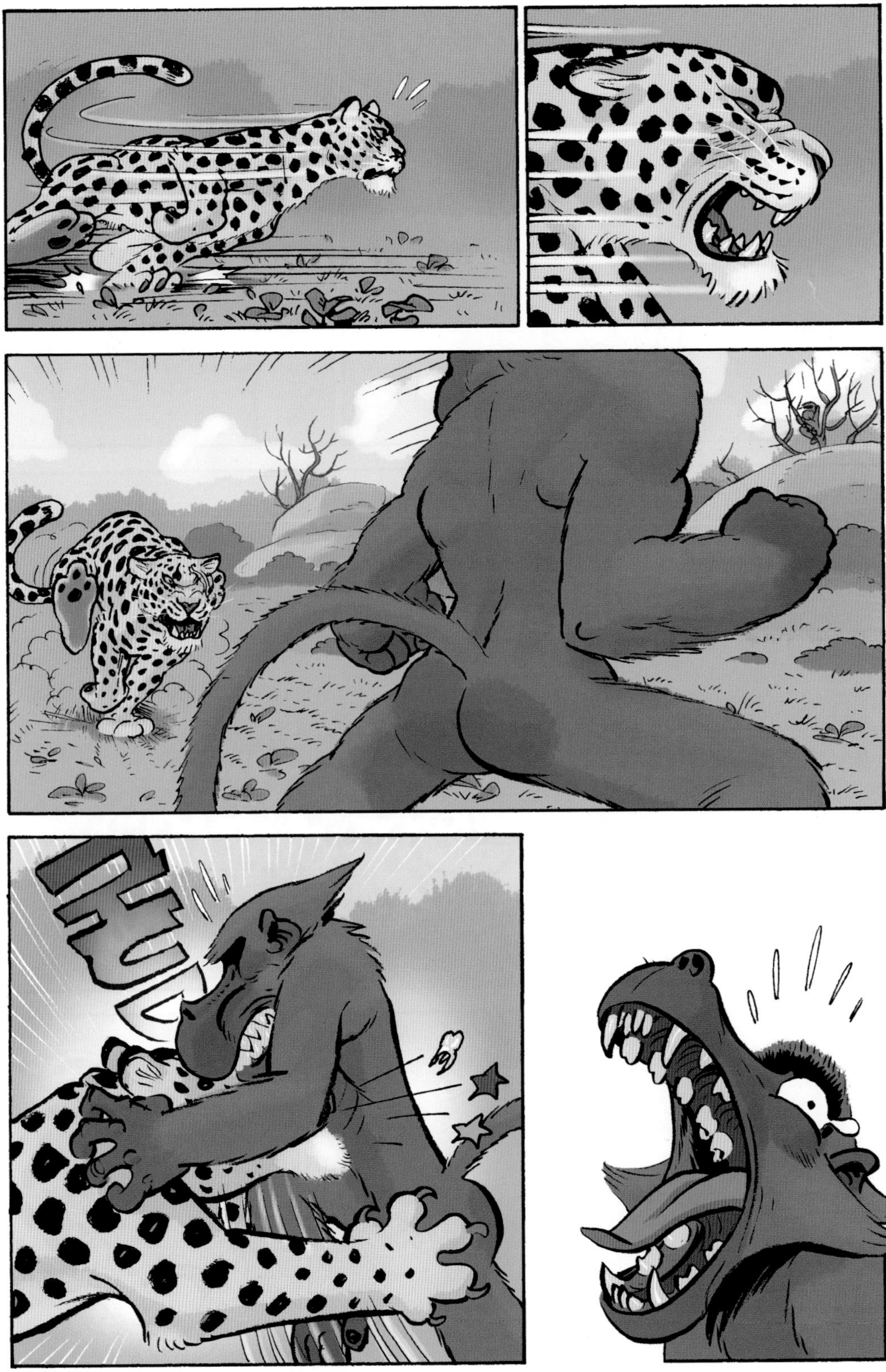
THUD

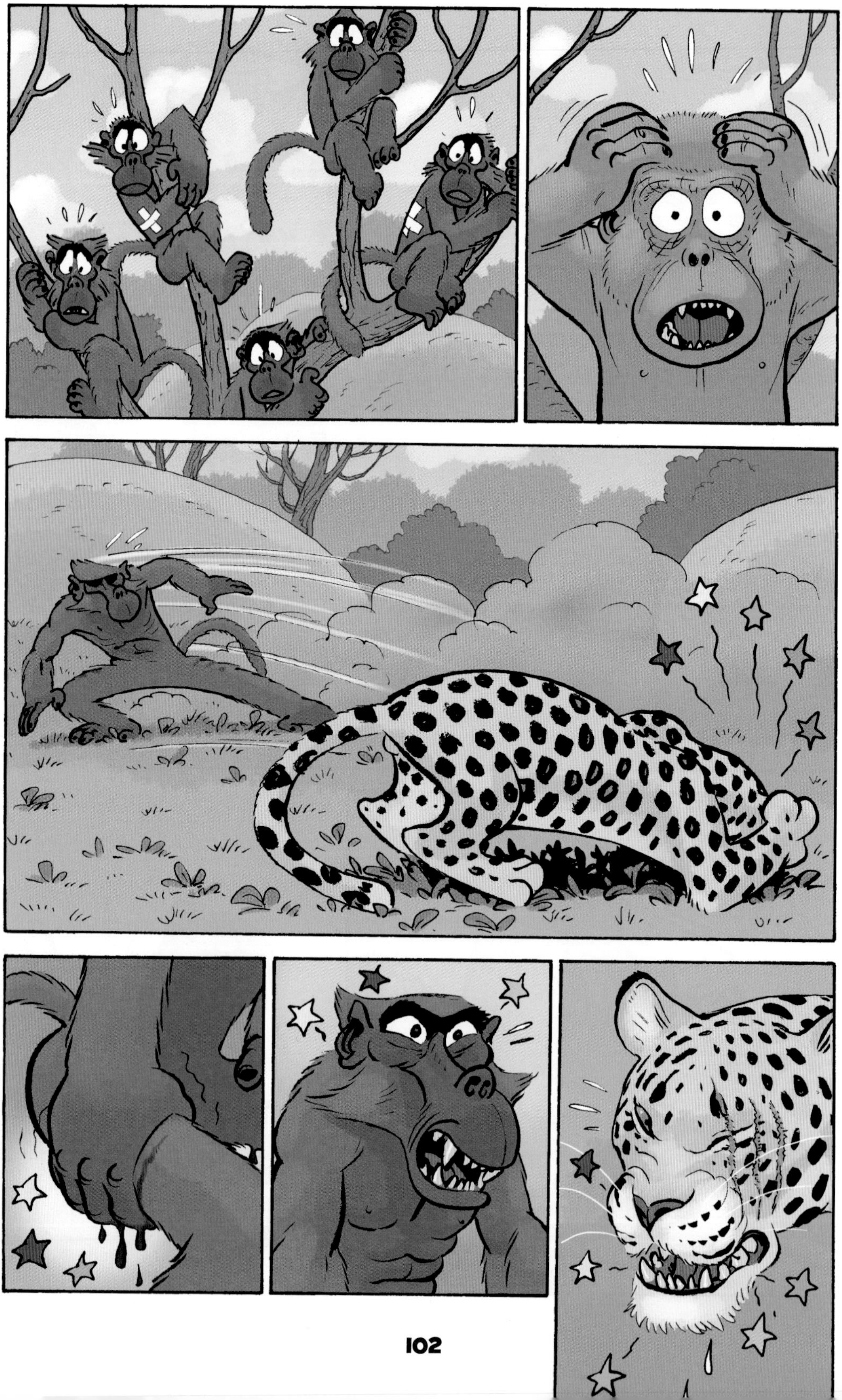

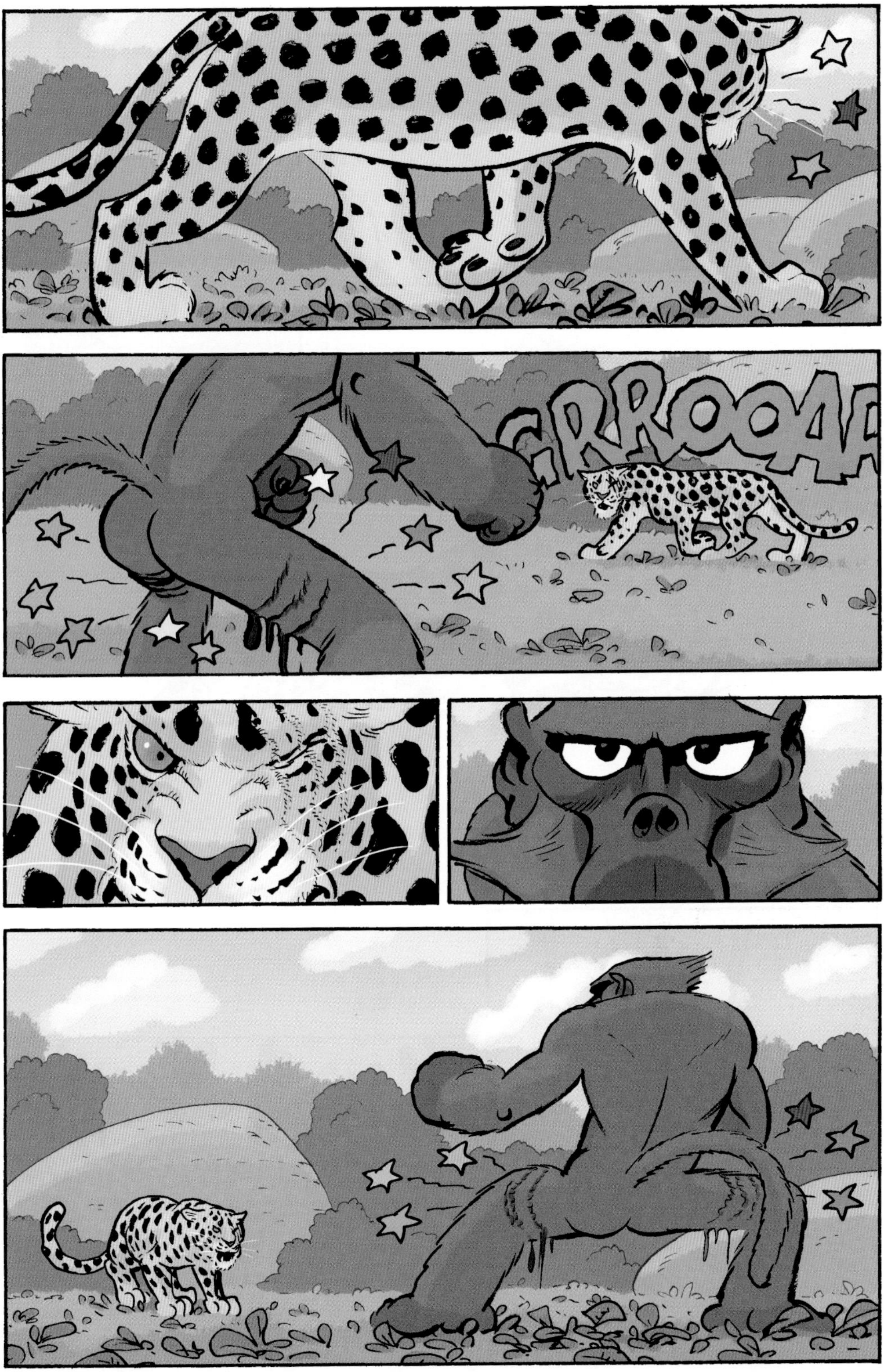
GRROOAA

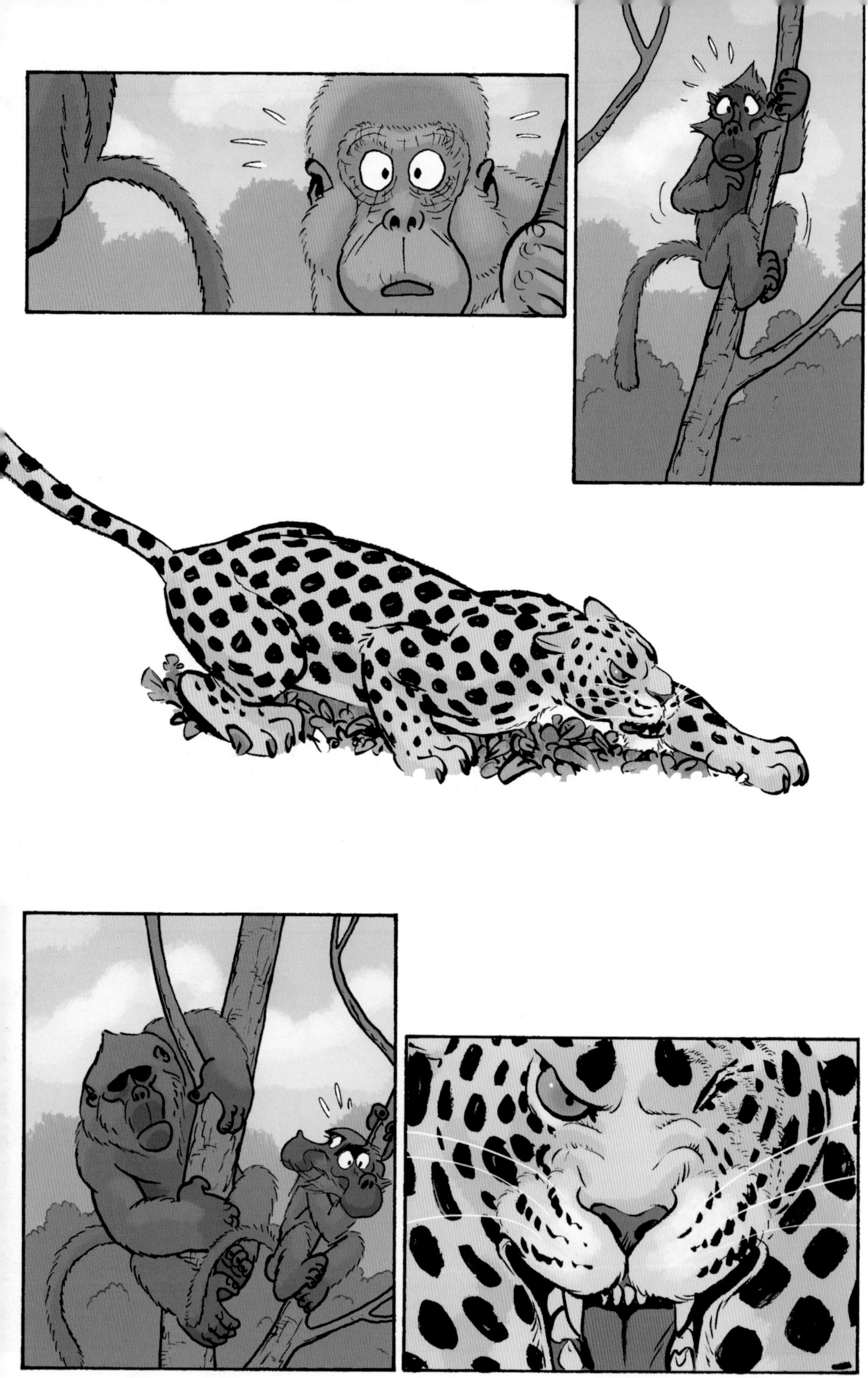

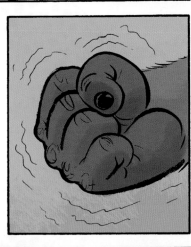

WAAAA

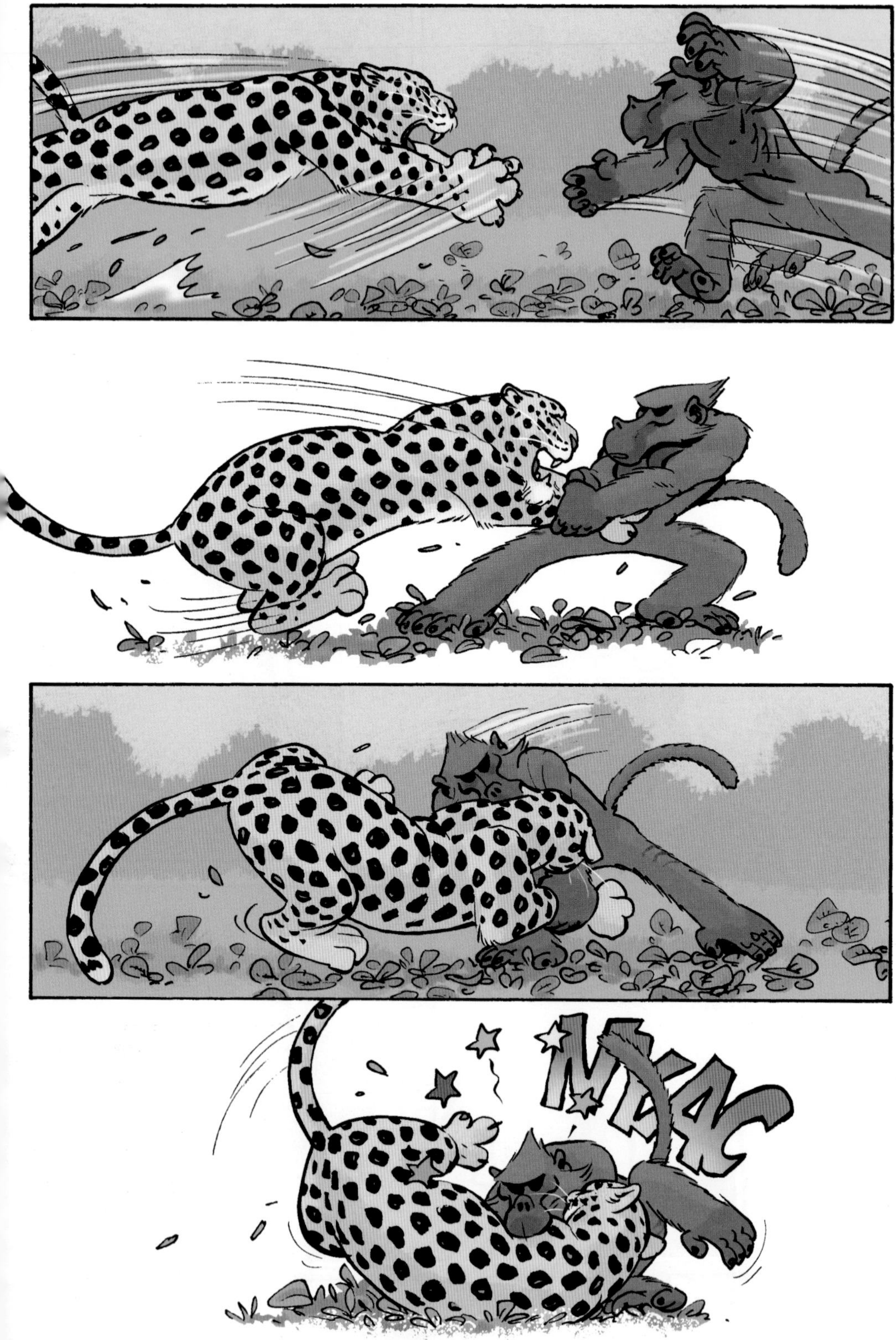

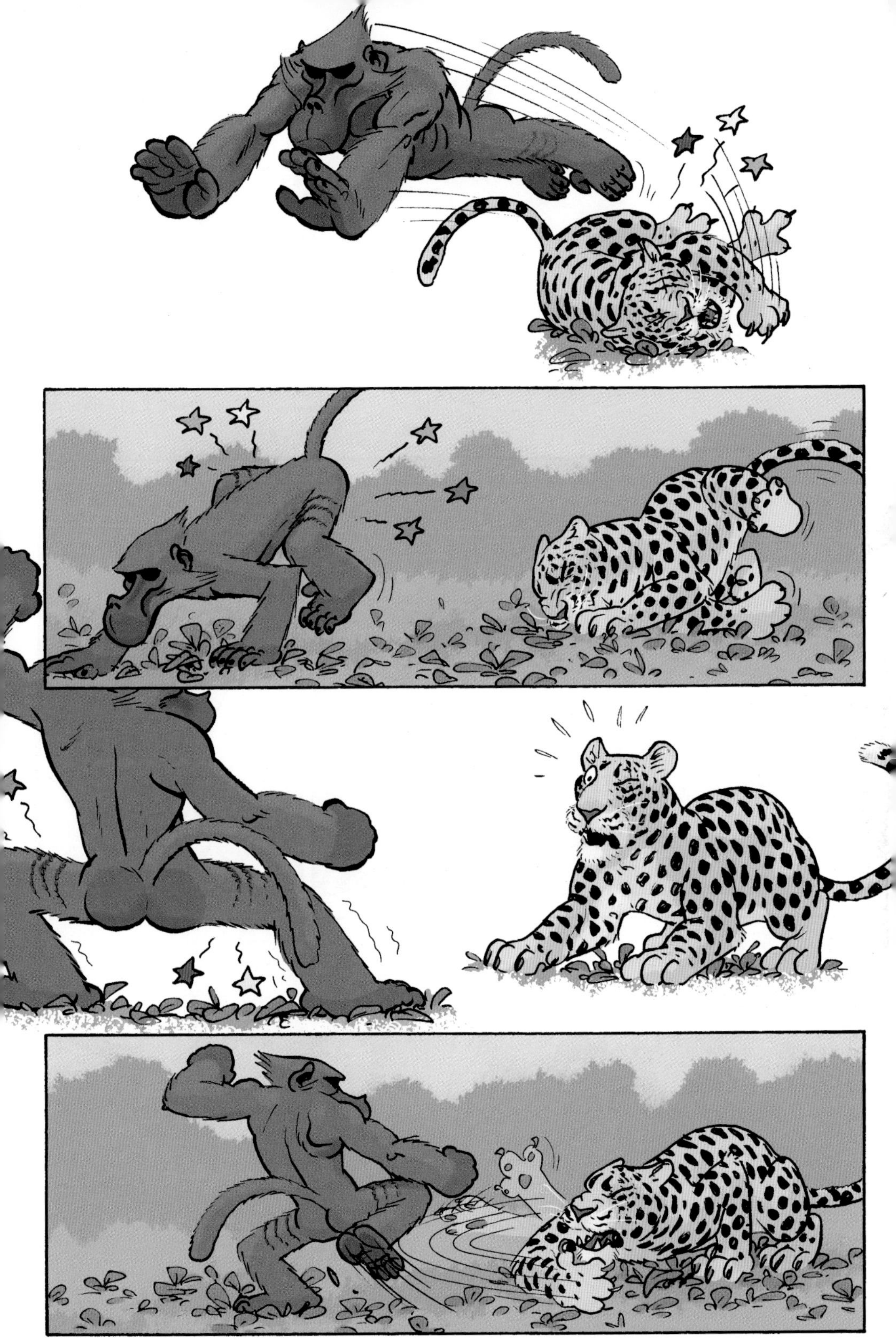

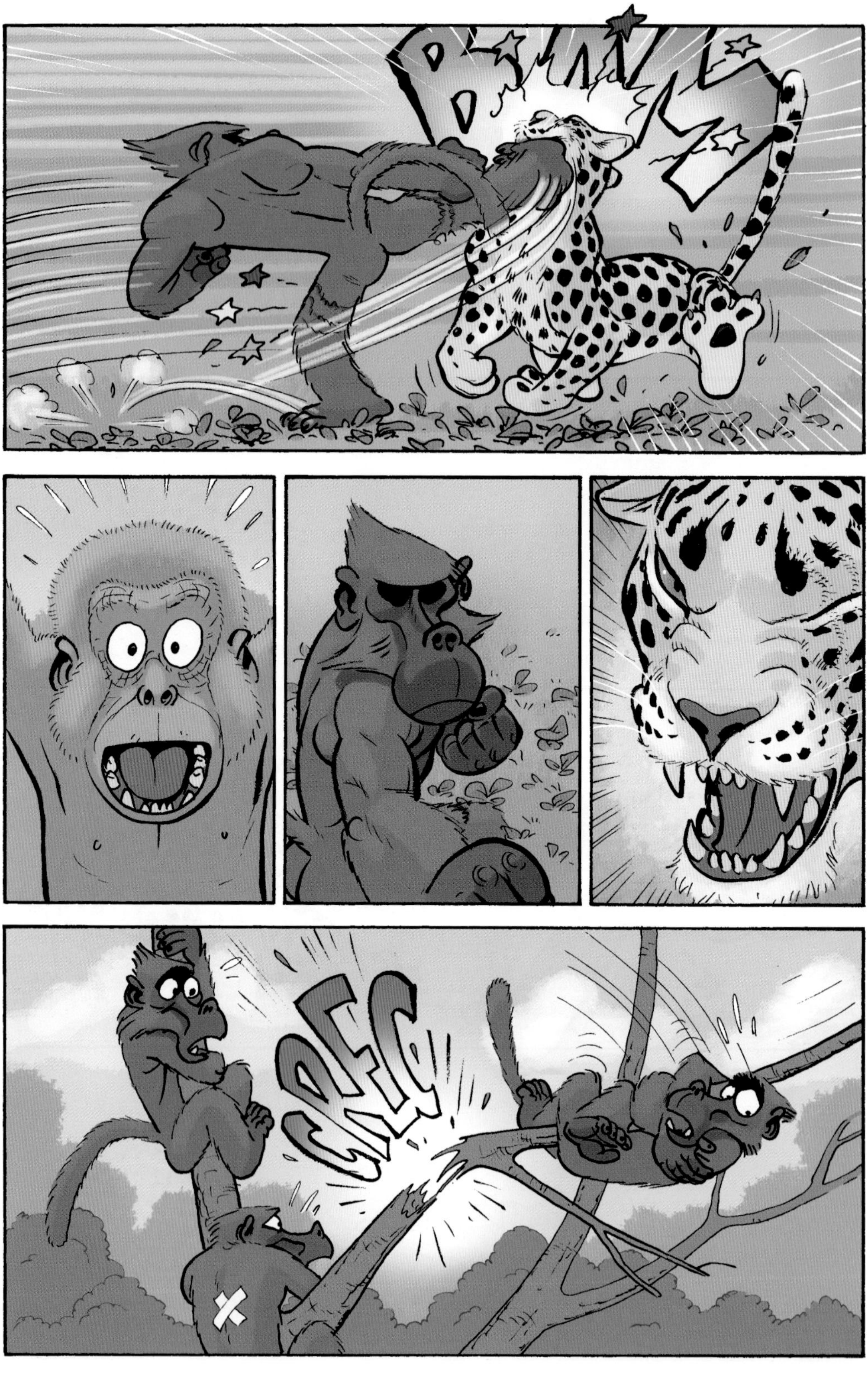

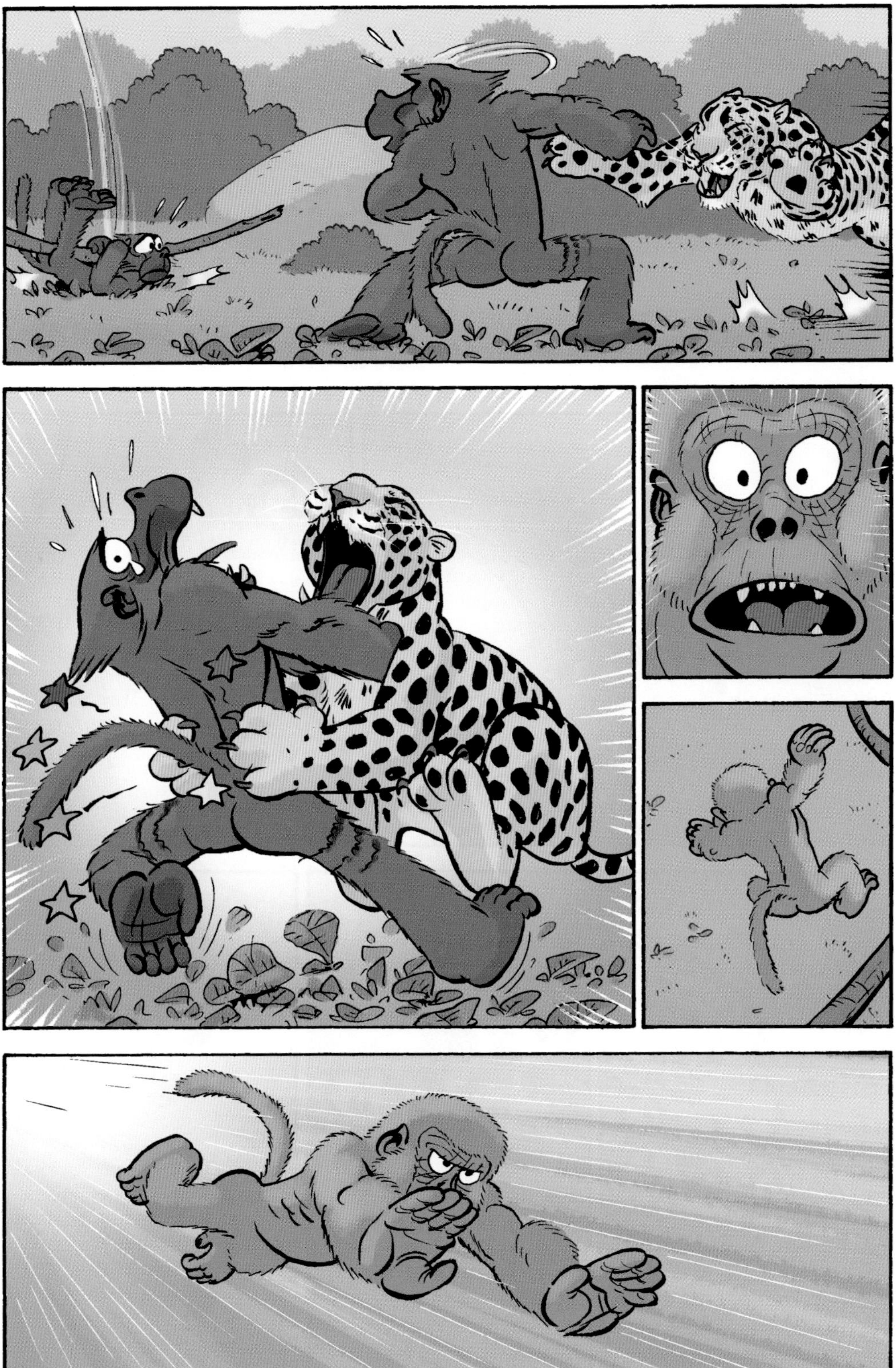

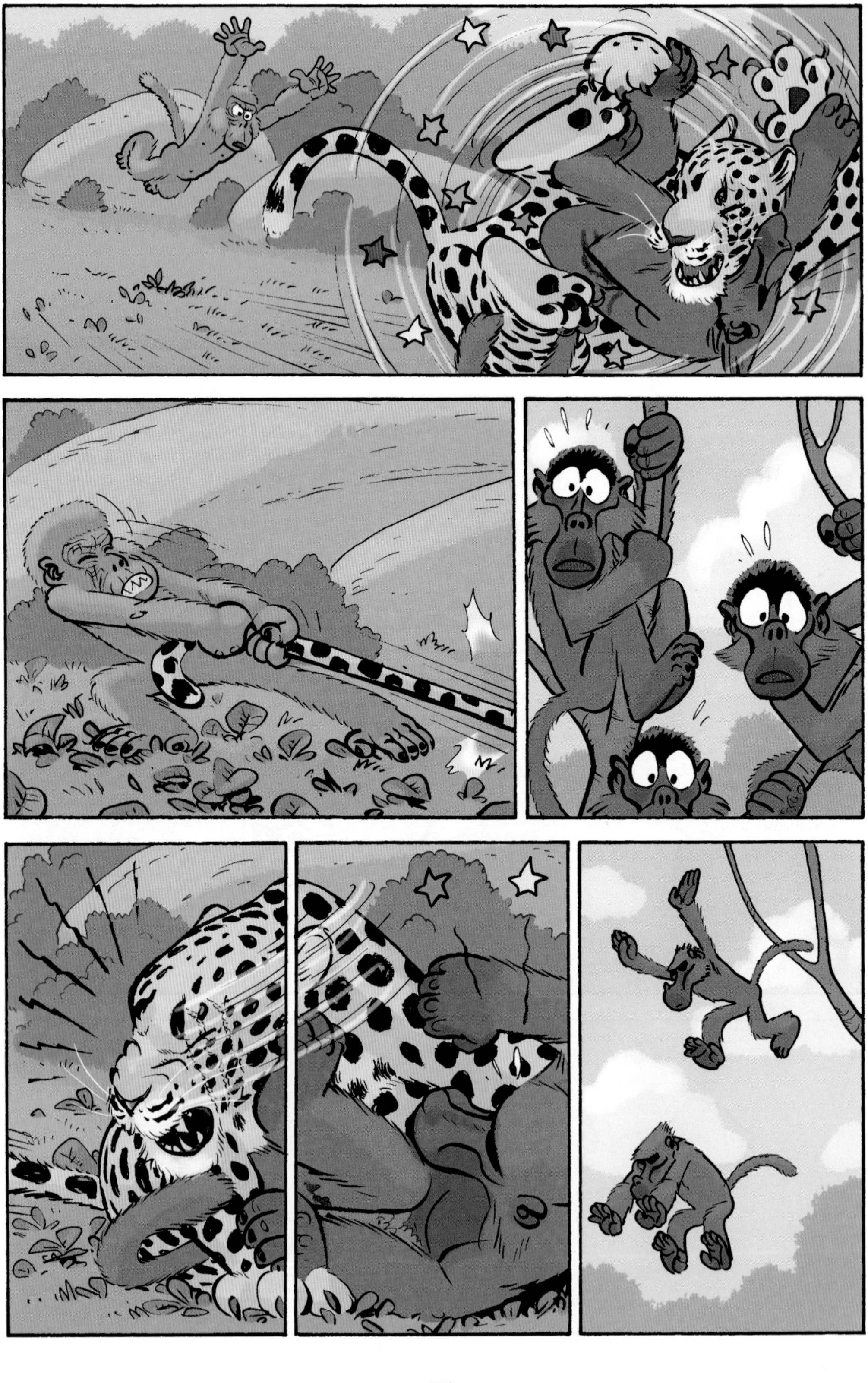

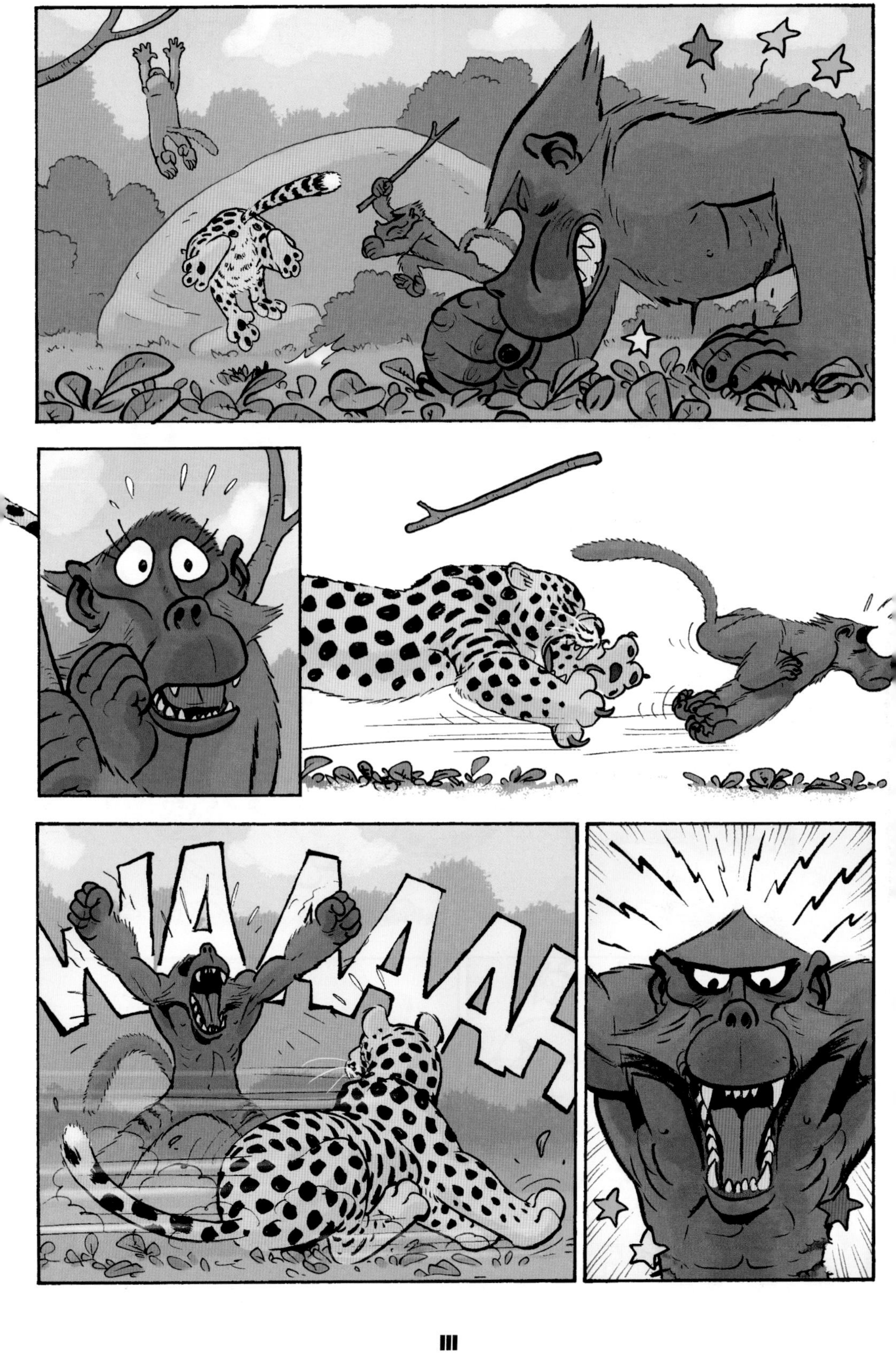
WAAAA

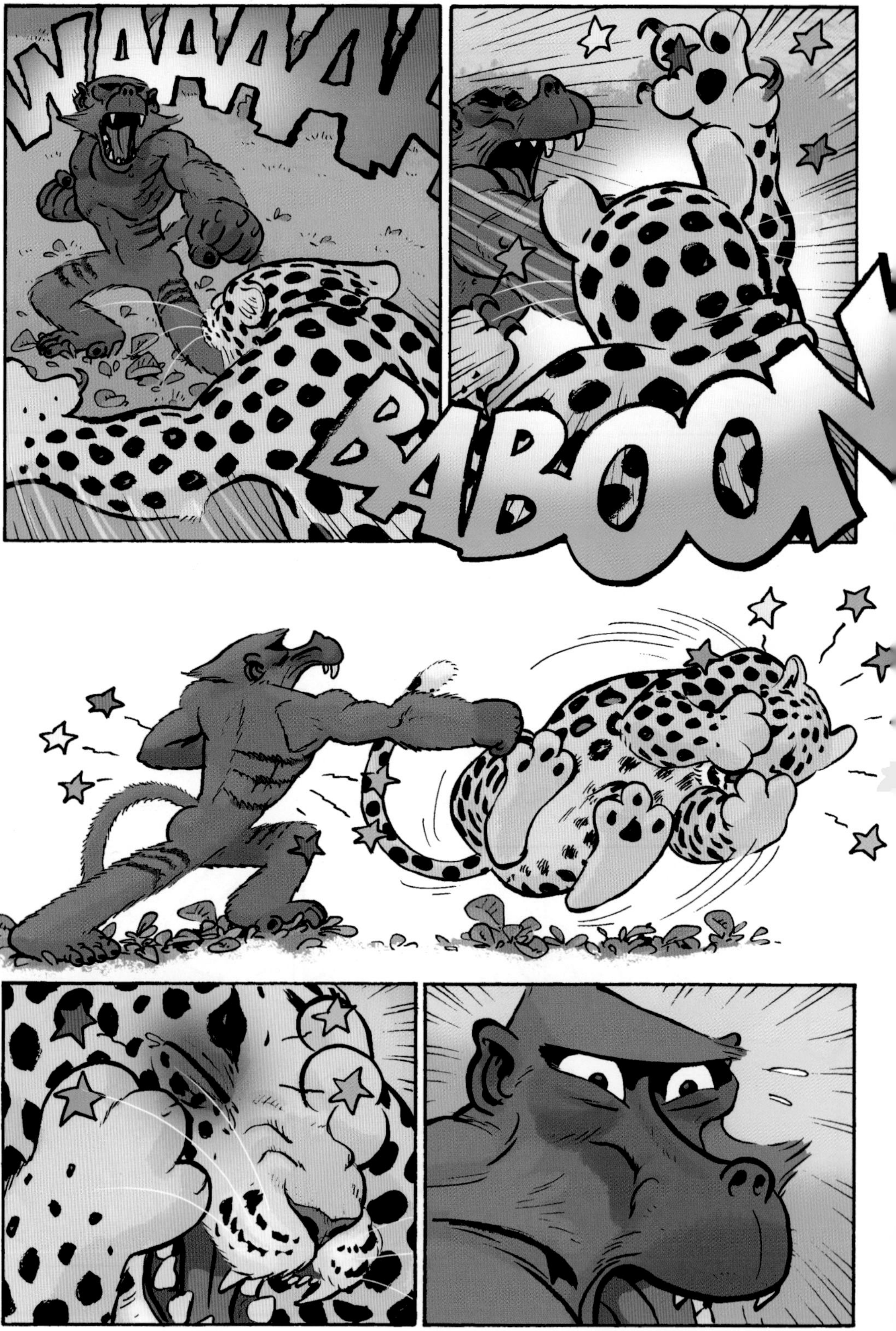
WAAAA!
BABOOM

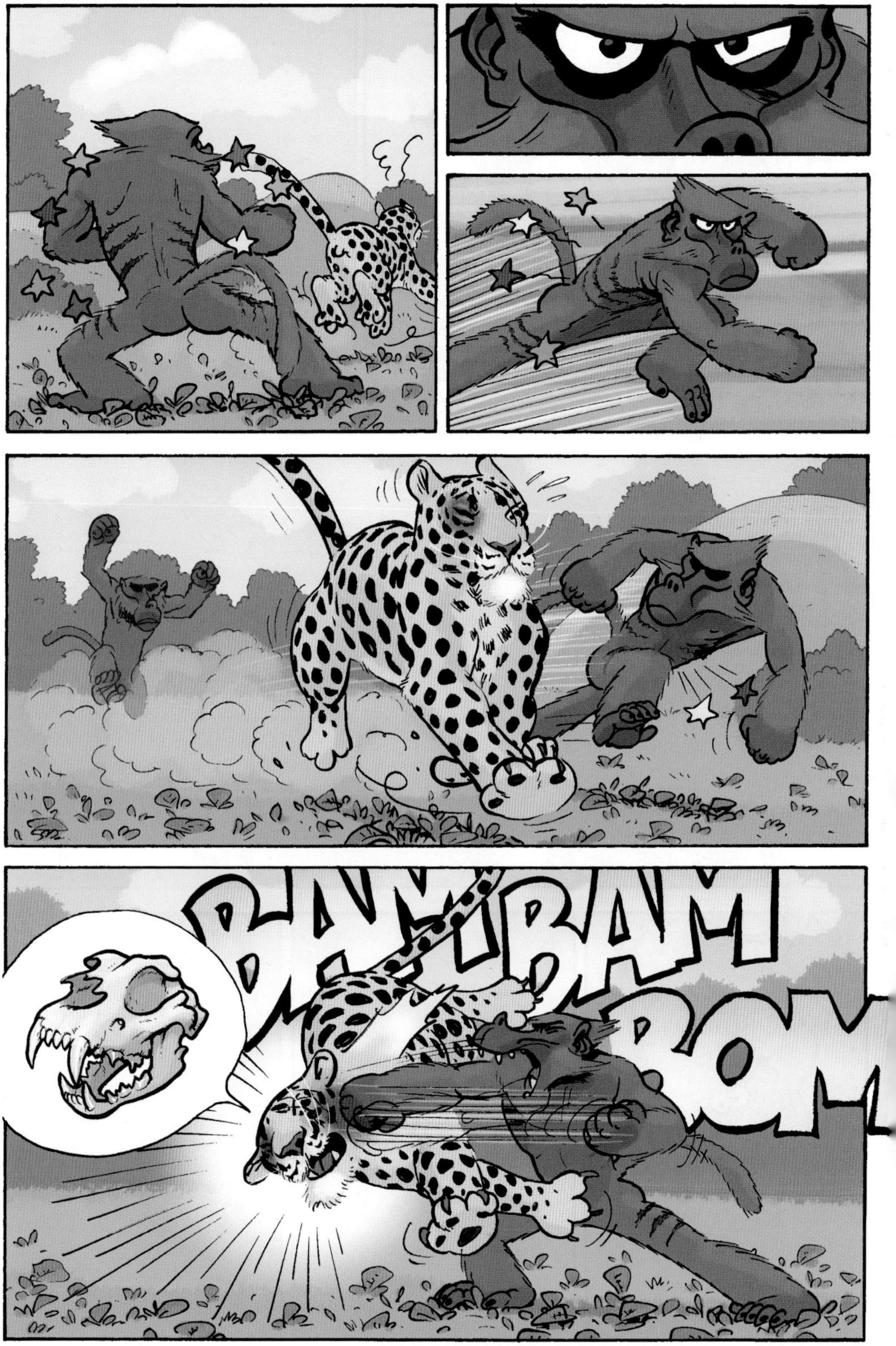
BAM BAM
BOM

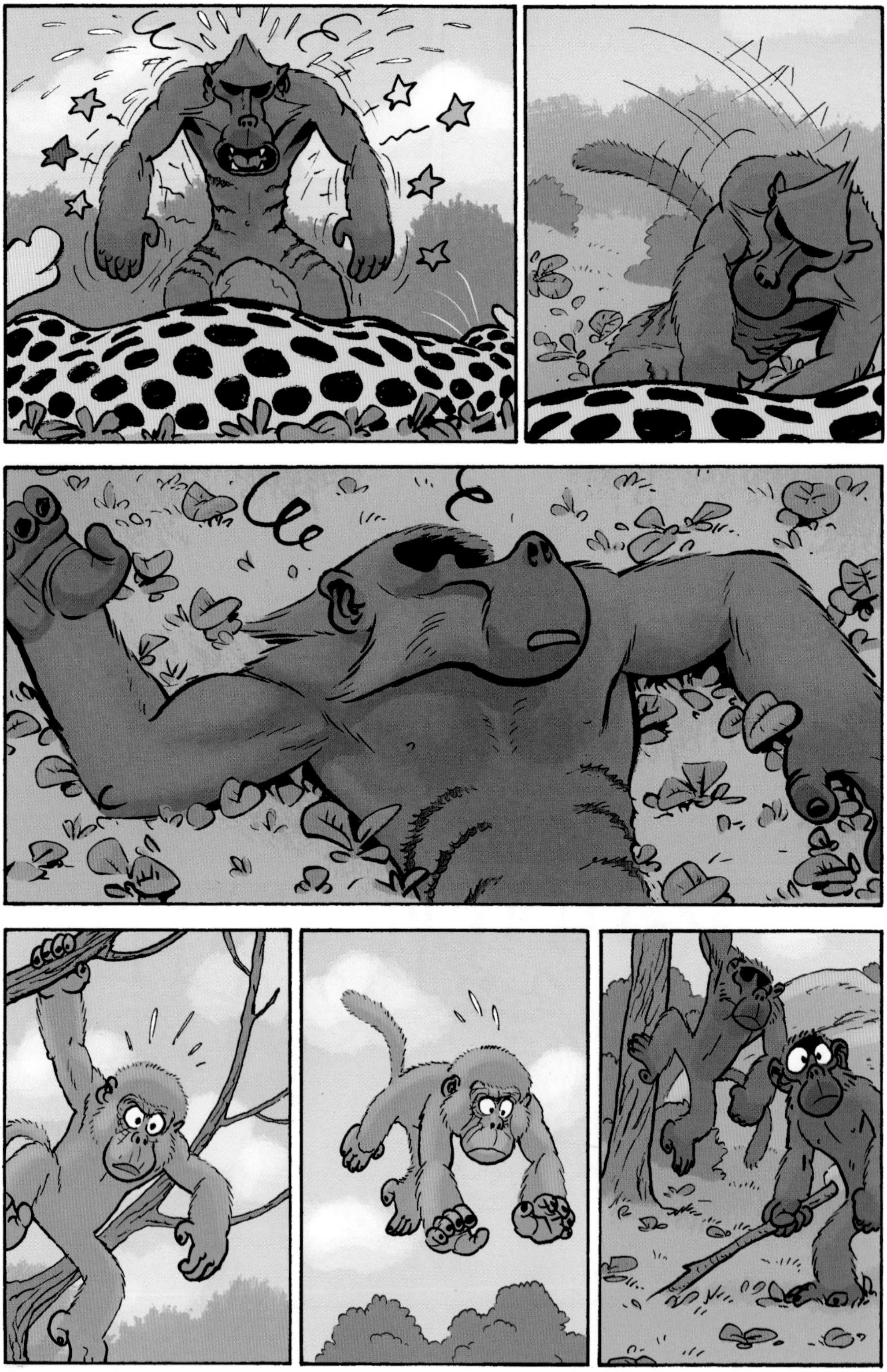

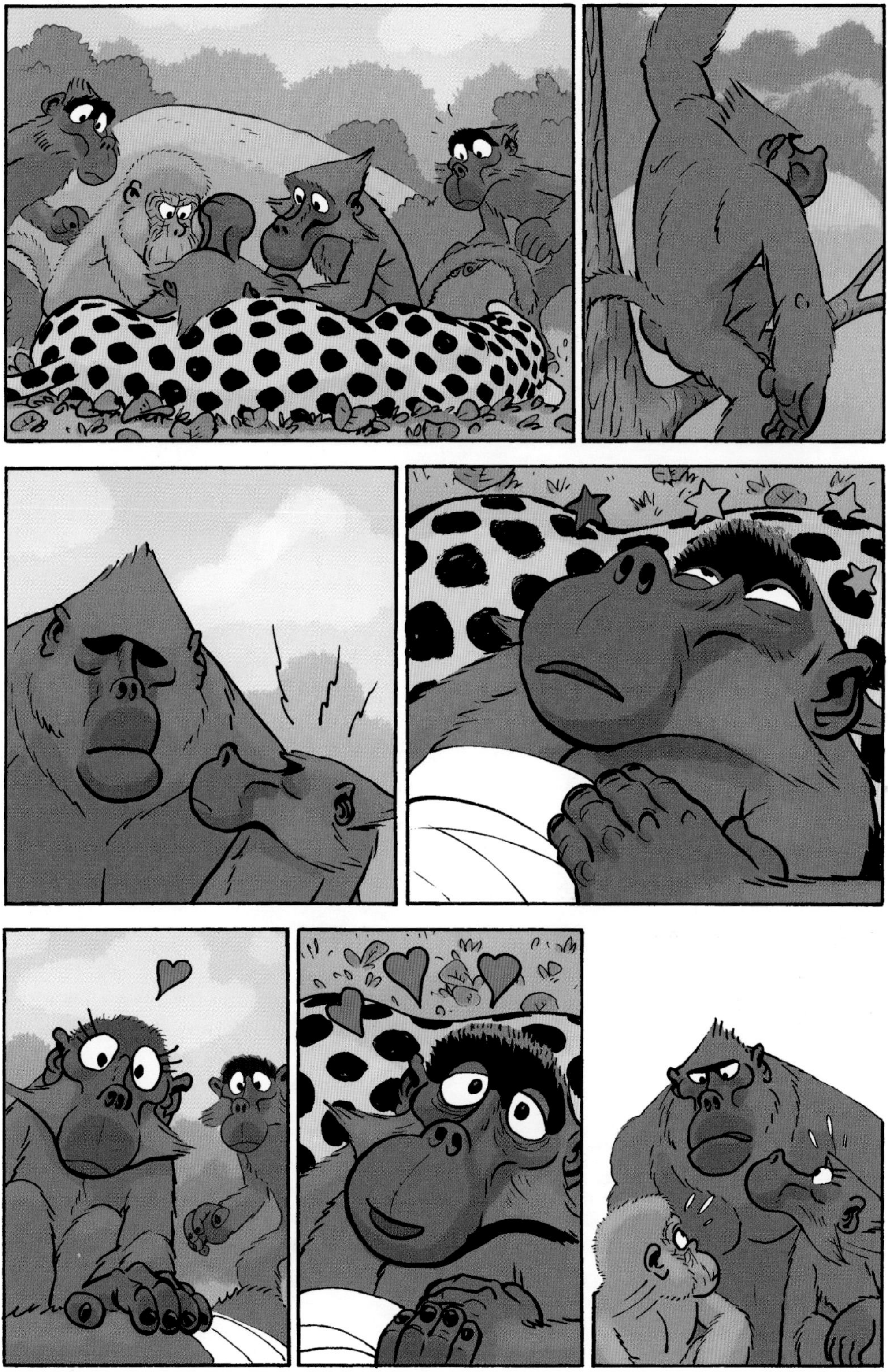

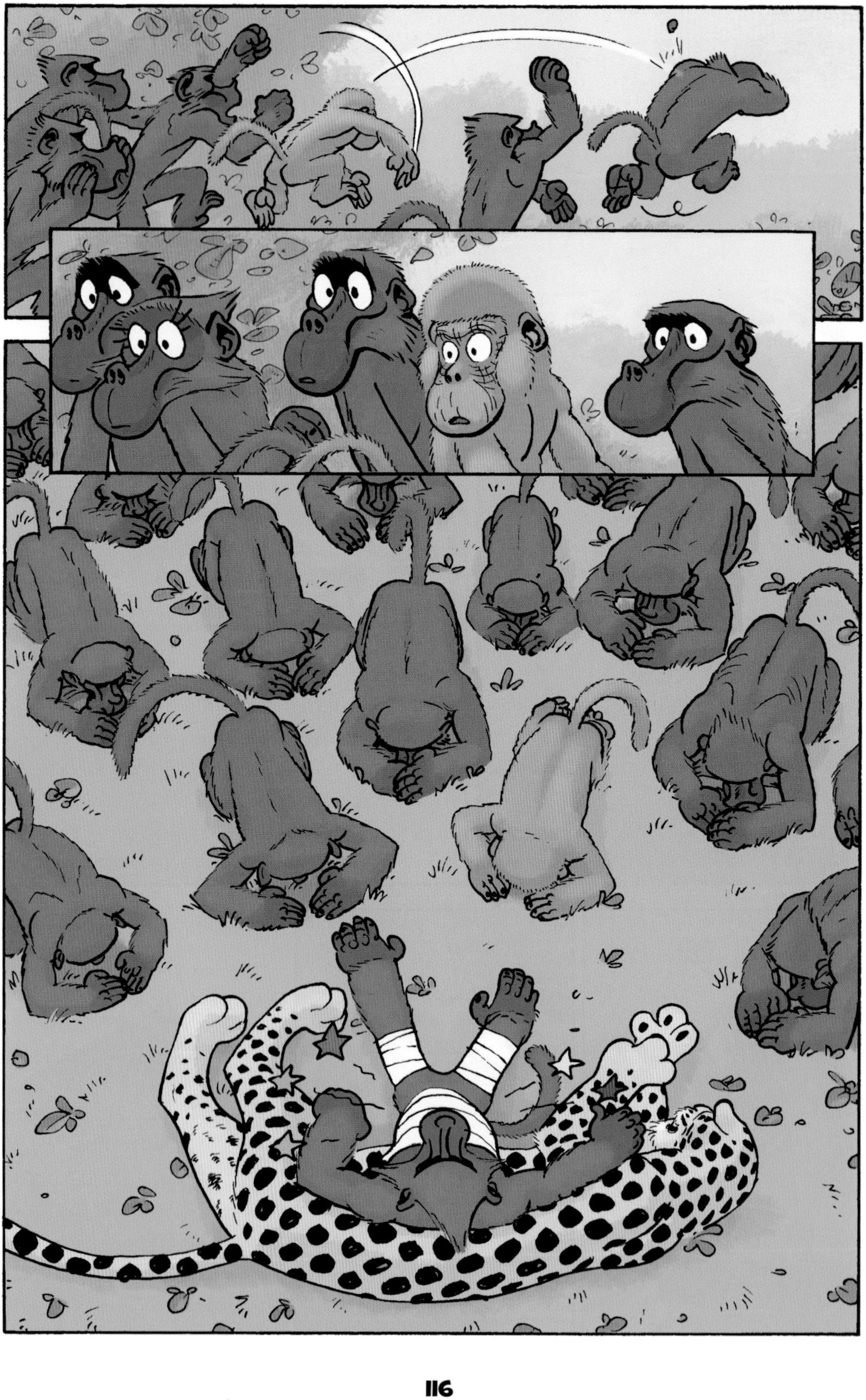

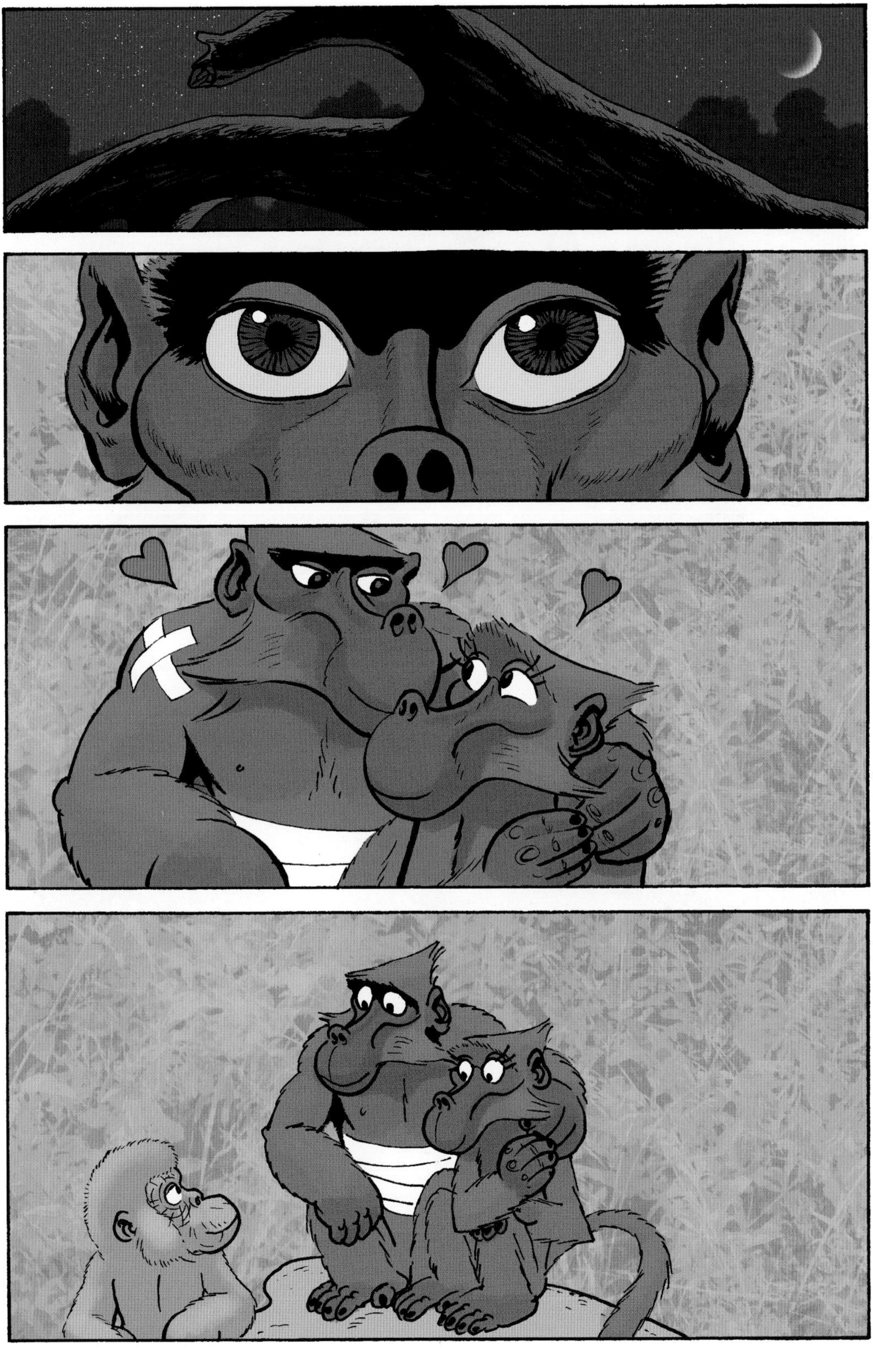

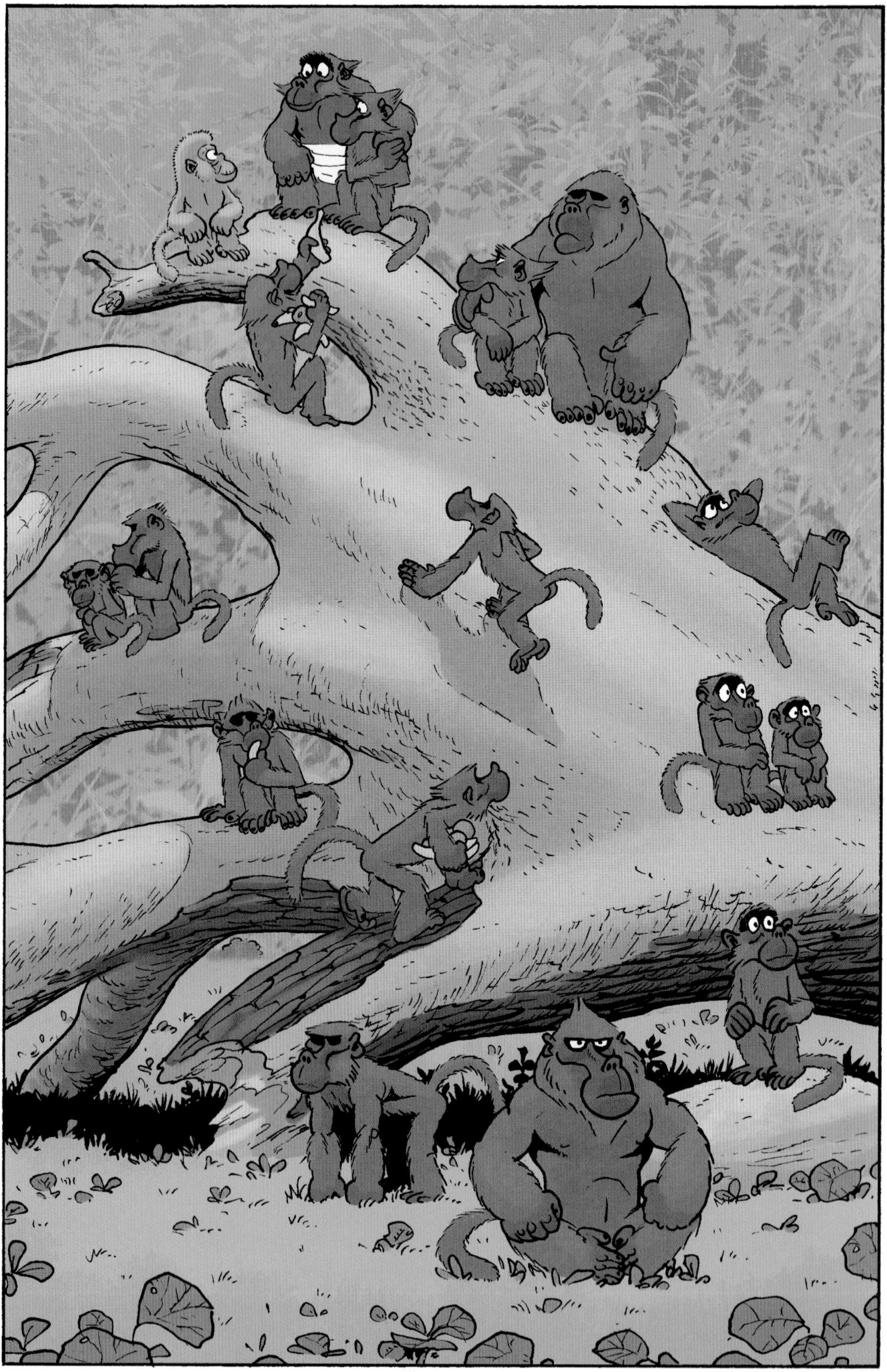

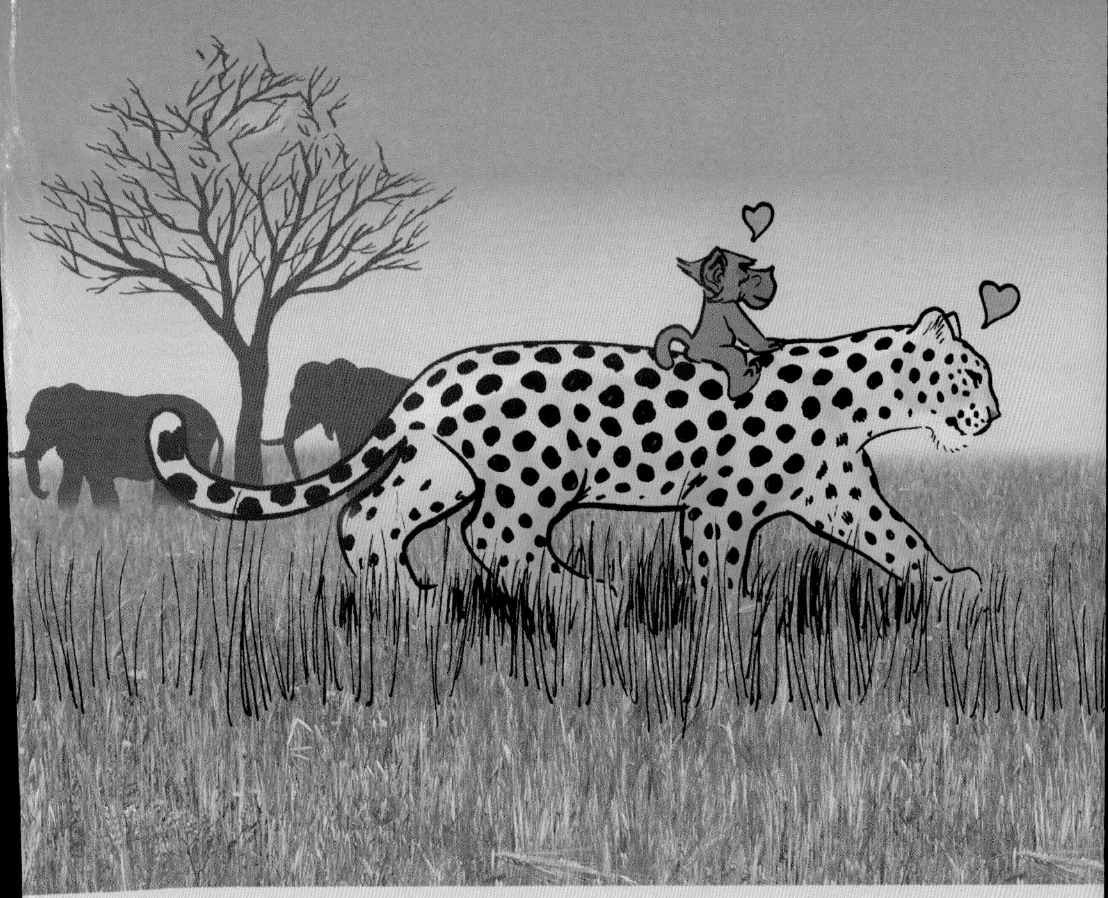

THANK YOU

I started to draw this book in 2008, before *Atlas & Axis*'s *Saga*, but never found a publisher, so it rested just a project. After finishing the saga I started my patreon.com/Pau site to show my most loyal readers the work I do day by day, and thanks to their support I could finish the story and publish it. This book is in your hands thanks to my dear patrons:

Åke Mora, Felipe Sánchez-Cuenca, David Vergara Munuera, Empar Rosselló Mora, Samuel Ellington, Guillem Bosch Roca, Shield, Bonnichsen, Cristóbal Mora, Michael Foertsch, Metrópolis Mallorca, Francisca Garau, Fernando Sánchez-Cuenca, Daniel Martín Peixe, Raquel Socías, Óscar & Zhuldyz, Nadal Galiana, David & Mauge, LT Fish, Germán Socías, Vicente Rodríguez Jiménez-Bravo, Mateo Vallori Nemeckova, Dapzcomic, Viktor Kalvachev Bernardo & Silvia, Jonathan D. Phillips, Jordan Mello, and José Carlos Cerro Garrido.

–PAU

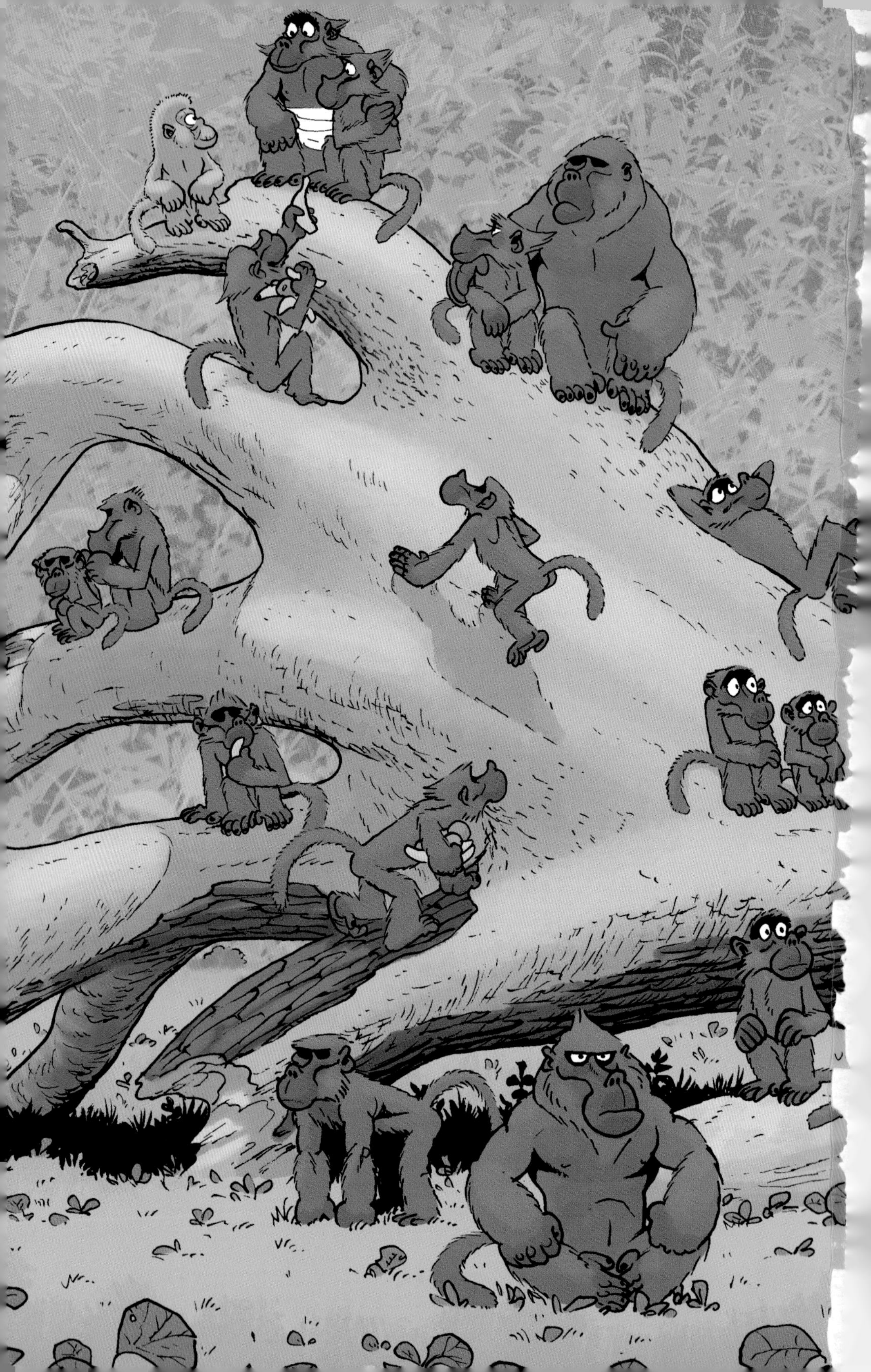